INTIMATE ENEMIES

OTHER BOOKS BY CARYL RIVERS

FICTION

Girls Forever Brave and True

Virgins

For Better, For Worse

The Mind Stealers

NONFICTION

Occasional Sins
(Originally published as *Aphrodite at Mid-Century:*
Growing Up Female and Catholic in Postwar America)

Lifeprints: New Patterns of Love and Work for Today's Women

Beyond Sugar and Spice: How Women Grow, Learn and Thrive

INTIMATE ENEMIES

CARYL RIVERS

E. P. DUTTON NEW YORK

Published in the United States by E. P. Dutton,
a division of NAL Penguin Inc.,
2 Park Avenue, New York, N.Y. 10016.

Published simultaneously in Canada
by Fitzhenry and Whiteside Limited, Toronto.

Library of Congress Cataloging-in-Publication Data
Rivers, Caryl.
Intimate enemies.
I. Title.
PS3568.I831515 1987   813'.54   87-9210
ISBN 0-525-24611-8

COBE

Designed by Michele Aldin

1 3 5 7 9 10 8 6 4 2

First Edition

Poem excerpts by Stan Platke on pages 195, 204, and 215, reprinted by
permission of *The Nation* Magazine, The Nation Company. Copyright © Decem-
ber 17, 1983 by *The Nation* Magazine.

To the memory of my parents,
Helen and Hugh Rivers,
with love and deep gratitude
for their unfailing support and love.
And to the memory of my brother,
Hugh Rivers, Jr.

ACKNOWLEDGMENTS

I want to express my thanks and deep appreciation to my editor, Joyce Engelson, for her continuing help, perception, and guidance. And to Elaine Markson and Geri Thoma, thanks for their friendship and untiring efforts.

I want also to say "thank you" to the members of my writers' group, who have followed this book from the first idea to the last period: Bernice Buresh, Diane Cox, Phyllis Karas, Diana Korzenik, Janet Robertson, Carolyn Toll, Sally Steinberg, and Barbara White.

I first became interested in the problems facing Vietnam veterans in the early seventies, when I had a magazine assignment to look into the issue. In the years since, I've followed the vets' struggles with continued interest. In addition to my own research, one book I found most helpful for its thorough treatment of the Vietnam generation was *Long Time Passing* by Myra MacPherson of *The Washington Post*.

INTIMATE ENEMIES

FROM JESSIE'S DIARY
(1963, AGE 13)

Dear Diary: I have been thinking, A LOT, *about what President Kennedy said, "Ask not what your country can do for you, but what you can do for your country." And I have decided that I am not going to be a veterinarian. That is kid stuff. I mean, somebody has to take care of sick dogs and cats and gerbils, but that is not what President Kennedy meant. I want to do something* GREAT *for my country, like be the first woman astronaut (except that I throw up on the Ferris wheel so maybe that is not the* GREAT *thing I am destined to do). But I am destined. I know I am. I am the only one of my friends who is, I feel it in my bones.*

Maybe I should go into politics, but I don't get votes very well. I finished last for treasurer in sixth grade. I even got less votes than Brian Shanahan, who farted in class all the time. You have to question whether you have a big future in politics if you can't beat somebody who farts. Vicki says I lost because I am a brain and I always show off, but what am I supposed to do, be wicked stupid when I have an IQ of 150? I saw it on Sister Rose Ann's desk, I

1

wasn't supposed to but I read it upside down and I am VERY SMART. *President Kennedy was smart too, and he was Catholic like me. I think we are very much alike. It's terrible that somebody shot him. I cried and cried and cried when he got shot and I made a promise, then, that I would always remember what he said: Ask not, etc. Maybe I will go into the Peace Corps and help poor countries be more like us. But my mom says I have a sensitive stomach, I have ever since I was two and I got the flu, and even the water in Rochester, where my aunt lives, makes me nauseous. I might have trouble out in Africa someplace if I was throwing up all the time while trying to help poor people. Throwing up seems to be the one thing that stands between me and being* GREAT. *But I will find something great to be that doesn't upset my stomach because I am* VERY SMART *and because I promised President Kennedy. Ask not, etc. I have to stop writing now. I have to floss.*

ONE

Jessica ("Jessie") McGrath, the youngest woman ever to be appointed provost of an American college of more than 5,000 students, took a deep breath and pushed the scrambled eggs to the side of her plate, feeling a decidedly unpleasant taste creeping up the back of her throat. She swallowed, hard. Throwing up on the white linen tablecloth right after the Rev. Geoffrey Dinsdale of the theology department intoned "Bless this bread, O Lord!" would not get the annual Board of Trustees meeting off to a jolly start.

She stuffed half a banana muffin in her mouth and tried to avoid smelling the eggs. Scrambled eggs had made her want to barf ever since the day she found her then-husband, Herb, making love to an American Studies major in the midst of the breakfast crockery. They had been so overcome with passion that they hadn't even bothered to clear away the dishes, so they both had little yellow globules—flecked with bits of dill—clinging to their respective behinds. Jessie had behaved in a truly bizarre manner, probably because they were *her* eggs.

3

She had crawled out of bed early on a day when the wind-chill factor at Logan Airport registered thirty-seven below zero and, in a little wifely act of love, had made eggs just the way Herb liked them, scrambled in butter, no salt, and a half teaspoon of dill.

She had dashed off to school, got halfway there when she remembered she had forgotten some important papers, and returned to find the scene of sexual bliss in the kitchen. When she saw the egg fragments, a blood-red cloud of rage descended on her senses, and she found herself whipping the little yellow blobs off their asses with a dish towel, shrieking, "Don't you dare screw in my eggs! Don't you *dare!*"

The American Studies major ran screaming into the bathroom, certain she was about to be garroted by a madwoman, cut down in the prime of her intellectual life before she was able to finish her thesis on the use of clothing as a metaphor for class structure in the *oeuvre* of Tom Wolfe. Herb just stood there, stricken, goose bumps popping up along with the egg bits on his bare behind. She might have forgiven him, but in an orgy of confession he admitted that there had been a Medievalist, a documentary film major, a candidate for a degree in Black History, and a lecturer in third world ecosystems before the present entanglement. Jessie was stunned. She had never guessed. Herb was screwing his way through every academic discipline in the catalog, from Arabic 101 to Zoology seminar, and she hadn't even known. And she had loved him, that was the awful part. Really loved him.

"And now, the annual report from the treasurer," said J. Arthur Byron, president of the Board of Trustees, who also happened to be Jessie's prime catch. He was head of a Fortune 500 company, and a dozen universities had been after him for their boards. Jessie charmed him, twisted his arm, made friends with his wife. He had connections everywhere.

"Report for the current fiscal year," said the treasurer, and Jessie's eyes glazed over. She knew it all by heart. She didn't want to think about Herb, but the eggs stared up at her, a bitter reminder. How could she not have known? Everybody else did. He might as well have had sweatshirts made up with the names of his inamoratas on them, except they wouldn't have fit on a sweatshirt. You'd need a goddam three-story banner.

How could a woman with an IQ of 150 have been so stupid?

She had trusted him, poor simple fool. She still believed in a lot of things that other people had outgrown. It came from being a Girl Scout too long—eight years. It did something to her psyche. Every time she had stood and said solemnly, "On my honor . . . I will try . . . to do my duty to God and my country," she had meant the words from the very fiber of her beating little heart. Deep down she still believed that *Good Housekeeping* inspected every product before issuing its Seal of Approval. She had believed Walter Cronkite when he said, each evening, "And that's the way it is." She trusted people, that was it. Like Anne Frank, she had believed that people were good at heart, despite considerable evidence to the contrary. Herb shattered that trust, broke it into a million tiny glittering fragments.

"Scholarship saw a considerable rise during the fiscal year, and our goal this year is to increase it even further—"

It was not the sex, so much, it was the lies. He wove them like a busy little spider, a network of lies intricate as lace: tales of meetings, seminars, out-of-town colloquia. At least if it had been for a grand passion, she might have understood, but it was only a series of quickie screws. Each of them, she realized now, siphoned away from Herb the little energy he had for loving, and in the end there was no emotional current left for her. The web of lies edged her farther and farther to the periphery of his life with an almost casual cruelty. But the worst was the trust. She didn't want to accept the most cynical female wisdom about men. In her mother's generation it had been "Smile, wear white gloves, and get the house and the car and the savings account in your name so the son-of-a-bitch can't get his hands on them"; in hers, it was "They're all chauvinist piggies with pricks where their hearts ought to be, so fuck it, why not consider a lesbian?"

She would never be able to trust a man again, she thought, that was what Herb had done. *That* was what she couldn't forgive. When she heard that he didn't get tenure at Brandeis she went out and bought herself a bottle of champagne. She was going to send him a sympathy card, *Thinking of you in your hour of sorrow,* but that would be demeaning herself. He knew she knew, and that was enough.

"Our provost, Jessie McGrath, would like to introduce some-one to you now," J. Arthur Byron said, and Jessie's attention abruptly snapped back to the present. "As you know," he went on, "ROTC returned to the Kinsolving campus two years ago, and

5

despite some early misgivings, the program has been a splendid success."

Jessie straightened her skirt. She was wearing her trustees outfit, a gray herringbone suit with a green silk blouse. (She had ripped the bow off the blouse; bows were coy, and trustees hated coy.)

She rose and moved to the microphone, and she said, flashing her most disarming smile, "I can tell you, there was a time in my life when I never would have believed anyone who said I'd be introducing the head of ROTC at a breakfast meeting." There were chuckles around the room. Everybody knew about her background. "I was one of the people who had misgivings. But I'm delighted to say that Major Mark Claymore runs a program that is academically sound, and he has been most cooperative in every way. He has been a real addition to the Kinsolving community, and I would like him to say a few words to you. Ladies and gentlemen, Major Claymore."

The major rose and came to the microphone. Jessie had been careful to seat him next to J. Arthur Byron, who had gone in with the first wave at Normandy: Omaha Beach. They had been chatting away intently.

"I'm honored to be here this morning," said Mark Claymore, "and I welcome the warm words of our provost. I do feel myself to be a part of the Kinsolving community, and that's a special privilege for me."

Mark would acquit himself well, Jessie had no doubts about that. She looked up at him as he spoke, a tall man with a military bearing and curly dark hair flecked here and there with gray. Men did look so handsome in uniform. Take some schlemiel, get him a haircut, and put him in dress blues, and he looks like fucking Eisenhower. Maybe if they did away with uniforms, made soldiers dress like garbagemen, maybe peace might have a chance.

"One of the great benefits of the ROTC program," Mark was saying, "is that it brings young men and women of talent to Kinsolving, students who would otherwise not have had a chance to come here. I went through college on an ROTC scholarship myself, so I have a special commitment to this program—as does the U.S. Army, another institution of which I am proud to be a part."

He was laying it on thick and they were lapping it up. Mark Claymore had come as a pleasant surprise to Jessie. She had thought they would dispatch some minor-league fascist to run

6

Rotcy, a posturing imitation Patton or some dull crew-cut captain with a midwestern twang and a soft spot in his heart for Joe McCarthy. But Mark was not only very bright and a genuine war hero, he had an acerbic wit that amused her. She was surprised to discover that he was working on his doctorate in history.

"Military history?" she asked him. "Tactics and that sort of thing?"

"No, modern Asian history. Post–World War Two."

"The army lets you do that?"

"They unlock the stockade door so I can work on my thesis. After I clean my M-16."

"You know what I mean. I didn't think you had all that much choice."

"Don't you read our ads? 'Be All That You Can Be.' The New Army is a great place. Plenty of options."

"What happens if there's a war?"

"A lot of people will be pissed. We don't say anything about *war* in our ads. Our market research says war is a downer."

Jessie had made sure that Mark got a place on the Provost's Council, a group of faculty and administrators who met regularly to set policy for the college. More and more often she had been marching Mark off, in uniform, to public functions. Too many people—prospective donors and parents of students she wanted to recruit—still remembered the days when Kinsolving was competing with Boston University for the title of the Berkeley of the East. Kinsolving, much smaller than BU, had to be more bizarre to get noticed. When the *BU News* raised hackles attacking LBJ over Vietnam, the *Kinsolving Call* had to go it one better. And not even the *News*, with its talent for bad taste, could top the *Call*'s page-one photograph, a very clever composite that apparently showed Lyndon Baines Johnson performing an act of oral sex upon Col. Nguyen Cao Ky. When the Weathermen went berserk in Chicago, Kinsolving radicals had their own Day of Rage, tramping along chichi Newbury Street breaking windows. The proprietor of a unisex boutique threw himself in a frenzy upon a Marxist-Leninist of the Maoist persuasion and nearly bit his thumb off. In those days, a most interesting assortment of people could be found wandering the halls of Kinsolving dorms, day or night: black drug dealers in superfly hats, radical lesbians in combat boots, undercover narcs looking uncomfortable in their love beads, stoned-out flower children, and crew-cut members of

7

the Spartacus League. One day in 1970, Kinsolving Hall was the scene of what the *Boston Globe* called "the biggest drug bust in the East in 30 years."

Clearly, this image was not a good market prospect in the eighties. One of Jessie's great accomplishments as provost was to quiet the echoes of Kinsolving's radical past while at the same time preserving the spirit of inquiry and experimentation that the World Humanist Foundation had wanted to foster when it started the college back in the thirties. (The Humanists were a quasi-religious group who found the Unitarians just a tad too stuffy for their taste.) The new brochures that went out under Jessie's imprimatur featured pictures of successful alumni: a Pulitzer Prize–winning poet, the head of a million-dollar high-tech firm, a famous trial lawyer. The brochures did not mention the porn star, the assistant managing editor at the *Communist Worker,* or the cocaine king doing twenty years in Sing Sing. After all, even Harvard had graduates hiding out in Rio from the Organized Crime Task Force.

Mark Claymore had become a very useful part of Kinsolving's refurbished image. His very presence soothed anxious moms and dads at college fairs. His picture in the local papers, giving out ROTC scholarships, blurred the memory of the famous LBJ photo, now a collector's item. Jessie was not above using a decorated veteran to increase the flow of applications to Kinsolving, and Mark, aware of what she was doing, was willing to cooperate. (Except that he wouldn't wear his medals to college functions. "It's tacky," he said.) Soldiers, these days, were as PR conscious as anyone, stung by the notion that the volunteer army was the alternative to jail or the funny farm.

After Mark gave his talk, the meeting droned on. But there were no threats to resign, no acid barbs thrown across the room, no incipient revolts. All in all, it was one of the calmer sessions. In the past, Kinsolving trustees had been known to hurl both objects and death threats.

When the trustees had all been packed off to cabs, Jessie walked with Mark down Beacon Street, toward her office.

"Can you make Parents' Night next Saturday?" she asked him. "It's going to be in the Student Union."

"Yeah, I'll be there."

"I really do appreciate your showing up at all these things, Major. It's above and beyond the call."

8

"Ours is but to do or die. You can walk faster."

"Not with these heels."

"Don't slow down for me. I go pretty fast."

"Yes, you do, Mark. Most people don't even realize you have an artificial leg."

"I get around just fine," he said testily.

"That's what I said."

"I just don't like to be patronized."

"Oh, shit, Mark, I wasn't patronizing you. Come on, don't *you* get surly on me."

"I'm a Vietnam vet. You're lucky I'm only surly, not homicidal."

"You *are* in some mood today. For the record, I think the way we've treated the vets is crappy."

"This from the former coordinator of SDS?"

"Also for the record, I never called you guys baby killers. I just thought the war was wrong."

" 'Hey, hey, LBJ, how many kids did you kill today?' "

"It worked. We got out. Or maybe you'd have been happier if we'd stayed."

"I think," he said, "we ought to continue this another time. I have a class."

"You're on. But not Saturday night. At Parents' Night, we're best buddies."

"*Oui, mon général.* You have but to command."

"Oh, fuck off, Mark."

He chuckled. "That's what I like about you, Jessie, you stand on ceremony."

"It's at eight on Saturday. Wear just one *little* medal. They photograph so nice."

"Sure. I'll wear my Vietnam Veterans National Appreciation medal."

"What's that?"

"It's a big gold screw."

She laughed. "OK, I get the message. See you Saturday."

She crossed the street to go to her office and Mark kept walking to the T-station, where he rode a couple of stops to the College of Liberal Arts building at BU. It was an interesting session of his seminar on modern China, on the events leading up to the Cultural Revolution. He was back in his office after lunch, trying to make inroads on a sea of paperwork. That was the only damn problem with the job, the paperwork—reams of it—and it was not his forte. He put it off too long and it piled up. What he did like was teaching his course in American military history and talking to students and advising them on their careers. That part of the job he found very satisfying.

It was dark by the time he was through, but the evening was pleasant, with a lingering hint of summer still hanging in the air. He walked back to his apartment, even though he could feel a slight chafing at the top of his thigh. He'd have to take care of that, fast, so it wouldn't turn into a sore. He didn't like being without the leg for any period of time. With the leg, he looked just like everybody else.

He walked into the apartment, the first floor of a brownstone owned by the college, grabbed a beer from the fridge, slipped out of his trousers. Then he unstrapped his left leg and flopped down in the chair. He aimed the channel gun at the TV, and it flickered to life. Robert Ryan crept out from behind a tree and waded a few feet through the green muck of New Guinea.

"War movie," he said. "Oh, what the fuck."

War movies amused him. They were so unreal. They never showed the boredom, the endless hours that grated on your nerves like the drip of water from a faucet. Of course it wouldn't be boffo box office, Robert Ryan and John Wayne just sitting there, scratching their asses, for hours in Technicolor.

He took a swig of beer. Why had he started in on Jessie McGrath this morning? She had done a lot for him—got him this apartment, the classiest place he had ever lived. He liked her. She had a fast mouth and could give him the needle right back when he gave it to her. She was a smart cookie. Smart and pretty and always in control. He hadn't known many women like that, and he decided he liked the type. Clingy broads depressed him. He had a theory that smart, pretty women who were always in control had untrammeled depths of passion locked away inside, and the right man could set them to blazing like tracer bullets in the night.

There was a male fantasy for you. Guess who, boys and girls, is the right man? You guessed it, Mark Claymore and his magic penis, the key to never-before-imagined heights of sexual delight. Who knew, maybe she had a thing for amputees. There were women like that. There was Helen, whom he dated for a while after the divorce, who used to kiss and fondle his stump with an

10

ardor that made him uncomfortable. He finally glommed on to the fact that it was the abnormality she dug, not him; *he* was the appendage. Helen just grooved on guys with parts missing. After him, she went on to a double amputee. Good old Helen. She'd be in hog heaven if she met a guy who'd had a head transplant.

But maybe it would have been better if Gerry, his wife, had been more like Helen. They had become a ménage à trois: Mark, Gerry, and the leg that wasn't there. She referred to the stump as "it," as if it had a life of its own. He was careful to keep "it" covered when they made love, but Gerry always knew it was there, like some sort of Peeping Tom, which made her nervous. Which made him impotent. Their sex life just faded away, like MacArthur's old soldier. Now and then they screwed, he out of desperation, she out of duty; that was about it.

The marriage dragged on for five years, until it just stopped one night, when he said to her, "Ger, what's the point? What the hell's the point?" He had a crazy hope that she would run to him and declare her undying love and they would make a new start, but she just sighed, a long deep melancholy sigh, and said, "You're right. What's the point?"

For about a year he went around in something like a trance. He had never really thought she'd leave. And she wouldn't have, if he hadn't given her the out. For five years she had kept at it, making the best of a bad bargain.

She had married a healthy farm boy, and he went off to soldier, but he came back as a man with moods and angers and a leg cut off just above the knee. The leg that wasn't there was a presence, like a crazy aunt locked in a closet.

He took a swig of beer and thought about her, which he did less and less often these days. It was a long time ago. When he did think of her, it was most often of her hands, which were small, but soft and well formed. She was vain about them. She often wore rubber gloves filled with Vaseline to keep them soft. He loved it when she stroked his forehead with her cool, soft hands. It helped him sleep, especially in the early days when the pain was so often there.

After the divorce, he went to prostitutes for a while. He stopped worrying about being impotent, but it damaged his self-esteem, paying for sex. The prostitutes made him sad. Some just went through the motions, and some tried to put on a good act. He didn't think they were dirty, like some men did. Growing up on a farm, he came early to the knowledge that sex was something natural. The girls sensed his acceptance, and they were nice to him. One young whore moved him especially, and with her he tried to be a lover. He wanted to hold her, to *reach* her. But afterward, when he wanted to cuddle with her, she drew away.

"No, you don't get that," she said. "You get all of this"—she gestured to her body, as if it were a separate thing—"but you don't get *me*."

"I don't want you to be just a piece of meat. I want you to be a person."

"Look, you're a nice guy, so I'll be honest with you. That's the worst thing for me. On the outside, I'm class merchandise. You like it, you buy it. If it's meat, OK. But you get to *me* and I'm not safe. Understand?"

He nodded. She just wanted to get out whole, someday. Like him. They had both sold their bodies for other people's purposes, and all they wanted to do was keep their heads down, avoid the incoming, and get out whole. He wished her luck.

After that, he gave up prostitutes. There had been other women, but it never worked. It went OK for a time, and then he would start to feel like he was in a closet, trying to suck air. He hated it when they pitied him, and when they said it didn't matter, he didn't believe them. He moved on.

He leaned back and watched Robert Ryan garrote a Jap. *Jap*. That was the word in that war. In his it was *slopes, dinks*. In Korea, *gooks*. Such lovely names for Orientals. He watched the Jap die and tried not to think about Jessie McGrath. Unsuccessfully.

He had peculiar fantasies about her, not at all like the sweaty ram-it-in scenario that was his usual thing. He saw her in a long white dress, her dark curly hair loose around her face, her bare shoulders as pale as the dress. He imagined kissing her—that was all—very gently for a long time, and her mouth was soft and sweet and tasted faintly of grapes. He snorted. She was a libber, a sixties radical; how she would laugh if she knew about his fantasy. Lord, she had probably done it six ways to Sunday; it was a wild time, then. He remembered sitting under a tree in 'Nam, reading *Newsweek*, picturing them, all the antiwar activists, fucking like rabbits, doing it in great tangled piles of flesh, and he wanted to toss a grenade at them and blow the whole pile to smithereens.

A Jap stuck his bayonet in Robert Ryan and Ryan started to

12

die, slowly, as Mark watched, and at the same time Jessie Mc-Grath's mouth still tasted sweet, of grapes, and he was kissing her, his tongue deep in her mouth, his body against hers, and he found, to his amazement, that his eyes were filled with tears.

Robert Ryan finally died and the violins played. And played.

"Oh, fuck," Mark Claymore said.

FROM JESSIE'S DIARY
(SOPHOMORE YEAR, 1969)

Dear Diary: Well, I did it. **Finally.** *I am not a virgin anymore.*

I was the only person on my whole floor at BU who was a virgin. That is like being the only kid in school who has to wear leggings or being the only girl who goes to the junior prom with her brother. My best friend and roommate, Andrea Margolis, lost her virginity in high school. I asked her how it was and she said OK but not great because high school boys don't know shit. Andrea told me to find an older, more experienced man to be the first.

"Just where do I find this person, Andrea?"

"You could find a professor."

"A professor! Andrea, that would be like—Doing It with a priest!"

"Jessie, even a high school boy would be better than a priest. And professors do not take sacred vows that they won't Do It."

"My professors are all so old they probably don't do it anymore anyhow."

"Men do it till they die, Jessie. I heard my mother say to her

14

friend Belle, 'If he thinks I am going to spread my legs, at my age, every time he gets his putz in an uproar, he has another think coming.'"

"Your mother doesn't like sex?"

"I think my father ought to make her pay for it. If she had to use her credit card to get it, she'd be at him night and day."

"I think I will want to have sex till I'm ninety."

"How do you know? You're a virgin."

"Don't remind me."

"It is sort of embarrassing, rooming with a virgin, Jessie. But it could be worse. You could be black."

"Andrea!" I said.

"I'm kidding, Jess. Jeez, where's your sense of humor?"

"Virgins don't have one. We just walk around thinking pure thoughts."

Andrea looked puzzled. "What's a pure thought?"

"Oh, you can think about martyrs or about Christ getting nailed to the cross."

"That's sick."

Andrea doesn't understand about Catholics. "Sure, it's sick, but it's not dirty. That's what's important."

"Thank God I'm Jewish," Andrea said. "When we want to think nice thoughts, we think about food. Bagels and cream cheese, noodle kugel, hot pastrami—"

"Andrea," I said.

"What?"

"Let's go eat."

But I finally did find somebody, Jeffrey Milliken, a junior. He's against the war so his politics are OK and he said he'd done it before. I pressed him on that point, and he swore on a stack of Bibles that he had.

So we went to his room and we started and it was neat for a while but Jeffrey was hot to trot real soon, and I wasn't ready for the big event that fast. I mean, I'd waited my whole life for this, and Jeffrey was just fitting me in before a chemistry exam.

But he was pretty nice, and he did try to make it good. But I don't think he had done it all that much because he fumbled more than the Patriots on a Sunday afternoon. I was prepared, I'd sort of stretched myself out with two fingers, which I'd read about in Cosmo, *because for sure That Cosmopolitan Girl does not want to shriek in pain when she flies off to Acapulco with her boss for a weekend of fantastic sex. Jeffrey had some trouble getting it in, though, and I couldn't concentrate on ecstasy when I was worried that my first Big Experience would be a flop and I'd have to go back to stretching, which is more boring than sit-ups.*

Then all of a sudden it was over and Jeffrey was looking all smug and he asked if the earth trembled. Now, that is very Harry High School; for chrissake, you are not supposed to ask. *But he looked so expectant, sort of like old Snapper does when he wants a Milk Bone, so I lied and said, "Yeah, it did a little." Then I said "thanks" and he said, "Sure, any time," and went off to his exam. And that was it. It is not the way it happens in novels. When the heroine lets the hero make love to her he is so awestruck that he turns into Lord Byron. "My darling, I will love you until the stars turn to dust," blather, blather, blather. OK, I didn't expect Jeffrey to gush, but "Sure, any time"? And when he saw me at dinner he asked if he could have my french fries because he knows I hate the school french fries.*

Andrea thinks I am making too big an issue out of this, and it's because I am—I mean, I was—a virgin. Next time, she says, it will be no big deal, it will be like brushing my teeth.

Oh, shit.

I want it to be a big deal. I want to have a tragic romance, I want a man to want to die because he can't have me, I want to meet in forbidden trysts on the moors, I want a lover to rip my clothes off in desperate passion, I want to leave deep, passionate claw marks on his bare back with my ruby red nails.

I do not think Jeffrey is quite up to this. I should have known. Chemistry majors lack a certain je ne sais quoi.

I think I will check out the English department.

TWO

"I saw you with what's-his-name, the major," Grace Darlington said. Grace was a professor in the classics department, the author of a book on female Celtic myths, and she had asked Jessie to share her apartment when the marriage to Herb broke up. "God, uniforms do turn me on. I wonder if Sylvia Plath was right. Every woman adores a fascist." Grace put the kettle on for tea.

"Sylvia Plath was a manic-depressive who killed herself. Not exactly the voice of Womanhood. Besides, Mark is not a fascist. He's a nice man, actually."

"A nice ass, have you noticed? And shoulders. No gut. I wonder how he is in the sack."

"I don't think he's your type."

"Why not? With a body like that, who cares about his politics?"

"He's only got one leg."

"What?" Grace nearly lost her grip on the box of orange pekoe.

"He's an amputee. Vietnam."

"Oh, God, thank heavens you told me. If I put my hand on his knee and it was *plastic,* I'd faint."

Jessie looked at her roommate. "You're serious?"

"Oh, yes. I can't bear to think of things like that. Losing a leg—ugh, I get goose bumps just thinking about it. Don't you?"

"No. Most of the time I don't even think of Mark as handicapped. Do you know, he even skis? It's amazing."

"Jess, could we not talk about this anymore? I feel nauseous."

"You're serious, aren't you?"

"I was a Candy Striper once. A lady burst a stitch and bled on the sheets. I just stood there and screamed. They fired me. Said I was not good for morale. Hey, I have a man I want you to meet."

"No thanks."

"So be a nun, see if I care."

"Oh, come on, I go out."

"The last man, Jess, was so old that he drank with U. S. Grant. You need to get laid, that's what you need. Lots of horny students around, with nice little buns."

"Do you know what the AAUP recommends for lady provosts who feel up nice little buns?"

"Boiling oil in the Student Union?"

"Just for starters."

"Men do it all the time."

"Yeah, well if *I* catch them, I light the oil. Universities have looked the other way at sexual harassment for too damn long."

"You're changing the subject, Jessie. Not every man is like Herb, you know. You're still gun-shy."

"I suppose. But sleeping around isn't my style. I went through that phase ten years ago."

Grace sighed, a long, deep, philosophical sigh. It was what they talked about, much of the time. As if their errant relationships with men could be cured by the balm of honey and orange pekoe.

"I'm thinking of changing my life-style. AIDS is so unchic."

"I've gotten to the point where I'm comfortable with just me," Jessie said. "It's finally OK that I'm not part of a matched set. Took me a hell of a long time."

"So it's the perfect time to plunge in again." Grace was an incurable optimist, despite a considerable history with disastrous men.

"No, I have to be careful. Men are like amoebas. They

18

swallow you up. You're nothing but a big bulge in their belly, if you aren't careful."

"There's a colorful metaphor."

"When Herb left me, I felt like nothing. Worthless. Here I was, the provost of a college, I'd run my own lobbying firm, I'd been an organizer against the war, I spent all this time in consciousness-raising, but I fell apart because a man didn't want me."

"An old story, Jess." Grace handed her a cup of tea.

"I just felt so obliterated. Alone, I was nobody. And I thought I was liberated."

"We all bought it, kiddo." She laughed. "When I was a kid, I remember my mother had a copy of *Ladies' Home Journal*. It had a self-help course on 'How to Be Marriageable.' You had to remake yourself, totally, to get a man. Because without one, you were worse than dead."

"It was such a struggle to get where I am now, Grace. Not needing approval all the time."

"It's easy to change up here"—Grace pointed to her head—"but not so easy in the gut. We're told from day one that we're nothing without a man. Of course we carry it around inside us, that idea."

She had stomped it out, Jessie thought. Crushed its head, like the Virgin Mary did to the snake. Or had she? That niggling doubt surfaced whenever a man came into the picture.

"Prince Charming comes along," she said, "and *zap!* I turn into a doormat. Some Fairy Godmother *I* have."

"But you don't have to stay alone, Jess. You don't have to get back in the same bind with a man."

"Don't I? Don't we all make the same mistakes all over again?"

"Sometimes. But we don't have to." They were quiet for a minute, and then Grace said, "You know, I'm starting to think about babies. I really think I want some."

"Some? How many did you have in mind?"

"Oh, I don't know. A couple. I've been looking at men lately, trying to picture them changing diapers. I used to just picture them without any clothes on."

"A naked man changing diapers? That's kinky, Grace, even for you."

"Don't you ever think about it, Jess? Kids, I mean, not naked men."

"Oh, sure, who doesn't? But I'm not going to go out and get

19

in a lousy relationship so I can have kids who will be miserable."

"It's too bad virgin births went out of style. It would save a lot of trouble."

"Grace, God has to get you pregnant for a virgin birth. It's not a do-it-yourself thing."

"I wonder if God has herpes."

"Of course She doesn't."

"Oh, good, Jess. *Very* good."

Jessie went into the bathroom, slipped out of her clothes, and stepped into the shower. So Grace was thinking about babies. Grace, the original free spirit! Good Lord, it seemed like everybody was thinking about babies these days.

She and Herb had decided no babies; they had their work and each other. (Herb, as it turned out, had considerably more.) It had sounded right to Jessie at the time, but in retrospect she realized that Herb just didn't want the competition. If there was love and pampering to be handed out, Herb wanted all of it.

There always seemed to be plenty of time, anyhow. But now she was facing a high canyon wall with the number 40 etched on it, only four years away. Soon it would be too late for children. When she was much younger, she had just assumed she would have children one day, and then there was Herb, and he made it sound so logical not to have them that she had to agree. She was two separate people in her years with Herb. There was the dynamic young organizer and executive, a rising star in academia, confident, a leader. And then there was this other person, Herb's wife, who could only say yes-yes-yes when Herb said he wanted to eat Chinese or go to the Vineyard for vacation or not have babies.

Jessie rubbed a handful of shampoo lather into her scalp with a vengeance. Superwoman and Superwimp, in the same body. No more. At long last she was comfortable with who she was, and with all the Jessies who had gone before. There were a few of them.

At eleven, lost in the romance of Catholicism, she had decided to become a saint. She put a plaster statue of the Blessed Mother on her night table and knelt and prayed an hour every night, the hardwood floor making little dents in her knees where the cracks were. Her mother got very upset at her.

"Jessie? Jessica Elizabeth, what are you doing in there?"

"I'm still praying, Ma."

"Jessie, you've been praying too long. Do your homework."

"It's important to pray. I may be saving lots of souls."

20

"Enough souls. There's already a line for heaven. Give God a rest."

"Ten more minutes. Then I will."

Being martyred made you a saint automatically, but to achieve that status, somebody had to kill you when you refused to deny your faith. She prayed to the Virgin to send her someone to kill her, but fast, so it wouldn't hurt much. A saint was a saint, after all. You got the title whether you were sent to your reward with one quick pang or suffered a real lot. Being shot was quick. She decided to get shot for God.

But who would do it? The Baptists up the street? She looked for signs of hatred of Catholics when she delivered their afternoon paper, but they only smiled and gave her a nice tip and never tried to martyr her.

The Communists? But the Russians might just decide to drop the bomb, and being blasted to smithereens—along with Protestants and atheists—probably wasn't a legitimate martyrdom.

Sainthood palled at the end of that year. Then there was her veterinarian phase. And then, of course, she decided on greatness. Going to Boston University proved to be the real turning point. She lost her faith freshman year, her virginity as a sophomore, and by the time she was a junior she was deeply involved in the antiwar movement. She knew early on that the war was wrong; knew what Johnson and McNamara and Rusk took a long time to understand, that the blood of the young men who sat beside her in classes was not meant to be drained off into the swamps of Southeast Asia, in a war most Americans didn't understand. She wasn't a pacifist; she believed in just wars. She was not a Marxist or a Yippie, and she didn't think Ho Chi Minh was a saint. She had a very clear head (once she got over her infatuation with martyrdom), and she felt there was a great moral choice to be made by her generation over Vietnam, and she wanted to be part of that choice. She was proud of her role in the movement, always would be, and she made no apologies. Interviewed for the provost's job, she didn't pull any punches when the chairman of the search committee asked her, "Ms. McGrath, you were arrested in Washington at a peace demonstration, is that correct?"

"Yes, at the Mayday demonstration. And once in Boston. Both times I was peacefully demonstrating. I believe both arrests were illegal."

"So you don't regret your criminal act?"

"No more than the Sons of Liberty regretted throwing tea in the harbor. I believe the war was a misguided adventure, and I will always be glad I spoke out against it. It was my duty as a citizen."

She thought she had blown the interview with that comment. She figured she was a long shot, anyhow. Her background wasn't academic. At the time she was director of a lobbying group called A Common Share that pressed for legislation for social change, and the nibble from Kinsolving came out of the blue. She was astonished when they offered her the job but was quick to accept. The idea of helping to shape the direction of a college appealed to her, and she had a Master's in political science by then, and a knack for administration.

She was appalled to find, when she took the job, that the college finances were a mess. The president, a pleasant but ineffectual man, had let everything slide. Jessie dug in and cleaned up the mess, and Kinsolving turned the corner. As long as the World Humanists kept the tap open, Kinsolving would survive, even with hard times for colleges ahead. Jessie made Kinsolving more marketable by putting in trendy courses in computers and TV production, without watering down the liberal arts program or gutting the pioneering programs in Black History, Women's Studies, and Ethnic Studies. Lobbying had taught her a lot about the art of leadership—how to charm, wheedle, be sympathetic, and twist arms when they had to be twisted. And she liked it. She liked making things run.

She stepped out of the shower, slapped some Jean Naté bath lotion on her body, and toweled off. She found herself thinking, inexplicably, about Mark Claymore. Standing next to him at Parents' Night, she had thought, suddenly, that he had the kind of face women love to touch—a sensitive mouth, full lips (sign of a passionate nature; Marlon Brando had them), and while he was clean-shaven, there was a hint of five o'clock shadow that she found appealing. She loved the look of a man who needed a shave—it was so *male*. (Except on Richard Nixon; on him it was just tacky.) She was sure, with his heavy beard, that he had a hairy chest, another turn-on. What was this thing she had with hair? Body hair had been a big issue in the women's movement for a while. Some people said real women had to be hairy, not plastic like Barbie. And men had lots of hair, beards, ponytails. Crew cuts were for fascists.

Mark was different from most of the men she had known. Under the patina of sophistication, the edges of the Maryland farm boy sometimes poked through. She imagined him as a teenager, lanky and rawboned, working on the engine of his father's truck, his dark hair curling damply on his forehead, the grease ingrained in the whorls of his fingers.

She had the sense that there were emotions in him that he rarely let surface. Anger was there, certainly; it flared, sometimes, unexpected as heat lightning, but it vanished. And it was often laced with wit. Sometimes, barely perceptible, there was a flicker of pain, but only when he was tired. It came and went so quickly she wondered if she just imagined it. He let you know, right off, that he could do anything anyone else could do, and probably better. What did it cost him, she wondered, to be an Iron Man?

Standing close to him, her shoulder next to his, she had begun to tremble, and the desire to touch his face—trace the outline of his lips, run her fingers down the straight blade of his nose—had been acutely visceral. It took her by surprise. When Herb left, she had turned that part of her life off with a determined twist of the tap. She had wondered when it would return. Apparently, now it had.

She slipped into her nightgown and chuckled at the scenario in her head: the Kinsolving College provost feeling up the head of ROTC over the punch bowl, in full view of the mommies and daddies. Given its artistic traditions, the *Kinsolving Call* would have a field day. She shuddered to think what the editorial board would come up with by way of illustration. One front-page blow job was quite enough, thank you.

She went into the bedroom, slid into bed, and pulled up the covers. She closed her eyes and there he was again, stripped to the waist, working on an engine—a teenager no longer—a faint sheen of sweat forming on the knotted muscles in his back, glistening lightly on the mat of hair on his chest, thick, dark curly hair—what the hell was this hair business anyhow?

She sighed and turned over. No point in thinking about Mark Claymore. He was the last man on earth she ought to get involved with. No danger of that, of course. No way was Mark going to cozy up to anyone who used to chant, "Hey, hey, LBJ, how many kids did you kill today?"

No way at all.

FROM JESSIE'S DIARY
(SOPHOMORE YEAR)

Dear Diary: I had a long talk with Andrea today, about not being a virgin.

"Andrea," I said, "I have been a non-virgin for two weeks, and I'm not any different."

"What do you mean?" she asked me.

"Well, I thought that after you Did It, you were very sophisticated. You got rid of all these moony romantic adolescent thoughts."

"Such as?"

"Would you die for love?" I asked her.

"Oh, Jessie, for heaven's sake, of course not."

"I didn't think so."

"Jess, nobody dies for love anymore, that went out with Tolstoy. These days, people get depressed for a couple of days and take a Valium; that's about it."

"I would die for love," I said. "If I was really, passionately in love with somebody, I would die for him."

"Would you die for Jeffrey?"

24

"Jeffrey? Oh, shit, no. I'd just give him my french fries. I'm not in love with Jeffrey."

"So who would you die for?" Andrea wanted to know.

"How do I know? Somebody I haven't met yet, that I will be passionately in love with."

"And why would you have to die for him, whoever he is?"

"Who knows? Maybe he's Jewish and his mother would strangle me, for being a shiksa."

"Jessie, I think you have a morbid streak," Andrea said, with a sigh.

She was right. "It's because I'm Irish. We're always morbid about love. A happy ending to an Irish love story is when everybody dies."

"What's a sad story?"

"Only one lover dies and the other one goes into a convent. And cries for ninety years."

"Jess, didn't you ever read any stories that ended, 'And they all lived happily ever after'?"

"I never believed them. I knew Cinderella got TB and died young. Rapunzel was sold into white slavery. Snow White got brain damage from a bad fall."

"Jessie, maybe you ought to go out and get laid again. Get rid of those dumb ideas about love."

"What is love, Andrea?" I asked her.

"Oy!"

"If it isn't dying for someone, what is it?"

"Will you stop with the dying business, Jess? Love is not terminal. Whatever it is, you don't have to do it in a fucking shroud." Andrea was annoyed, I could tell.

"I don't want love to be just sacking out in some guy's pad. Just doing it and saying 'See ya.'"

"That is sex, not love," she said.

"Well," I said, "there has to be some happy medium between throwing yourself in front of a train for love and screwing some guy just because he's on your floor."

"The guys on this floor, I think I'd take the train. It would be long and slow and horribly repulsive."

"Getting hit by a train?"

25

"No. Sex with the guys on this floor."

"I can see, Andrea," I told her, "that you are going to be no help."

"Jess, what the fuck do I know about love?" she said crossly. "I've been to bed with three guys. One was scared shitless, the other was drunk, and the third one said he loved me but he got mono and was sent home to New Jersey."

"Maybe I ought to ask Talia," I said.

"Talia has decided to be gay."

"She has? Why?"

"Talia is very radical chic, Jess. It's chic to be a lesbian. Everybody's doing it."

"I don't think I will," I said. "I'm having trouble enough with not being a virgin. I don't think I could handle being a lesbian too. I think I'd just like to meet one man I could love forever and ever."

"I think that's ambitious," Andrea said. "How about one you can love until senior year?"

"See, that's just what love is today. If a couple lasts three semesters, people think they are Heloise and Abelard."

"Who?"

"Great Catholic lovers."

"I never heard of them," Andrea said.

"They were madly in love. He got himself castrated to stay a monk and she went to a convent."

"Oh, my God, Jess, that's awful!" she said, making a face.

"It's more romantic than 'Your place or mine?' A great, doomed love."

"Jess, do not tell that story to guys, unless you want to go to a convent too. Guys do not think castration is romantic. It makes them nervous."

"Oh, Andrea, I want to have a flaming, passionate love affair, but the guys I meet just want a joint and a fuck. I think I was born in the wrong century."

"In any other century, Jessie," Andrea said severely, "you couldn't vote or own property. You would be chattel."

"Yeah, that would really suck, wouldn't it."

"You bet!"

26

"But there must be guys around, Andrea," I said, "who want to fall in love, not just screw."

"Yeah," she said, "and they're all twelve years old. Face it, Jessie, romance is dead. Fucking is where it's at. The sexual revolution is on."

Oh, Dear Diary, I am afraid she's right! If Camille were alive today, on her deathbed, between coughs, she'd say to Armand, "Hey, time for one great fuck before I croak." Liz would write to Robert Browning, "How do I love thee? Let me count the ways: On top, missionary, sideways, sixty-nine, French."

Dear Diary, I have this great big well of love inside me, I know I do, it's just sloshing around there, not being used. There's enough of it to last a lifetime. As much as Saudi Arabia has oil. But I am afraid nobody will want it, Dear Diary. All this screwing around everybody's doing, it's like musical chairs, you don't get to rest for very long before it's up and at it again. I don't think people get to know other people, really. I mean, what will Jeffrey think about me in years to come? He said I had great boobs. There will be a little memory cell in his brain marked Jessica McGrath: French fries, boobs, carbon molecules. That's it. Oh, Dear Diary, what if nobody wants the love I have to give, and it just stays there forever, a wasted natural resource? I think a terrible doomed love would be better than a lot of quick fucks where two souls never touch, never meld, only pass like two ships in the night. But I will wait, dear diary. Somewhere, someday, I will find a man who can love me the way I can love him. It may take a long, long time. But I will find him, someday. I will. I know it. I hope. Maybe. Well, at least there's a shot.

THREE

Mark leaned back in his chair, in his office in the Arts and Sciences building, and glanced at the pictures on his wall. There was Gavin, his idea of what a general should be. Gavin, wearing his stars, jumped with his men into France, a real honest-to-God combat jump. And there was Ike, wearing five stars and his famous grin—Ike's picture hung there because he was a farm boy from Abilene. Westmoreland wasn't there. The stories that had filtered down about Westy had made Mark want to puke, stories about the general sitting in his tent in his undershorts, not wanting to ruin the crease in his trousers. In 'Nam, for chrissake! Fighting the last war, twenty years too late.

Mark had a firm sense of what he wanted in a general. He despised the technocrats, the trimmers, and the political schemers. A good leader had to have mud on his shoes. He had to understand what was happening at the operational level, where the dying went on. Wars were lost because people didn't sweat the details, and that led them to make small miscalculations, which

28

turned into bigger ones. Good generals weren't hard-charging bulls. They were foxes, crafty, sly, and with a gift for the unexpected. Westy, he thought, didn't make the grade.

He glanced at his watch. On Wednesdays he had office hours, to hand out handsome four-color brochures and to talk to prospective recruits. Business had been brisk lately, because Kinsolving, like all the other colleges in Boston, had just announced a tuition hike for next year.

There was a rap on the door and a young man stepped in. He was dressed in a suit and tie, his hair was neatly cut, and his face scrubbed and shining. An eighties student, dressed for success.

"Major Claymore?"

"Come on in. Can I help you?"

"I'd like to Be All That I Can Be. Great song. Great. Better than Lionel Richie for Pepsi, even."

"Uh—thank you. Can I answer any questions about the ROTC program on campus?"

"Yes, sir. Do you have stock options?"

"I beg your pardon?"

"There was a guy here last week from Xerox, and he said employees can buy stock, at good rates, after six months with the company. Does the army do that?"

"Well, the army doesn't actually give—stocks."

The boy's face clouded. "It doesn't?"

"No. The army is nonprofit."

"It is? Shit. Oh, excuse me, sir."

"But you can buy bonds."

The student seemed to brighten at this prospect. "Oh, that's good. What's the interest rate?"

"I'm not sure. About six percent maybe?"

"Six percent? I get ten on my mutual funds. I mean, six percent, sir, that sucks."

"Well, you could think of it as an investment in your country."

"I'm a business major, but my father thinks I should spend a couple of years in the army. He was in the army, and he says it made a man out of him."

"Well, that's probably true. It is a maturing experience," Mark said.

"Six percent. Couldn't the U.S. government do better? You can make a lot more on Krugerrands. My father has those."

29

"Krugerrands? You mean from South Africa?"

"Yeah, right, good investment, gold, my dad says."

"You don't care about apartheid?"

"Is that a multinational?"

"No, it's—ah—a system of racial segregation. In South Africa."

"Oh. That must be the stuff some kids are demonstrating against, right?"

"Right."

"I'm not interested in politics. It's boring. Sir, if I go into the army for a couple of years—well, I don't want to fight or anything. I'd like to learn some engineering, high-tech stuff."

"We do have a broad range of engineering programs, actually."

"Invading someplace like Grenada might be fun. But I don't want to get my ass shot off in Central America."

Mark cleared his throat and gave his standard answer. "I think it's rather unlikely that we will have combat troops in Central America. Not in the near future. But that's only a personal opinion."

"Could I get Heidelberg?" the boy asked. "I'd like that."

"There should be a good chance of getting Germany if you put in for it. We have a lot of troops there as part of our NATO commitment."

"Neat people, Germans. They make great cars. Do you have any color brochures? I'd like to show my father."

"Sure." Mark handed the student a stack of brochures showing men and women doing exciting things in the army. They were having such a wonderful time you knew perfectly well there wasn't a war on. "If you have any questions, feel free to give me a call. I'll be happy to explain the options to you."

"Thanks. I appreciate that, sir. Oh, by the way, what branch do you get to drive tanks in?"

"Armor. You'd be training in tanks the summer after your junior year. Probably at Fort Knox."

"We have tanks in Germany, right? Panzers?"

"Well, actually, the Panzers were German tanks. World War Two."

"But I saw a movie about this guy Rommel, on TV. He was on our side, wasn't he?"

"No. Erwin Rommel was a German general."

"But in the movie, he was real smart."

30

"He was. They called him the Desert Fox. A brilliant tactician."

"Yeah, that was the name of the movie. You're sure he wasn't on our side?"

"I'm sure."

"I guess you're right. It's been a couple of years since I saw the movie. Well, thanks a lot."

"Any time."

The student left and Mark sighed, a long, deep, martyred sigh. What in hell were they teaching kids today, anyhow? He looked up at Eisenhower and said, "What are you laughing about? If he *had* been on our side, North Africa would have been a breeze."

There was a whole lineup of students to see him, all very serious and interested in careers. Nobody wanted to be John Wayne. They asked about graduate degrees and computer science and even retirement. Patiently, Mark explained all the options. By the end of the day, he was fatigued, with an ache through his back and shoulders. All the talking was more wearing than physical activity.

He felt better after he had worked out for half an hour with his weights, and then he debated what to do about dinner. He had gotten to be quite a good cook, out of necessity, but tonight he thought he'd just throw some frozen fried chicken in the micro-wave. The chicken wasn't half bad, and he had a lot of reading to do for his seminar. They were well into the Cultural Revolution now, a strange and ferocious time in modern China.

He relaxed, had a beer while the microwave was zapping the chicken with death rays, whatever the hell it did, and looked around, with pleasure, at his apartment. It was his taste, completely. There were several very good Japanese prints, one of them quite old, in bamboo frames, several pieces of Thai art, an Oriental rug. Japan had captivated him, on his first leave from 'Nam. He loved Japanese design and style, because it was so serene, precise, un-cluttered. His life, he thought, should be like that. He had bought a lot of stuff and shipped it home, but Gerry only tolerated it, stuck it away in places where it wouldn't be noticed. She liked frilly curtains and prints with tiny flowers in them and fake wildflowers— a decor he thought of as Country Phony. So he got to take all the stuff from Japan, after the divorce.

After 'Nam, he had started reading history because he

31

wanted to know what happened, how it had all gone wrong, step by bloody step. He *had* to know. It was his way of dealing with the experience, trying to make sense of it. If things made sense, you could control the future. If not, you were adrift in a sunless sea, with no compass points to steer by.

Reading had always been a refuge for him anyway. His mother, a former schoolteacher, taught him to read when he was three. He remembered the smell of her powder, a warm, sweet smell, as he nestled against her and proudly sounded out the words. She died when he was seven, hit by a drunken driver as she crossed the street to a local store to pick up some oleomargarine and a can of V-8. His father saw it happen; Mark remembered standing in the little Baptist church beside his father, while everybody sang "Amazing Grace" and his father cried, holding tightly to his hand. His mother had a friend named Grace, and he wondered why she was Amazing, and why they were singing about her, and when could his mother come home from heaven. But he saw his father crying, and he thought it best not to ask.

His mother's death shattered his father. He was a tall man, with a laugh that came from deep inside his belly. His father's laugh had been one of the familiar sounds of Mark's childhood. He heard it no more. His father seemed to be trying to resist some force that threatened to pull his being apart, scatter it to the ends of the earth. Holding himself in one piece claimed all his energy, and when he sat and stared into space, Mark knew he was replaying in his head what happened on the street that day.

Caring for a young son seemed beyond his capacity, so much of the time Mark ran free, roaming among the scrub pines that bordered the farmhouse on Maryland's Eastern Shore. It wasn't much of a farm, just a few chickens, but Mark loved to go in the henhouse early in the morning and put his hand under a hen's warm feathers and come out with an egg. It always seemed like a miracle. His father had been planning to raise chickens on a large scale, but after his wife died he lost heart, so he barely made ends meet by doing odd jobs and carpentry and hauling things with his pickup truck.

Mark read constantly, picking the volumes from his mother's library, and he would sit, in tattered jeans, his toes digging into the sandy soil, as he pored over the classics his mother collected: *Ivanhoe* and *Treasure Island* and *Jane Eyre* and *Wuthering Heights*. He identified with Heathcliff, the wild boy who never fit in

32

anywhere. Sometimes he got so lonely he would dig a hole in the warm sand, lie in it, and cover himself to the neck with sand, and for a while he would feel as safe and warm as he had in his mother's arms.

But he was not an unhappy child, all in all, because he was used to the outdoors and his own company and all his friends— the characters in the books he read. Solitude became a habit, and he was a loner in high school, not disliked but close to no one. He had no idea of what he would do with his life, but he had a vague idea that he would like to write a book one day, and he was quick with words. His English teacher, an ex-Marine, suggested he try for an ROTC scholarship. So Mark applied, and got a full scholarship to the University of Maryland, and went Infantry. He met Gerry in his junior year and loved her right away. She was warm and kind and bubbly, a nice contrast to his shyness. She chattered, like a little bird, and had those lovely soft hands. They were married, and after graduation they spent nine months at Fort Bragg before he shipped out to 'Nam. Gerry was distraught about it.

"Mark, isn't there any way you can get out of going?"

"It's only a year, Ger. Before you know it, I'll be back."

"You could be killed."

"I won't be. I know I won't. I promise."

"Why are we there, anyhow? What do we care about those people?"

"It's like dominoes. One country falls, then another. We have to be there."

He wasn't gung-ho, but going where the action was excited him. The lifers, most of them, wanted to get to 'Nam in the worst way. It was the only war they had. It was where you got promotions, climbed the career ladder. Mark wondered, too, if he could cut it. His father had been in the Pacific. He didn't talk about it much, but he was proud to have been part of the war. It was a rite of passage, for a man.

But Mark had been in 'Nam only a short while when he realized it was all wrong. Everybody lied. Body counts were the way you kept score, and you could keep the brass happy by keeping the figures high. So you exaggerated—ten bodies, twenty, and the guy above you added a few more, and it kept going that way, up the line, and the people at the top heard what they wanted to hear. Except if you believed the figures, we'd have wiped out half of Asia, never mind the VC.

A lie lived at the heart of it all, so things got corrupted, fast; it spread like bacteria in a carcass. The men didn't know what the hell they were doing there and they got strung out on dope, the people in the cities sold their sisters as whores, and a village culture that had existed for centuries was wrenched apart and uprooted. Mark saw the puzzled looks on the faces of the villagers—as the Americans set about winning hearts and minds—and he wondered if this was how the Indians had looked, as they were herded off to reservations. It seemed not to make much sense. No one was sweating the details. The politicians in the cities got greedy and used the Americans to hold on to power, and the Americans desperately tried to prop up one cardboard pol after another. Everybody jerked off everybody else. It was a mess.

So Mark decided the thing to do was to control what he could, and stay alive, and keep his men alive. If you narrowed the circle of things you cared about, you could have some control.

At first, 'Nam was just long stretches of boredom punctuated by terror. But he got the hang of it, developed an almost uncanny knowledge, in the field, of when something was going to happen. He had an edge over the city boys; all the years running free in the woods gave him an extra sense. It was as if mortal danger had a scent, like an oncoming storm, and made his nose twitch. He had an instinct about things; he sniffed out trip wires and trails that gave off the faint effluvia of ambush. The men in his outfit understood it, and he became their talisman. They died, of course, many of them, but not so many as in other units. He began to believe, too, in his power, after a while, though he tried not to. He wondered if he had been dipped, like Achilles, in some water that made him invulnerable. He had a wild urge, one day, when the streams of gunfire whipped through the tall grass like a scorpion's tail, to just stand up and defy the deadly hail of metal. He was convinced, for an instant, that the scorpion's tail would lash to the right and to the left of him but leave him untouched, the way the angel of death passed over the houses of the Israelites.

In the next instant he was shaking because he knew how totally crazy that was, how close he had come to being sawed in half. He tried to will the old terror to come, because the terror made you keep your ass down. When you lost the fear, you stepped over some invisible line, and then death owned you. It was only a matter of time.

He had seen men who had crossed it. They were too cheerful, the way a suicide acts when he has made up his mind, in the limbo of life before decided death. Such men were light as air; they seemed to say, What the fuck, I'm dead. And inevitably, they were. Being scared shitless at least meant you were alive.

Years after 'Nam, when he read S. L. A. Marshall, the historian, the man's words rang true. What men feared most, Marshall said, was killing. Breaking the primordial taboo, the sin of Cain, was an act drenched in terror. At first.

Mark saw, close up, the first man he knew he killed, a VC sniper. He had picked the man off, as he was running, with a burst of rifle fire. Standing over the dead man, he thought how quickly death claims dominion. The man seemed only a husk— silent, empty, and still. By then, Mark had seen enough of death so that it was no stranger, but now he stood over a man whose life he had claimed. He trembled, but he had no regrets; the man would have killed him, given the chance. But he felt no exhilaration either, and he breathed a sigh of relief. He had seen men who grew to like killing, who did it as casually as stepping on a bug.

He thought a lot, in 'Nam, about killing. From the dawn of time warriors killed for a reason—homeland, glory, God, king. Foolish reasons, often. But only murderers killed for sport. 'Nam made it so easy for men to murder: the body counts, the free-fire zones, the suspicion—no, the knowledge—that an eleven-year-old boy could kill you. If you killed from terror or duty or patriotism, you stayed human. Beyond that lay a circle of darkness, and the men who entered it were cut free, somehow, like astronauts floating in space. There were so many siren songs luring you into the darkness. When all the rules you lived by were abrogated, you had to call on something inside yourself to stay human, some inner homing device such as a bird uses to stay on course. The drugs, the heat, the paranoia all conspired, in 'Nam, to destroy a man's moral radar.

Some men touched the edges of the darkness and afterward went mad or repented or blasted their minds with drugs. Others sunk into it, silently. He wondered what would become of them. Some, addicted, would roam the world as mercenaries, killing until they in turn were killed. Others would be returned to the everyday world, where they would never fit. Like the wooden circles of a child's pound-a-peg, bent out of shape, they would never go back through the opening by which they had come. Death or madness would claim then, eventually—those who had the imagination to understand. The stupid ones, maybe they didn't feel much to start with, so they'd fit back through the openings just fine.

In 'Nam, time began to lose its meaning. He wondered if the rest of life were only a dream, if nothing existed except the choking heat and the high grass and the *whomp-whomp-whomp* of the helicopter blades. The Vietnamese lost their strangeness. At first they had seemed unreal, weird little people from an alien planet. But one time he was squatting down in a hooch, trying to talk to a village elder, surrounded by small, fine-boned golden people, when an American sergeant walked into the hooch. His first thought was, How big he is!

It was with a shock that Mark realized that the sergeant was not a big man at all: at least two inches shorter than himself. For a moment, he was seeing with *their* eyes.

And he didn't want to. He didn't want time to disappear, he didn't want to be drawn like some onrushing star into the black hole of Vietnam, because this world was full of death and the other one wasn't. He tried to keep that other world clear in his mind, but it kept fading away, like that town in the musical, what was its name? *Brigadoon.*

He chuckled to himself, quietly, and Wolfson, from Detroit, asked him what was so funny. Mark just shook his head. He had been thinking of Gene Kelly and Van Johnson wandering in the Scottish highlands and stumbling into a firefight, as the Mekong Delta suddenly materialized on a moor. He saw Kelly dancing with a chorus line of VC, tap-dancing through a rice paddy, and coming on Cyd Charisse in front of a hooch, wearing a dress slit up her thigh. Kelly did a buck-and-wing, and Cyd dropped a grenade down the back of his pants. Welcome to Vietnam, MGM, and kiss your ass goodbye.

So he floated toward the black hole, knowing it, not able to make the other world come clearer. The belief in his invulnerability tightened its hold on him. The gods did protect some men.

He only had two weeks left when it happened. He was walking across a field, Wolfson to his right, and then he was in the air, which was very odd, because the air was not where he was supposed to be. Then he was on the ground and his first thought

36

was, No, this can't happen to *me*. Something is all wrong. Then he noticed how blue the sky was, blue and fair. He stared at it.

Everything was strange, fragmented. His mind was working, but in a peculiar manner. It occurred to him that he had been damaged. He grabbed for his penis and said, "Thank you, God," when he found it was still there. Then he saw his leg. What was left of it.

"Shit," he said.

He must have been in shock, he figured out later, because at first he felt no pain, only a sensation like needles prickling all over. It was only when the medic crawled over to him that he felt it, a wall of pain like nothing he had ever known, and he screamed. The medic gave him a needle and things got fuzzy and the pain went someplace far away. In the chopper, he heard somebody say, "Poor bastard, the leg's fucking gone," and he thought, No, he has it all wrong. That certainly can't be me.

The ring of the telephone startled him, jolting him out of memory. He was disoriented for an instant, so real had been the memory of the heat, the sounds, of 'Nam. He reached over and picked up the phone. It was Jessie McGrath.

"Mark. I hope I'm not disturbing you."

"No. Not at all."

"Several faculty members have requested a special meeting of the Provost's Council tomorrow morning. Ten o'clock. Are you free?"

"Yeah. I have an appointment, but I can change it. What's up?"

"The usual tempest in a teapot. There seems to be a problem with the annual Kinsolving lecture. I think we have to talk about it."

"I'll be there. The conference room next to your office?"

"Right."

"Listen—"

"Yes?"

"How would you like to come to dinner some night. I cook great Chinese."

"You do? My, you do have unexpected talents, Major. I'd like that. When?"

"Thursday?"

"Thursday would be fine. Thank you."

He hung up the phone and sat still, astonished at himself. He didn't know he was going to ask her to dinner. Why in hell did he do that? What on earth would they have to say to each other once they got beyond the small talk? And if they did get beyond it, they might end up bludgeoning each other.

He picked up his book and started to read, about the Red Guards and their part in the revolution. But her voice, and his peculiar invitation, had unhinged his thoughts, and suddenly there she was, waiting for him, Jessie with the dark brown hair, floating like a zephyr on the summer air, only it was he who was floating, he had two legs and he was running the way he did as a kid along the sandy shores of Chesapeake Bay, graceful as a gull. It was deep summer, and there was a bedroom with a large overhead fan and white curtains and crisp sheets on the bed, and her skin was as pale as the sheets. She lay close to him, her hair smelling of sunlight, and his legs, both of them, were tanned and whole. They made love, slowly, beautifully, as if the whole thing had been choreographed by some artsy soft-focus porn director who said at press conferences, "I make *art,* not filth."

He had taken to observing her, lately, when she wasn't looking. He watched her as she walked, shoulders back, her jaw thrust out just a bit, like a kid determined to get someplace in a wind. She bit her nails; there were ragged, chewed places on the edges. She had a few freckles across her nose, and one front tooth had a little chip in it. Just under her chin was a small white scar; he had asked how she got it and she said, "Sliding into second for Immaculate Conception and not keeping my head down."

He liked the imperfections—the nails, the tooth, the scar. They made her vulnerable. Another image hove into his mind. They were walking by the edge of a windswept sea, the sky was as gray as nails, and he was wearing a greatcoat, with a cape, and he folded the cape around her like some huge dark bird, and she was safe inside it and he could feel the beating of her heart. Her lips tasted salty.

He groaned and got up to get another beer. His brain, obviously, was turning to mush. Time to go out and pick up a couple of copies of *Penthouse* and look at the crotch shots and jerk off to a little uncomplicated filth. Two bucks and you got T and A, nice and vulgar and perfect for self-abuse. No violins, just flesh, nipples, and pubic hair. He tried to focus the image in his mind, some broad with her legs spread wide, but it didn't work; all he saw was Jessie's face, close to his; she was wrapped in the coat, her heart beating, with the chipped tooth and the little white scar.

He popped open the tab of the beer can and took a swig. That's what came of reading *Wuthering Heights* at fifteen, when normal kids were drooling over Miss September, the sociology major from UCLA with the tits you would not believe. Some men were Hugh Hefner, and he was stuck with Heathcliff.

What the fuck.

FROM JESSIE'S DIARY
(SOPHOMORE YEAR)

Dear Diary: Oh, I am such a coward coward COWARD. *We talked about our fantasies in our women's group today, and I lied. Talia says that since the personal is political, our fantasies have to be politically correct. This is very hard. I mean, you can't control your fantasies, you take in so much garbage from the culture it just has to come out somewhere. Isn't it better to have regressive fantasies—which are harmless—than turn into Phyllis Schlafly, wearing your hair in a bun and trashing women because you're scared shitless to trash men? I mean, I bet that deep in his heart Stokely Carmichael wants to tap-dance. He doesn't* want *to want it, but I bet he just can't keep the tappy-tappy out of his toes, in his dreams. It is* not *his fault.*

That's what I should have said in group, but I lied. I made up this fantasy where I was carrying a whip and all these men were galley slaves and I was just whipping the crap out of them. Talia was very impressed. So was Andrea. Andrea said to me, "Jessie, that is a dynamite *fantasy. I could never have a fantasy like that. It's probably because you're Catholic."*

"Because I'm Catholic?"

"Oh, yeah. Tacking people to the cross and all that. Your religion is sort of bloody."

"Yours isn't? I mean, God sends frogs and blood and plague and then kills a lot of firstborns, and you folks celebrate with dinner?"

"You have a point. But whipping is not a big thing with Jewish-American princesses. We have sulking."

"Sulking?"

"A good sulk, Jess, is better than ground glass under the fingernails. Make people guilty and they're yours for life."

"I think the Jesuits said that too. Or maybe it was Sister Mary Immaculata."

And then I changed the subject. I didn't want to talk about fantasies anymore. How could I tell Andrea that I don't really think a lot about whipping people? Feeling up bloody welts seems sort of unsanitary. But I couldn't tell everybody, especially Talia, about my real fantasy, Rafe. Rafe is such an unliberated fantasy.

First of all the whole setting is really weird. I'm in this bar, someplace flat and dusty, and I have these enormous boobs and I'm wearing a white peasant blouse and a chintz skirt, the kind of stuff you make slipcovers out of. The boobs are great but my taste is vomitous. The blouse is Dacron, for chrissake. And then Rafe comes in with his gang.

Rafe is all in black leather, and he has these bedroom eyes. He has to be right out of The Wild One that I saw at Vicki's house on the "Late Show," when I was fourteen, which is a bad age to see Brando in black leather, your glands are too impressionable. He comes to this place where I'm the bar girl and he orders whiskey and I lean way over to let him see the whole vista—these boobs that look like silicone jobbies, but they're real.

Well, Rafe's eyes go right out of their sockets—boing-boing-boing—like Sylvester the cat's used to do when he was chasing Tweety—and he doesn't say a word, he just grabs me and kisses me hard. Rafe's body is all muscle; he has to spend half his life pumping iron, with a body like that. Without a word we walk out of the bar together, Rafe and me with his gang of bikies following, all of them mad with passion for me.

41

They don't really look like bikies, though, or smell like them. I mean, in real life, bikies have beer bellies and smell like old gyms and have the IQ's of Mr. Ed. If I went near a real bikie I'd spray myself with Lysol for weeks. Rafe's gang members are all built like the chorus in the American Ballet Theatre, muscular but lithe, and they smell like guys who shower every day with Lifebuoy but who've just worked up a nice little sweat. They're musky, but they don't stink, *for heaven's sake.*

Well, to make a long story short, we ride on the cycles for a while and then we go into this green glade and I Do It with all of them, and they're just mad with passion but they all know more than Dr. Kinsey, it's not wham-bam. I mean, this part is not too realistic. How many bikies have read up on clitoral orgasms?

So you see, how could I tell this to Talia, the most liberated person I know? A bikie fantasy; how regressive can you get? How in the hell do I make this fantasy correct? Is it possible?

Well, let's see. Maybe, after we do it, we can all sit with the Harley Davidsons in a circle, and I can read to them from Mary Wollstonecraft. Then Rafe can lecture them on social class and the patriarchy and they will become so liberated that they will roar through small towns, terrorizing citizens into signing a petition demanding an Equal Rights Amendment. On their jackets, their metal studs will spell out The vaginal orgasm is a myth.

Oh, Dear Diary, I feel so much better. I have a correct fantasy. See what a little imagination will do? I knew I could do it, because I have an IQ of 150.

I will tell Andrea; she will be just knocked over. I don't know about Talia. I think I will have to work up to that.

But I feel so much better. It really is important to take your fantasies in hand and make them correct. Talia was right.

The personal is political!

FOUR

Jake Siegel and Brian Kelly were known, in the halcyon days of the sixties, as the Gold Dust Twins. Only Abbie Hoffman and Jerry Rubin were better at grabbing headlines. Jake and Brian were the ones who put the huge papier-mâché head of Ho Chi Minh next to Teddy Roosevelt on Mount Rushmore, an engineering feat that the National Park Service hasn't figured out to this day. Dressed like Henry Kissinger and Alexander Haig, they tap-danced into the Senate chamber singing "Side by Side." They were on the cover of *Time* and *Rolling Stone* and were interviewed several times on the "Today" show.

Fame, alas, is fleeting, and most of the freshmen entering Kinsolving had never heard of the Gold Dust Twins; if pressed, they would have guessed it was a heavy metal band featured on MTV. Kinsolving, with its reputation for iconoclasm, had proved to be a haven, in the eighties, for many sixties radicals. Yale, after all, would hardly have welcomed two guys who danced naked—except for Nixon masks across their privates—in the streets of Miami during the Republican convention.

Jake and Brian had gone their separate ways as the seventies had rolled inexorably into the conservative eighties. Brian finished his PhD in political science and taught courses called "From Marx to Mao" and "The Counterculture." He wore jeans and love beads, and he still pulled his graying hair back into a ponytail (the same style he wore to chat with Hugh Downs on the "Today" show).

But Jake, always the first one of the twins to sniff the prevailing winds, was into success. His degree was from the BU School of Management, and he taught corporate strategy and management techniques. On weekends he ran success seminars, touting a mixture of pop psychology of the Be Your Own Best Friend variety, Japanese business philosophy, and a dash of est. Jake wore three-piece suits copied from Lee Iacocca, and his haircut was classic boardroom conservative, parted on the side and blow-dried to conceal an incipient bald spot.

Needless to say, these disparate life-styles frayed the edges of the twins' friendship. Brian said that Jake had sold out to corporate greed, and Jake decreed that Brian was still working out adolescent problems held over from toilet training. Both had been elected to the Provost's Council, which often proved wearying to Jessie. Their constant bickering could try the patience of a saint. On the other hand, they were both excellent teachers, and they were never dull.

"Hello, Brian," Jake said, waltzing into the conference room next to Jessie's office. "Great threads." He flipped Brian's African tribal beads. "Planning to buy Manhattan?"

"I wish I could look like you, Jake, but the Dress for Success boutique at Sears is too rich for my blood."

"The guy who's really chic," Jake said, pointing to Mark Claymore, "is him." Mark was wearing regulation green trousers with a black sweater and shoulder boards, the army's casual look. "The military style is in these days, Major; you're really hip."

"My tailor thanks you," Mark said.

As the other members of the council began to drift in—punctuality was not a Kinsolving tradition—Jake turned to his old friend and said, "Hey, Brian, guess who I saw last week? Ed Moscowitz."

"Molotov Moskowitz? My gosh, how is he? I remember the day he torched three cruisers in half an hour."

"Me too. Molotov was a fucking artist with a Coke bottle and a little gasoline."

"What's he doing?"

"Regional sales manager in Connecticut for Data General."

"Molotov with Data General? I can't believe it!"

"Yeah, makes you feel old, doesn't it? But he says he can still hit a moving target at fifty yards."

"Big talk."

"No, he says he practices." Jake grinned. "His neighbors in Greenwich get a little pissed, though."

As the last member of the council wandered in, Jessie took her seat at the head of the table. Coffee and Danish, served by her secretary, were waiting. In addition to Brian, Jake, and Mark, there were Liz Hailey, head of the Afro Program and the college's affirmative action officer, and Wendell Phelan from the classics department, whose pipe seemed a fixture between his teeth. Wendell's great disappointment in life was that he wasn't a Cambridge don—a difficult career goal to achieve when you are born in Paramus, New Jersey. Completing the group was Norman Wineberg, from chemistry.

As the council members slipped into their seats, Jessie said, "Wendell, since you asked for this meeting, I would appreciate it if you would explain the situation."

Wendell always needed a bit of stroking. He really was wonderful in his field, but when he felt the least bit neglected, he began to pout. He once pouted through three semesters of Chaucer. But Jessie had learned how to push his buttons: make him feel important, but never give him anything resembling real power. Real power made him depressed.

"It's the Kinsolving lecture," he said, "a tradition great with age. To see it demeaned is to see the past itself demeaned." Wendell always talked as if he *were* at Cambridge; nobody much minded.

"Wendell," Jake said, "the Kinsolving lecture got started the same year the Studebaker came out. We are not talking Magna Charta here."

Wendell turned on Jake, his eyes flashing. "Do you take anything seriously, Siegel? It's all a big joke to you, isn't it? Well, some of us on this faculty take our mission to educate the younger generation quite seriously indeed!"

45

"Jake is just joshing you, Wendell," Jessie said, kicking Jake under the table. "Please go on."

"The list of Kinsolving lecturers is a distinguished one," Wendell said. "We have had Margaret Mead, Benjamin Spock, Ralph Nader, Betty Friedan—"

"Tiny Tim, Gordon Liddy, and *Mr.* Spock," Jake continued. "Come on, Wendell, it's just a bunch of kids inviting somebody they want to hear."

Jessie said quickly, "This year the students have already invited the speaker and he has accepted, isn't that right, Wendell?"

"Yes, unfortunately."

"Who is it?" asked Brian. "If it's Prince, I will vomit."

"Could we make a rule, nobody with purple hair?" Jake said.

"This is serious!" Wendell sputtered.

"Who is it, Wendell?" Liz Hailey asked.

"It is Herman Mannering, the author of an odious tome called *The Good Life after Nuclear War.*"

"You're kidding," Liz said.

"I saw him on 'Good Morning, America,' " Norman Wineberg said. "His book is a huge bestseller."

"He's a survivalist," Brian Kelly said. "He's one of these nuts who says so what if New York and LA get blown up, we can all live happily in caves."

"Hardly one of the great thinkers of the Western world." Jake snorted.

"At least he's not a fascist, like the guy you had in your management seminar last week," Brian snapped at Jake.

"The Chairman of the Board of Baby Gro Products is not a fascist."

"He sells baby formula all over the third world, and mothers give up nursing to give their kids that crap. It kills babies."

"Oh, it doesn't kill them. Only stunts their growth a little."

"Can I ask a question?" Mark said, turning to Jessie.

"Of course, Mark."

"Have the students always chosen the lecturer?"

"Yes. The student council decides. The administration has never interfered, although it has disapproved sometimes."

"The man is nothing more than a huckster," thundered Wendell Phelan. "Have you seen the stuff he's planning to pass out?" He opened up his briefcase, took out a sack of color brochures, and tossed them on the table.

46

Liz Hailey picked one up. "What's this?"

"Apocalypse Towers. In the Utah salt flats. Sixty stories, straight down."

"He can't be serious!"

"Oh, yes he is. He claims he's got five thousand tenants signed up already. Look at these brochures."

Brian picked one up and flipped through it. "The Oppenheimer deli? A dating bar called the Manhattan Project?"

Mark leaned over Brian's shoulder to peer at the gaudy brochure. "A tanning center called the Wernher von *Brown?* This man has a way with words, folks. Look at this. 'Decorator colors for every unit, ranging from Plutonium Pink to —Survival Gilt?' He's putting somebody on."

"Look, Liz," Jake said. "It says that Apocalypse Towers will not discriminate on the basis of race, creed, or sex."

"When Martin Luther King said he had seen the mountaintop, Jake, I don't think he meant sixty stories *down.*"

"He's actually building this stuff?" Norman Wineberg asked.

"Looks like it," Mark said. "He's selling pretty cheap. Condos go for fifty grand. A steal."

"You *would* defend this . . . warmonger!" Brian snarled. Brian seemed to regard Mark as personally responsible for every military atrocity in history since Attila the Hun. For his part, Mark delighted in needling Brian, watching Brian flush red to the roots of his ponytail. Jessie would probably kick him under the table, but he couldn't resist.

"Well, Brian, when the Big One goes off, I'd rather be there than here. Better Plutonium Pink than dead."

"We have to come to a fast decision," Jessie reminded the group. "The lecture is scheduled for next Thursday. I think one thing we certainly can do is not allow Mr. Mannering to pass out these commercial brochures. He can talk about Doomsday all he wants, but he can't peddle condos to the kids."

"Yes," Liz Hailey agreed. "I think the parents would be angry at us if it looked like the college was helping some guy sell them real estate."

"However," Jessie said, "I think we would set an unfortunate precedent if we tried to ban him."

"He's not a felon," Mark said. "He's not inciting to riot. He may have a screw loose, but banning him would only give him a barrelful of publicity."

47

"Yes," Jessie said. "I don't like this man's ideas, but the students are using student fees for this. It may be a silly choice, but after all, a college is a place where a lot of voices can be heard."

"He is trivializing nuclear war!" Wendell said.

"Do we really want this—crypto-fascist on the campus?" Brian asked.

"This has always been an open campus," Liz Hailey said. "There's a strong tradition of letting the marketplace of ideas flourish. The bad ones get weeded out, in the end. We hope."

"I think we should take a vote," Jessie said. "We know what the issues are."

Heads nodded around the table.

"All in favor of allowing the lecture to proceed, please say Aye."

"Aye," Mark said. He was joined by Jake, Norman Wineberg, and Liz Hailey.

"Opposed, No."

"No!" thundered Wendell Phelan.

"No," added Brian Kelly.

"I vote Aye," Jessie said. "The Ayes have it. The motion carries. I would urge you all to talk about this lecture with your classes, if it's appropriate. Bring up some of the issues it raises. Maybe the controversy can prove to be educational after all."

After the meeting, Jessie had to walk across the "campus"— a tangle of streets and buildings in Boston's Back Bay—to the classroom where she was doing a guest lecture on the evolution of the women's movement. Mark joined her.

"Thanks for your help in there," she said. "These meetings can get pretty fractious."

"Democracy in action."

"Yes, that's one of the things I like about this place. We're much less wedded to the chain of command than other institutions, the 'Me boss, you peon' kind of thing. It takes up a lot of time, and it can get silly, but it makes Kinsolving a lively place."

"Would you draw the line anyplace? Would you let anyone speak?"

"I think someone who advocated hate or violence could be seen to be violating the civil rights of our students. The head of the Klan, for example. But I'd rather err on the side of freedom than of censorship."

"You handle yourself pretty well," he said.

She chuckled. "A little of the velvet glove, a little of the iron fist. *Foot,* actually. I had to kick Jake to get him to lay off poor Wendell. I *nearly* kicked you."

He grinned. "I have to admit, being on this council is a lot different than I thought it would be."

"You thought it would be Great Minds debating Cosmic Issues?"

"I thought the army had a corner on Mickey Mouse."

She laughed. "There is more Mickey Mouse in academia than in all of Disneyland. And the battles! The classics department thinks the political scientists are plotting to get their building. Chemistry thinks Biology is going to use germ warfare against them. They're like a bunch of warring tribes, always going at it."

"I'm pretty good with a mace and broadsword," Mark said.

"Don't laugh. I may take you up on it, one of these days."

After her class, Jessie met Liz Hailey for lunch to talk about the new affirmative action guidelines, and then she dashed into the Store 24 on Commonwealth Avenue to pick up shampoo and deodorant. As she stepped to the register, she noticed, in line ahead of her, a man with a familiar set of shoulders. Oh, no! Her ex-husband, Herb. Standing beside him was a young girl with straight blond hair, wearing jeans and a backpack. She looked, Jessie thought, about twelve.

Don't let him turn around, Jessie thought, but he paid for a pack of cigarettes and, of course, turned around.

"Jessie!" he said, surprised. "It's good to see you. You're looking great."

"Hello, Herb." They were civilized people, after all, not the sort who tried to rip out each other's tongues and beat each other about the face and head with fire tongs.

"Jess," Herb said, "this is Mary Alderidge. She's in film studies at BU." He told the girl, "Jessie is the provost at Kinsolving." He said it proudly, as if having an ex-wife who was a provost belonged on his résumé.

"Nice to meet you," Jessie said. "How have you been, Herb?" She bit her lip and didn't add: Too bad about the tenure.

"Oh, fine, fine. I'm teaching a couple of courses at Met College, but I'm spending most of my time on my book. Really working on it."

"That's nice," Jessie said. "Best of luck with it." She paid for the toiletries and hurried out onto the street. She sighed. There was no avoiding it. Boston was such a small city, and the academic community so inbred, she was bound to bump into him on occasion. He did look good, she thought, with another sigh. He had sandy hair and the kind of tousled good looks that women adored, of the Robert Redford variety. He cultivated his diamond-in-the-rough appeal carefully, wearing faded-out designer jeans and Irish hand-knit sweaters because they gave him that boyish-but-rugged look. He had often picked out clothes for her. The things he bought inevitably looked better than what she chose for herself.

She bit her nails as she walked down Commonwealth Avenue. How old was that kid with him anyway? Nineteen, maybe? The way Herb was moving through the city's women students, he'd be down to junior high school soon. The next time she saw him—at Steve's Ice Cream or in the BU bookstore—the girl with him would be carrying *My Weekly Reader* and snapping Grape Dubble Bubble.

She sighed again, bit another nail. She thought she had Herb figured out now. He had a constant need for adulation, which was why he always chose women who were no intellectual match for him. The power all had to flow one way. He could dazzle younger women with the sheer wattage of his intellect. Herb, she was sure, would never be so gauche as to grab a coed's tush in the hallway or threaten her with a D if she didn't settle in for a spot of fellatio in his office. Herb used his brain as an erogenous zone. The problem was that Herb's brain wasn't so dazzling to anybody over twenty-five. He was a canny lecturer, but once you got past the jokes and the bon mots and the verbal pyrotechnics, what was left was fairly banal, most of it cribbed from the text or from other people's work. He had been writing his book—on American politics in the Kennedy years—for twelve years. At first Jessie believed what he had said about it, that it would be a masterwork that would set the academic world on its ear. They talked about it constantly, his great *oeuvre*. But slowly it began to dawn on Jessie that in fact Herb was terrified of making the kind of leap the book would require, exposing his ideas and his scholarship to the judgment of his peers. It was safer to stick with the students, who didn't know too much and therefore could not challenge him. He was charming and quick on his feet, so he had quickly developed a good reputation among the students. His classes were always

50

packed. He had been careful to make the right connections in the right places. Jessie found herself giving (catered) little *intime* dinners for deans and academic vice-presidents. It was the perfect setting for Herb to shine, and it was understood that he was to be the star, displaying his wit along with his knowledge of impertinent little French wines. If Jessie grew too voluble under the spell of a dry little Chablis from Pont-Neuf, Herb would glare and she would button her lip. Herb figured it would work for him; it always had.

But when the time came for tenure, it all fell apart. His publications were thin, and those that did exist were mediocre. The two chapters of the book he had hurriedly finished for the committee were really a hodgepodge of other people's research. The tenure committee saw how he looked on paper, where the charm and the bon mots were not there to sparkle, and turned him down flat. Even his friends in high places couldn't save him, sorry as they were. He hadn't given them any ammunition.

A cloud of depression settled on Jessie as she walked down the street. Despite the fact that she had Herb's compulsions neatly charted in her mind, in the pit of her stomach the conviction lay, like an undigested meatball, that the breakup of the marriage had been *her* fault. She was a woman who couldn't hold her man. If she'd had big tits, if she'd been wittier and dressed better, if she had been able to find her G spot, Herb wouldn't have run around. She knew that wasn't true, of course. She could have had the face of Meryl Streep, the body of Suzanne Somers, and the sexual skills of an entire Hong Kong bordello, and that wouldn't have stopped Herb. He needed more adoration than a cloisterful of nuns could provide.

Still, the damp tendrils of failure pressed against her skin, and seeing Herb in all his tousled glory only made her more aware of them. If he had a pattern, she had one too. With Herb she had done the same thing she had done with other men, stepped humbly to the back of the bus and let his life be the important one. In all the years with Herb, the conversations always centered on *his* books, *his* battle with the department chairman, the seminar *he* was giving on Kennedy. Her life, which was really much more interesting, only got mentioned in passing. Herb's eyes glazed over when she talked about trying to convince the state senator from Acton to vote for the plant-closing bill. As far as Herb was concerned, that wasn't the sort of politics that

51

mattered. His political concerns were Olympian. Anyone below the level of subcabinet member was not worthy of his attention. She fell into the habit of tending to her own life as if it were a secret garden, little flowers blooming away from his view. The more visible she became, the more Herb avoided the subject. One day her picture was on the front page of the *Globe,* right under his coffee cup, and he didn't even mention it. Instead, he worried about why Sam Hillerman, who taught an excruciatingly boring course on foreign policy (according to Herb), got invited to speak at the Political Science convention and Herb, who was the undisputed star of the department (according to Herb), did not. It was probably because Hillerman, who had been an ambassador, pulled rank with his old cronies.

"But they're interested in the Middle East, and he was ambassador to Jordan," Jessie said. "That's probably why they asked him."

"The man is out of touch, Jess. A has-been. He's pathetic, really. The students all go to sleep in his class."

"Herb, let's go out tonight, to celebrate. We just got the plant-closing bill passed. We've worked for a year on this one."

"Oh, Jess, not tonight. Tonight I have to lecture at MIT. I told you that."

"No, you didn't tell me."

"I did too. You just forgot to write it down. You always forget things."

"Well, how about afterward?"

"I'll be too exhausted. You know how these things drain me. We'll do your little celebration tomorrow night. Or Wednesday. OK?"

"Well, I—"

"Jess, I have to run. I have to be in class in twenty minutes. Don't wait up, I'll be late."

What was it about her, Jessie wondered, that made her crumble like a Toll House cookie whenever she got serious about a man? How had they managed to convince her that their precious, fragile egos had to be tended like hatchlings? And she, poor fool, why had she done it, always tiptoeing around, trying to puff them up, protecting them and never, for God's sake, even daring to suggest that they weren't gods? She sighed again. Were there men who liked bright, strong women? Were there men who were sure enough of their own strength that they didn't have to be adored? The Father, the Son, and the Holy Ghost were enough deities for one person to contend with. A fourth Person of the Trinity, in the form of some guy and his blessed ego, was just too much worship for one woman to manage.

She thought, then, about Mark Claymore, all of a sudden inviting her for dinner. She had seen him staring at her in a peculiar way lately. He was very unlike the kind of men she usually associated with—leftish intellectuals from the academic world. She had been noticing something about those men, more and more. They had a lot to say about hating racism and sexism and went on about how their hearts bled for the oppressed masses, but at dinner parties not one of them got up to clear a dish. They'd moan about how downtrodden minorities had to do society's scut work, but it didn't bother them a bit that the women they lived with did their ironing. Left-wing intellectuals were all for liberation—until it interfered with their creature comforts.

One thing she had observed about Mark was that he listened to her. Really listened. And there was a quiet strength about him that she liked. Not a macho "Me Tarzan" thing, but the sense that he was comfortable with what he knew and what he could do. Of course, he had been through a lot; getting a leg blown off in combat made you grow up in a hurry. The leg had not interfered with her fantasies about him, in which he was always naked to the waist and doing some kind of work that brought a nice little sweat to the muscles in his back. She must be outgrowing her Irish Catholic repression, fantasizing about sweat. Sometimes he was wearing his army fatigues, his dog tags clanking on his bare chest, hammering, digging, sawing.

The flush of desire was so intense that she dug her nails into the palms of her hands. This was ridiculous. He was getting to be a habit with her unconscious, popping up when least expected, with his sweat and his hairy chest and all the damn sawing and hammering. He had probably built an entire condo, in her mind.

She thought about his eyes, a grayish blue, of how they could harden, like balls of ice, and then thaw again, in an instant. She wondered, as she had before, about the anger. It was there, and it was under control, but she had to admit it frightened her a little. The other men she had known all expressed anger verbally, used words as weapons. She had learned to deal with that. His anger lay coiled inside, silent as a snake, always ready to strike.

She wondered how it would happen. Or if. He kept it there,

behind his eyes, and she had only seen a glimpse of it. She didn't think she wanted to see much more. But there was something else as well, a gentleness that she saw in the way he worked with the students. He didn't try to curry favor, he could be firm when need be, but there was a concern that radiated from the way he looked at them, listened to them, patiently explained things to them.

Paternal, she thought. It was the word she was seeking. It must have made him a good soldier. The hallmark of a good soldier, she had read, was that he cared for his men, that in a game of death he had concern for life. He had been, she thought, one of those.

And he cooked Chinese. He was handsome, witty, fun to be with, and he cooked Chinese. It sounded too good to be true.

Especially for her.

FROM JESSIE'S DIARY
(SOPHOMORE YEAR)

Dear Diary: I am facing a moral issue. It is—don't laugh—about shaving. The personal is political, remember. We spent two and a half fucking hours in our women's group today talking about shaving our legs and armpits. Talia, who is the most liberated person I ever met, says shaving reduces us to Barbie dolls, little female eunuchs who destroy our real womanhood by making our skin look like polyurethane. Being hairy is real and female, Talia says. Andrea and Talia had quite a go-round on this. Andrea says she doesn't care if it's real or not, Jewish-American princesses are just not hairy, period. Talia sneered and asked if she wanted to be a JAP forever, and Andrea said, no, she was going to be a JAR, a Jewish-American radical, but she didn't see what being hairy had to do with being liberated.

In my heart of hearts, I know Talia is right, but my cultural conditioning is very hard to overcome. In eighth grade Mary Jane Alessandro didn't shave her legs and Richie Ryan called her a gorilla, in the lunchroom. I would have died if he called me that. So I went out and bought a tube of Nair and I put it on my legs and it got caked real hard and it had this sort of blue color, and I thought, What if it never comes off? I would have to go through life with hard blue crud on my legs, which is worse than stubble, which you get when you shave. But the worst thing was it smelled like a stink bomb and my mother came upstairs to ask what the awful smell was.

I stood in the closet, so my hard smelly blue legs wouldn't show, and I stuck my head out and I said, "Smell? What smell?" And she looked all over the place, in the medicine cabinet and around the tub. My mother had told me I shouldn't shave my legs because I was too young to get stubble, but no way was I going to be called a gorilla. The Pope could have come to my house and personally ordered me not to use Nair with a papal bull (Non Nairius Hairius?) and I would have done it anyway. Being excommunicated by the Pope would have been better than being called gorilla by Richie Ryan. I know I ought to be hairy and a true female, but every time I don't shave my legs for a week it's not Gloria Steinem's voice I hear but Richie Ryan's rotten little tenor, screaming, "Gorilla!"

So I've really copped out, Dear Diary, and I shave my legs, which is why I wear leotards to group, because all in all, I'd rather have a personal letter of excommunication from the Pope than have Talia yell at me for betraying all the liberated women in the Western world.

I do not, however, shave my armpits, which gets itchy, but here too I am a coward. Ronald Finklestein, who I have been sleeping with for three months (It's all right, he's a resister), likes hairy armpits but finds hairy legs disgusting. This is peculiar, I admit, but Ronald is also a victim of cultural conditioning. He is from Manhattan, and when he was sixteen he fell in love with Sylvana Mangano in Bitter Rice when she sweated away in the fields as an Italian bracero. Ronald is very avant-garde in his cultural tastes. He said it was the first time he ever saw unshaved armpits and he thought it was unbelievably sensual. He just sat there, in his seat at the Thalia Theatre, and he wanted to lie down in the fields with her and lick her armpits, which may be a big turn-on for him but I find a tad revolting. Licking sweat is not my idea of a romantic evening. Ronald says it's my Irish Catholic anal retentive upbringing, and he

56

may be right, because the smell of Ivory soap turns me on, which is also sort of weird.

But back to Sylvana. I am pretty sure her legs were hairy, because Italian peasant rice pickers don't have Lady Schicks lying around, so why didn't Ronald find that disgusting?

It is male cultural conditioning, that's what it is, deciding which body hair on women is OK and which is not, according to some dumb black-and-white movie with subtitles viewed in a burst of pubescent fervor. Why do I go along with it? I who am committed to the overthrow of the Patriarchy?

I am not part of the solution, so I am part of the problem. I am gripped in the chains of my cultural conditioning, and I am not strong enough to break them.

But someday, I will be.

FIVE

Jessie pulled the car into the Charles Center garage in Harvard Square and hurried toward the Harvest, where the nabobs of Cambridge often met to graze. You might spot the winner of last year's Pulitzer or next year's MacArthur Fellowship dallying over coffee or crunching spinach salad. Jessie and Andrea—now Andrea Margolis Lefkowitz—met there often for lunch. Andrea was on the verge of a partnership in a high-powered consulting firm in Boston, telling CEOs how to spend their millions. After seven years as a city planner, with a specialty in low-income housing, Andrea had been burnt out, exhausted, and still making less than the average bus driver. She moved on to the private sector, where her star rose with startling speed. She found it easy, after the years in a pressure cooker; in the high-rise tower she didn't have to twist the arms of recalcitrant local pols, or plead with irate citizens who felt the poor should all live someplace else, or make end runs around sleazy developers.

Her income was in six figures. She and Ira had a big house in Belmont with a pool and a Mercedes.

Andrea had been the matron of honor at Jessie's wedding and she'd bought the booze the night the divorce decree became final, so the two of them could get tearily blotto. Jessie was the unofficial godmother (goyishe godmother, Andrea called it) to Rachel and Noah, Andrea's children. They had been friends since the first day of freshman year at BU when they had been thrown together as roommates. They had muddled through every life crisis together. Each somehow made the other feel right. As one moved a step higher on the ladder of the great (and male) world, she could look over and see the other on the same rung. It was comforting; a familiar face among the alien corn.

When Jessie arrived at the Harvest, Andrea was waiting for her, wearing a navy suit with padded shoulders and a green silk shirt. She had graduated from Loehmann's to the Corporate Woman shop at Filene's. Looking JAPy was a no-no in the Prudential tower. For Andrea, giving up mascara had been like stripping in public. "Only goyim go out with naked eyelashes," she told Jessie. "In a month I will be eating white bread and I'll change my name to Buffie. I'll send pro-PLO letters to the *Times*. I'll join the Weston Country Club."

But Andrea had her mascara on for lunch at the Harvest. One couldn't withdraw cold turkey from Max Factor, after all. The shock to the system was too great.

"What's the salad?" Jessie asked Andrea as she slid into a chair.

"Chicken and cashews in plum sauce. Two?"

"Right. How was Dallas?"

Andrea sighed, a philosophical sigh that indicated a world-weary wisdom about the realities of corporate America.

"A hassle. The vice-president for marketing kept trying to pinch my tush. My plane was four hours late getting out. And Rachel is pissed at me because I missed her dance recital."

"Couldn't Ira go to that?"

"No, he was in the goddam wind tunnel again. I wish MIT would sell that thing and use it for a hair dryer."

"You look tired, Andrea. Maybe you ought to take a vacation. Just you and Ira."

"I can't. I'm so stacked up with work that I'm playing catch-up. How's it going with you?"

"Oh, Jake and Brian are driving me nuts, as usual. But I think the science center is going to come through. We need about five million to do it right."

Andrea chuckled as she took a sip of Perrier. "Would you listen to us! You're talking five million, I've just been dealing megabucks in Dallas. Jessie, would we ever have thought it would turn out like this? When we were out trying to tear down the Establishment?"

"We were going to change the world, weren't we? Make it all perfect."

"We thought we owned the world. Or rather, they owned it; we'd take it away from them."

"We did some good things. We stopped a war. Whatever else happened, we had a part in that."

Jessie wondered if her generation would always measure their lives against that time. Could life ever again be so tumultuous? As if Andrea could read her thoughts, she shook her head.

"I sometimes think, Jessie, when I'm up in that tower, that it's not where I wanted to end up. I was going to rebuild the cities."

"You still do a lot of pro bono."

"I know. But I hope I don't get like so many of the guys. There's so much money floating around, you get sucked into the life-style. It's so easy."

"Not you, Andrea. You are a Jewish-American radical."

"Jessie, look at me. Did Trotsky wear a power suit?"

"Those shoulders are a bit much. Refrigerator Perry doesn't have shoulders like that."

"I thought in my power suit I wouldn't get my ass patted. I might as well have been wearing Fredericks of Hollywood, as far as this guy was concerned."

"It's a way for men not to take you seriously."

"I know. And I can't complain to Ira, because he'd be shit-faced. He'd think my business trips were orgies."

"I've never been on one that was."

"Yeah. I always used to think that guys who traveled at lot on business were out screwing around all the time. But all you want to do at the end of the day is take a shower and go to bed. Alone."

Jessie and Andrea often swapped stories of what it was like in the male world, as Jesuit explorers might have shared hand-drawn maps of some alien wilderness. It kept them from getting lost in the underbrush. The only thing they talked about more was men.

"Which reminds me," Jessie said. "I saw Herb the other day. With his latest."

"Was she in Pampers?"

"Just about. What is it with these guys, Andrea? Why don't they want to grow up?"

"Who wants to grow up? Especially our generation. We ruled the world for a while. Our music, our causes, our life-style. Maybe it's harder because of that."

"*We* did it, Andrea. And I like being a grown-up. I like being in charge of things, making things happen."

"Don't you miss the old days, Jessie? The excitement of it all?"

"Sometimes. But I know who I am, now. I'm—formed. I wasn't, then. Not all the way."

"Any twinges when you saw Herb?"

"Oh, sure. I mean, I don't want him, but I don't want those teenyboppers to have him either. They make me feel like Grandma Moses."

"A taxi driver in Dallas called me ma'am. I was depressed all day."

"In that suit, I'm surprised he didn't call you *mein Führer*. Besides, in Texas they call everybody ma'am."

"Sometimes, Jessie, when I'm up in one of those glass towers, I get the sense that it's all unreal. That the conference-room door is going to open and it'll be my mother, telling me to clean up my room."

"With me it's Father Riordan. He's going to show up at the trustees' meeting and say, 'Jessica Elizabeth, go to the principal's office.' And I'll say, 'Yes, Father,' and I'll go."

"I wonder if men feel like that? Or is it just us, because we're so new at it?"

"At least men have other guys to look at. Figure out how to behave."

"Yeah. I sure as hell can't be one of the boys. But I did learn about football."

"You? Andrea, you hate sports. You were the only person I

61

ever met who was nineteen years old and still thought Babe Ruth was a candy bar."

"I know. But you have to learn their language. They think you're a Martian if you don't. It's bad enough that you've got boobs."

"You think you can make them forget the boobs with stats from the NFL?"

"No, but it helps. I used to think a tight end was colitis. Now I can talk about yards gained rushing and who won the Super Bowl."

"What's a hat trick, Andrea?"

The flush of triumph faded from Andrea's cheeks. Jessie grinned. They liked to quiz each other, to see who wasn't keeping up. Andrea always won on designer labels, Wall Street gossip, and movie stars. Now she frowned.

"A hat trick? Oh, shit, I don't know that one. And I read *Sports Illustrated* all year."

"It's hockey."

"Hockey? People sit in freezing rooms and watch guys hit each other with sticks? Jessie, that's dumb."

"Football is intellectual?"

"Of course not. It's really boring. Except for the tight pants. Joe Montana has such a cute ass."

"I hope you don't say that in board meetings."

"Give me credit, Jessie. They'd freak out. Guys can talk about women's bodily parts all they want, but let one of us call a guy's tush cute and they hang a scarlet A on us."

"And it doesn't stand for Alabama."

"Alabama. Bear Bryant."

"Very good!"

"For me, it is. All those southern places are one big blob to me." She sighed. "Oh, Jessie, when does it get easier?"

"I don't think it does."

"Hey, I have a guy I want you to meet. He's a friend of Ira's."

"Oh, good, we can neck in the wind tunnel."

"No, he's into gene splicing. You can take penicillin showers together."

"No, thanks."

"You can't keep on being a hermit."

"Actually, Mark Claymore asked me over to dinner."

"The major? The ROTC guy?"

"Yes."

"You, Jessie, going out with a soldier?"

"Funny, isn't it?"

"Remember the day we phoned in the bomb threat to the ROTC office at BU?"

"Yeah, that was fun. We cleared out the whole communications building."

"They canceled my final in Organizational Communications."

"Andrea! I thought you were acting from pure pacifist motives."

"I gave peace a chance, and I got an A minus at the same time. I was the realist, Jessie. It was you who were the idealist."

"I guess I won't mention that little episode to Mark. At least not till dessert."

"What will you and Rambo talk about? Or does he just grunt?"

"He happens to be going for his doctorate in Asian history." Jessie realized that her cheeks were warm. She was blushing, like a junior in high school who just told her best friend she had a prom date. Andrea raised an eyebrow.

"A soldier philosopher? That sounds interesting."

"He lost a leg in Vietnam. I think he's pretty ambiguous about the war. Knows it was a botch, but he's proud of having served."

"They're still getting screwed, the poor bastards. They got shipped off to the wrong war, and everybody blamed them. Including us."

"I know. And now people want to forget it all happened. They want to bring back all this macho-hero horseshit. They're lying again about what war really is."

"I have a son that I love as much as my daughter. I wonder, will we have to do it all over again someday? Keep on marching?"

"Christ, with our Supp-Hose and our pension checks, getting hit by nightsticks again?"

"It gets the blood flowing to the brain. It'll cure our Alzheimer's. Hey, do you really like this army guy?"

"I think I do. You could have knocked me over with a feather when he asked me to dinner. But we'll probably end up yelling at each other."

"If you don't, we could be a foursome again."

"That never really worked, Andrea. Herb and Ira only pretended to be friends. Herb was always trying to be more intellectual than Ira. It *killed* Herb that people said Ira was going to get the Nobel before he was forty."

"Ira always tried to be witty when Herb was around. Ira has no sense of humor. He thinks quasar jokes are funny."

"Is that what those were?"

"Yes."

"Herb always laughed. He didn't want Ira to think he didn't understand them."

"Ira knew Herb didn't understand. He knew Herb would laugh anyhow. It made Ira feel very superior."

"Why did Ira need to feel superior? He has forty-seven degrees."

"Oh, men get into that stupid shit. They're always sizing one another up. Mine's bigger than yours. It's a relief not to have one. You don't get so anxious."

"You know, that's something I like about Mark. He doesn't seem to be into that competition bag. He seems happy with who he is. He's not like a lot of the guys in academia, always jostling for position."

"When you've been through what he has, maybe it all seems stupid."

"Well, I don't think it will come to anything. I wonder if I'm permanently scarred from Herb, anyway."

One nice thing about Andrea, Jessie thought, was that she could go on about Herb at great length and Andrea would never tell her to shut up. She understood that talking about Herb was one way of exorcising him; though it did take the shade of Herb a very long time to skulk off into the mists.

"Come on, Jessie, not all men are Herb."

"Good thing, for America's second-graders."

"You've been alone too long."

"I'm not unhappy."

"But horny."

"Sure. I got sort of numbed out after Herb left. But I am definitely thawing."

"How about a quickie?"

"No, that's not me. My body would love a quickie, but my

64

psyche would be moving my undies into his drawers and hanging posters."

"We used to believe it was all so simple. We'd just be liberated and that was that."

"We also believed in worldwide revolution and Consciousness Three."

"Funny, isn't it, how things turned out."

"So who's laughing?"

FROM JESSIE'S DIARY
(SOPHOMORE YEAR)

Dear Diary: I am just so mad and so hurt. You would not believe what Ronald has been pulling. The other night, in our organizing meeting, he kept interrupting me, as if nothing I had to say was important at all. I see this a lot. The guys want to take over and do all the talking, and when the women try to talk it's like we're invisible, we don't count. But what was worse was that I wrote the speech that Ronald gave at Marsh Chapel. It was all my ideas, I worked for weeks on it, polishing it so it would be just right for him to deliver. And he just took it and read it and never gave me any credit. He got all the applause, everyone was calling him such a great speaker, and never once, not once, did he say I wrote the speech.

I thought it was supposed to be this great joint venture, we were going to do it together, and he just took it and never even said thank you. He acted like it was perfectly OK for him to do that, to take my work and pretend it was his. You should have seen him, all smug and fatuous, puffed up like a blowfish, when everybody came up and congratulated him. He just shoved me aside, didn't even look at me. Why did he do that? I wouldn't do that to him. It isn't fair! I didn't mind that he gave the speech, but not to get any credit at all, it isn't fair! And Ronald is supposed to love me. Is that how you love people, you steal things from them and ignore them and then say they're being bitchy when they try to say how hurt they are?

And then last night, oh, that was the corker! Ronald announced very grandly that it was the law of nature for men to be leaders and women to be followers. He's studying rats in his psychology course and he said that female rats, when they see male rats, they crouch down and present their rumps in a gesture of submission. Well, that did it! I told Ronald that if he would like to present his rump that very minute I would kick his asshole through his teeth, so much for that male-chauvinist-pig crap. I said if he wanted laws of nature, what about bees, where the males get to screw the queen once and then they die, that's all they're good for; and spiders, when they mate, then the female has the male for lunch; and did you know, Ronald, that all fetuses start out female but the not-so-great ones don't make the grade, so they get penises? The Adam and Eve story is backward, it's females *that come first, so go tell that to your stupid rats, and who wants a rat for a role model anyhow?*

Well, Ronald was really shocked, because usually I am this nice person who just holds his hand and tells him how great he is. He didn't understand what he had done. He said, "So you helped me with the speech; you're supposed to, you're a woman." Helped! *The whole speech was mine, every fucking word. Ronald is dyslexic, it's a big deal if he can get "Run, Spot, run" down on paper. But in his mind, he did it all. He really believed that.*

I told him this and he sulked, which he does a lot. He just kept on sulking and giving me that pathetic wounded-deer look, which he is so good at. And then I felt bad and offered to make up. But he said he didn't want to sleep with me that night, which is supposed to be some big punishment? He gets on his high horse and takes his penis off to a corner like it ought to be gift-wrapped or something. Ronald has this idea that he is a great lover, that whenever he wants to stick it in somebody they ought to genuflect out of sheer gratitude. I saw the way Sonia was making sheep eyes at him, after the speech. That would kill *me, if my speech sent Sonia into a sexual frenzy and she*

67

wound up Doing It with Ronald, after falling in love with my *mind. A sort of Cyrano de Bergerac story. If she tries it, I will rip her hair out by the roots.*

Ronald said that if I wasn't careful I would wreck a beautiful relationship with my selfishness. I thought about that. I mean, I get great ideas and Ronald takes them, and when he sulks it's my fault, and when he talks I'm supposed to listen but he doesn't have to listen to me. When Ronald wants to screw, we screw. When he is tired, and I want to do it, he says I am demanding and castrating. This is a beautiful relationship?

So I said maybe we ought to split up and Ronald panicked and said he loved me, he'd always love me, and if I left him he would sign up for Vietnam where he would never fire a shot, just walk into a barrage of bullets with his gun unloaded. And he looked at me with his dying-deer look and his big beautiful brown eyes and I decided to give him another chance, because if he got killed in Vietnam I would never forgive myself. I said I was going to give my speeches from now on, though, and Ronald said that was all right, he would let me.

Let me! *I started to yell at him but then he looked up at me with those brown eyes. He's a jerk a lot of times, but he* is *cute.*

So we didn't break up.

SIX

Mark picked up the trash bag, tied it with a plastic strip, and took it to the back door for the morning pickup. He tossed the green, shiny bag into the row of similar ones that lined the alley. It was a warm, muggy early fall night, with a light rain falling, and as he stood there, it happened. The bags, gleaming wetly under the streetlights, became, without warning, body bags.

He had thought, as he watched, that it was an odd reversal of snakes shedding their skin. Men died and grew a new covering—smooth, wet, green, and silent. The men were stacking the bags like cordwood, very quietly, getting them ready for shipment. And then suddenly, he was inside one of the bags, where the air was dark and warm and the vinyl stuck wetly to his face. He couldn't speak; he tried to croak out a noise but no sound would come, and his fingers clawed at the shiny green material. He was buried alive in the damp green skin, like a pea in a pod, and he would rot there like a pea gone soft, all gray and squishy, dead inside the pod.

The world turned again, like a kaleidoscope, and 'Nam vanished. He was standing on a street in Boston, the rain falling wetly against his cheek as he looked at a row of trash bags. He thought of a line from a poem a vet had written about the body bags, row upon row of them: a nightmare awaiting the Man from Glad.

His heart was beating wildly, an odd contrast to the stillness of the night. Flashback. He hadn't had one in ages.

He walked back into the apartment and opened a beer, his hands shaking as he did so. It had seemed so real. It was terrifying when the world slipped out from under you like a bathroom rug and you went tumbling back into the past. He couldn't stop his hands from shaking.

It must be all the anniversary stuff, that had to be it. The TV was full of it, you couldn't turn around without it staring you in the face—the gunfire, the scenes of Saigon crowded with men in uniform, the ever-present choppers floating over the greenery like mosquitoes. And there were the pictures, dredged up and on the front pages all over again: the little girl running naked, screaming, down a street after being burned with napalm; the suspected VC being shot in the head, his brains spraying out in an explosive cloud. Oh, what a lovely war.

He went back into the living room, his body still trembling. Christ, he had thought he was through with *this*. With a herculean effort he willed his body into stillness. Control. You had to control things. Then it would be all right.

He had been smart enough, when he got back from Vietnam, to know that he couldn't just bury it all in a hole someplace, like a pet bird that had died, and walk away and forget it. He chose to use his head as a sifter, to sort it all out. The anger could be understood by knowing where it came from. Thinking was what kept him sane. There was another part of the equation, of course, all the other feelings that came with the experience, but they were dangerous, a tar pit from which some men never returned. Those emotions were best left to lie fallow, decompose. The tar pit had depths no man imagined.

He walked over to his weights and began to work out, using his arms, powerful now from the steady exercise. He did a series of curls, went to a hundred push-ups. His body rebelled, but his will insisted. His body fell into line. He made it do what he wanted it to. It swam, it worked out, it skied, expertly. The skiing had been so hard that he wanted to give it up after more headlong plunges into the snow than he could count. The farm boy from

70

Maryland had never seen skis until he was twenty-six. His wet, sore, aching body had cried out for him to stop but he had been firm with it, and eventually the persistence paid off, because on skis, twisting down the black diamond trails, he felt as free as he once had as a kid on the shores of the Chesapeake Bay. Walking, with the leg, he had to try to keep up with a world that hurried by him. On skis, few people could pass him.

He had always taken his body for granted, before 'Nam. It was just *there,* always reliable. But on the plane coming home his body tormented him with the sort of pain he had never known existed, an eternity of it, mingled with the steady droning of the engines. Mark wasn't sure which was worse, the pain or the drugs. When the pain got bad he hollered for the morphine, which put him into a drugged limbo filled with phantoms. The drugs popped the lid off the suppressed memories, let them roam at will through his dazed brain. He saw ruined faces, entrails crawling with maggots, an inferno more vivid than Dante's; he had *seen* his hell, while Dante only imagined. Next to him, a young infantryman moaned, on and on, a low whine that had a predictable pattern, until the sound nearly drove Mark mad. Then it stopped, suddenly. Mark was relieved, until the realization sliced its way into his foggy brain: The man had died.

"Dear God, please don't let me die," Mark prayed. "Not this close! God, please!"

He was a zombie for a while, alternating between painful wakefulness and the phantoms. He had three operations for repairs on what was left of his leg, and when he had recovered sufficiently they shipped him off to a VA hospital in the South that had a first-rate limb trauma center. As he was wheeled into his room, which he was to share with two other vets, he was greeted by a young man with dark curly hair and a big grin on his face, who said, "For chrissake, another goddam gimp. We were hoping for a guy with the clap who could at least make the booze runs."

"I got the clap too," Mark said. "Those operating room nurses are fucking animals."

The young man introduced himself. He was Eliot Feldman, aka Hebe, and the other man in the room was Julio Colon, known, of course, as Spic. Before the day was out, Mark was christened Redneck. On the ward were Spade and Pimp and Mick and Hunkie and Swede. The jokes were the most basic ones: racist, sexist, insulting, and demeaning to every ethnic group, and above

71

all there was gimp humor. The official ward pinup girl was Helen Keller. The savage humor tore at self-pity, mocked it, chewed it up, spat it out. The ward saved his life, Mark realized later. It kept him from despair, made the pain bearable, started him back on the road to the world that everybody else lived in.

After the activity of the first day, Mark began to sink into a deep pit of depression as the reality of his situation dawned full upon him. He was a man without a leg. Eliot hovered over him those first few days, needling him, making him keep busy, not letting him go down in the bog. The men in the ward were like a pack of dolphins; when one of their number got too exhausted to swim any further, they huddled close and buoyed him up with their bodies, all the while being funny and foul and plotting ways to beat the system. Eliot Feldman decided that one way to get nice trips would be to form a singing group, the Gimp Tabernacle Choir. Dutifully, the group practiced every day, and Eliot, as musical director, selected the repertoire. There was a selection of Filthy Favorites, such as "Gonorrhea Leah" and "Saigon Sue," but the choir's specialties were Gimp Golden Oldies, or "Goldies," with lyrics by Eliot. The choir's theme song was "My Funny Valentine":

> My funny Valentine,
> Sweet comic Valentine,
> You make me smile with your heart.
>
> Is your mouth a little weak
> Since the Slopes shot off your cheek?
> When you open it to speak
> Are you smart?
>
> But don't change a hair for me,
> Don't leave your chair for me,
> For you're my favorite legless geek.

Eliot had a manic energy that infused the ward, and he was its undisputed leader. He had lost both arms in a chopper crash, but he informed anyone who cared to listen that he regarded this as merely a minor setback in his plans to make a million dollars before he was thirty-five. When Mark wheeled himself back into the room one day after recreational therapy, Eliot was lying on his bed with his feet in the air, waggling his bare toes.

"What the fuck are you doing?" Mark asked.

"I saw a guy on TV, no arms, paints with his toes. I mean really nice stuff, sunsets, boats. Toes are really flexible."

"You want to be Rembrandt?"

"No, I have other plans."

"Yeah?"

Eliot wiggled his toes. "Foreplay."

"Foreplay?"

"Eliot Feldman and his erotic extremities. Let Eliot titillate your titties with his talented toesies."

Mark laughed. "Better than a fucking watercolor, Hebe."

"You bet. We were lucky, Redneck, didn't get the old putz shot off. Ever think about that?"

"Yeah, first thing I grabbed."

"If I'd had it blown off, I'd have killed myself. Imagine walking around with a hole where your prick used to be?"

"Instant sex change. Who needs Denmark when you've got Da Nang?"

Eliot chortled and waggled his toes again, lasciviously. "Let me see your rash, sweetie. Don't worry, it's not syphilis, just athlete's foot. Put a little Absorbine Junior in your douche."

It was Eliot who dreamed up the Great Escape Caper. The VA hospital, while medically excellent, was about as far away from civilization as it was possible to get in a non–third world nation. "In the goddam boonies," as Eliot put it. The only nearby watering hole was a joint called Diamond Lil's, which was off limits to VA staff and patients, ever since a jealous husband pumped a bullet into the lung of his wife's lover one hot midnight.

One muggy night, morale was at a low ebb on Ward L-15. The men had been getting on each other's nerves all week. Even a new Helen Keller joke—"Why does Helen Keller have a yellow leg? Her dog's blind too"—could barely eke out a chuckle. Eliot, fidgeting as he sat on his bunk, got Mark to pour a cup of cold water over his head and said, "I'm goin' nuts. We got to bust out."

"The Birdman of Alcatraz." Mark snorted. "We'll swipe some morphine and *fly* out."

"Can you drive?" Eliot asked him.

"Of course I can drive. What kind of a question is that?"

"We snatch the hospital van. Nobody watches it."

"You're crazy," Mark said.

"No, it's easy. You steer and do the brake. I do the accelerator. Spic can hot-wire anything."

"True?" Mark asked Julio.

"If it's got wheels, man, I can make it go."

And so the die was cast. Under cover of darkness, Mark and Julio wheeled out the back door and Eliot trotted beside them, into the lot. With Eliot bracing him, Mark lifted Julio, who had lost both legs, into the driver's seat. They waited nervously as Julio fiddled with the wires.

"Hurry up, dammit," Eliot said. "We're pretty conspicuous out here."

The engine of the van coughed and then rumbled to life.

"No sweat," Julio said. He pushed himself across the seat and Eliot and Mark climbed in. Mark took the wheel and pulled the van out of the lot, and then they were tooling down the highway toward Diamond Lil's, singing a Goldie at the top of their voices, "You'll Never Walk Alone."

They made something of an entrance into Diamond Lil's, Julio riding piggyback on Eliot, his arms around Eliot's neck, and Mark hopping on his good leg. They settled at a table, and a waitress came over to take their order.

"Hey, y'all from the VA hospital?"

"No," Eliot said, "we're the U.S. ski team. Had a real rough season."

"The last hill was a bitch," Julio said.

They had a fine time, drinking and talking to the bar girls. Eliot took off his shoe and demonstrated how he could drink a Bud, holding the bottle with his foot. Julio sang a maudlin song in Spanish about his beautiful homeland, Puerto Rico, and they all lustily cheered the energetic—but not exactly rhythmic—efforts of Sarah Jane, the go-go dancer. After one exuberant number, Sarah Jane sat down and had a drink with them. She turned out to be a local girl, a sweet kid whose one ambition in life was to get to Caesar's Palace.

"See, I'm tall, five ten, and I could make four hundred dollars a week out there. I'm saving up, to go. They have the most beautiful costumes. Do you think I could make it out there?"

"Absolutely," Mark said.

"In a minute," Eliot added.

74

"You're as good as any of 'em, Sarah Jane," Julio said, and belched. He was half in the bag already. "Good thing I'm not driving."

It was then that Eliot was struck by inspiration.

"Hey, listen, Sarah Jane, we'll pay you a hundred bucks if you'll do a show at the hospital tonight."

"Well, I don't know—"

"Two hundred," said Mark.

"Except you got to know," she said, "I don't take off my G-string and I don't let anybody feel me up or anything like that. I want to go to Caesar's Palace, so I have to keep my reputation."

"No funny stuff," Mark said. "Just dancing, that's all."

"You promise?"

"Scout's honor."

Sarah Jane giggled. "OK, I'll do it."

They were a peculiar-looking group, heading back in the van: Mark steering, Eliot on the accelerator, and Julio singing drunkenly in Spanish. In the backseat, Sarah Jane, wearing a raincoat over her purple-and-green pasties and G-string, kept an eye out for the fuzz.

"Are y'all going to get in trouble for this?" she asked.

"Oh, no," Mark said, "the VA has a big dance therapy program."

"We were going to get the Alvin Ailey troupe, but they couldn't come," Eliot said. "So you'll have to take their place."

Sarah Jane giggled. "You guys sure are crazy. But you're a lot of fun. Are you all like this?"

"Gimps are the greatest," Mark said. "We are just tee-riffic."

They smuggled Sarah Jane into the ward through the back entrance, and the word spread quickly that there was going to be a big dance show in Eliot, Mark, and Julio's room, which was the biggest on the ward. Everybody crowded in and met Sarah Jane; then they shoved the bunks to the wall. Spade had brought his tape recorder, and Eliot gave a formal introduction: "GTCP— that's Gimp Tabernacle Choir Productions—presents a colossal night of entertainment. Straight from sixteen weeks at Diamond Lil's, the incomparable ecdysiast, the Ginger Rogers of the South, Miss Sarah Jane Gridley!"

Everybody applauded and cheered and whistled, and Sarah Jane began her dance. But she had only taken a few steps when

75

the tape in Spade's machine snapped and the music halted abruptly.

"Shee-it," Spade said. "That was my only tape."

"Don't worry, we'll sing," Eliot said. "The entire Tabernacle Choir is here."

Out of respect for Sarah Jane, they didn't do any of the Filthy Favorites, but "My Funny Valentine," very up-tempo, worked passably well, as did a few of the other Goldies, and Sarah Jane almost danced to the beat, so inspired was she by such an enthusiastic audience. When the choir had gone through its entire repertoire, they launched into a speeded-up version of their one patriotic number, "The Star-Spangled Banner," and Sarah Jane go-goed to "the rocket's red glare" with Eliot conducting. At that exact moment, the door flew open and in strode Dr. Gerald Greeley, the medical director of the unit, who had been alerted by a nurse to some unusual goings-on in L-15.

"What in the name of God—" Dr. Greeley sputtered.

"Dance therapy, sir," said Eliot. "This is Miss Sarah Jane Gridley. She's from Alvin Ailey."

"Culture, sir," Mark said. "She's doing *Swan Lake*."

"Right, man," said pimp. "She is one fucking A-One swan. Sir."

"A swan in purple pasties?" Dr. Greeley said.

"It's modern dance, sir," Eliot said. "A new version by Agnes de Mille."

"Young woman"—Dr. Greeley sighed—"have you ever even heard of *Swan Lake*?"

Sarah Jane wrinkled her cute little nose. "I think so. Give me a few bars and I'll see."

Sarah Jane was unceremoniously hustled out of the ward, but she was two hundred dollars richer, and the morale problem was solved. The Great Escape was the talk of the hospital for weeks afterward. Word of the caper traveled upward through the ranks of the VA; it later passed into legend, to be mentioned reverently at veterans' gatherings everywhere. When the story reached the ear of a brigadier general, he called Dr. Greeley, fuming, and demanded that the men involved be severely punished.

"Look, General," Dr. Greeley said, "between them, they've lost three legs and two arms. What else can we do to them?"

Not long after the Great Escape Caper, Dr. Greeley told Mark his new artificial leg had arrived. It was newly developed, rushed into production for veterans of Vietnam. The latest in prosthetic devices, it was plastic, lightweight, and mobile. Mark nodded, not really very interested. The world beyond the hospital seemed very far away. Gerry had come down several times, but it was a long, tiring trip, and the sights at the hospital depressed her. To Mark, she was like a visitor from Mars who had just dropped in from her alien planet. He had settled in to life on the ward. He liked the Gimps, he didn't mind the therapy too much, now that the worst of the pain had gone, and he had endless time to read. He didn't want to think about what lay beyond the hospital, perhaps because he was afraid to think about it. So he just went through the days on the ward, uncomplaining.

A physical therapist tried to explain the functions of the new leg to him, showing it off proudly. Mark watched and listened, bored. But something happened the first time he strapped the leg on, pulled his trousers over it, and hobbled to the mirror. He stared, astonished, at the image that greeted him: a tall young man, standing, looking at himself.

When he had first come to the ward, he avoided mirrors more assiduously than Count Dracula. While the vampire saw nothing in the glass, what Mark saw was worse—a man with a ragged stump where a leg used to be. When he forced himself to look, not to turn away, he gradually got used to it: a one-legged man, in a chair or on crutches.

But now, it was suddenly different. The new image took his breath away. He looked—whole. It was as if he had stepped into a time machine to inhabit his former self.

"Shee-it," he said, wonderingly. "I'm not a gimp."

For the next few days he practiced with the leg until the flesh on his thigh was raw and bleeding. At first he felt as if he were dragging a board that had been attached to his thigh; he despaired of ever getting any natural motion. But gradually he began to get the hang of it, and as he did so, the world beyond the ward started to slide into focus. Things at the hospital that had never bothered him now began to chafe: the bland food and the incessant jokes and even Eliot's frenzied energy. One day he came to a practice of the Gimp Tabernacle Choir fully dressed,

77

wearing the leg and walking well. For the first time, he was aware of an uneasiness between himself and the other men. Eliot's new lyrics for a Goldie, clever as always, seemed flat to his ear. Spade kept looking at him strangely. He was no longer one of them. It was time to go.

Later, in the room, Eliot said to him, "You're leaving, aren't you."

"Yeah."

"A leg is easy," Eliot said. "Knee, ankle, two joints—that's it. Arms are something else."

"There's a lot of new stuff."

"You ever *seen* it, Redneck? Rube Goldberg. Christ, I tried the damn things. Took me half an hour to pick up an ash-tray."

"You got to do it, Eliot. You can't stay here."

"I'm scared, Redneck. I'm fucking scared. I can't even brush my teeth alone. I haven't got any fucking *arms!*"

Mark's eyes widened in surprise. "Shit. You know, you're right?"

Eliot grinned.

"Hebe, you got brains," Mark said.

"Not much help in opening a can of Spam, Redneck."

"Spam sucks. Eat out."

And Eliot began to cackle and Mark started to laugh and then they both collapsed on the bed in laughter, and they laughed until it seemed their sides would split open. When the laughter was spent, Eliot said, "We are fucking going to make it, Redneck."

"Fucking A we are!" Mark said.

Mark was ready to head home two days later. Before he left he had a talk with Dr. Greeley, who wanted to sign him up for a therapy group when he got back to Maryland. Mark declined.

"There are a lot of things you haven't wrestled with, Mark; you keep things inside. There's sadness. Anger."

"I'm not pissed. I just want to get on with my life."

"You're going to be angry, Mark. Don't try to wrestle with it all alone. A lot of people want to help."

"I'll be OK."

"Don't be a hero."

"I'm OK."

"Have you thought about what you're going to do?"

"Yeah, I think I'll stay in, Doc. I can qualify for an MOS in communications. I hear the army needs information specialists. I don't need a leg to type."

"Sounds like a good idea. You're young, Mark. You have a good life ahead of you."

"Fucking A," Mark said.

FROM JESSIE'S DIARY
(SOPHOMORE YEAR)

Dear Diary: Well, I am not the same person as I was yesterday. Today I am an ex-con. A jailbird. I have been in prison.

We were on the Boston Common, protesting the war, peacefully (we burned an American flag, but it was only a little one), and this bunch of guys started to make trouble. One man actually spat at me. I had never seen anyone look at me with such hatred. It's funny, these guys seem to hate the women protesters more than the men. Maybe it's because we're stepping out of our "place." We're not being good little girls and saying yes, yes, yes, while Big Daddy, the government, lies to us about this immoral war. You know, they teach us all these things in school, about how the Founding Fathers threw tea in the harbor and resisted tyranny, but they must think it's all a fairy tale, somehow. They teach us about freedom of speech, and then when we act on the things we've learned, they hate us for it. Those guys out there yelling at us, they would have yelled the same way at the Sons of Liberty. What good is having liberty if you don't use it to speak out when your government is wrong? I couldn't live with myself if I just turned my head, hit the books, and went on with my life as if what is happening in Vietnam didn't matter. I think we will turn the tide of this war. I believe it. We are a force no one can stop.

But anyhow, back to jail. These guys started beating up on us, and the cops waded in, and who did they start clobbering? Us! I saw one girl get hit over the head so hard that the blood just gushed all over her, in her hair, down her shirt. One cop came at me with a club and I kicked him in the balls, the lousy fascist. But then a couple of other cops grabbed me and dragged me off to the paddy wagon.

I kept thinking of this book my father used to read to me when I was a kid, about Officer Bear, kind and fair, who keeps us all from harm. The picture was of this bear in a policeman's uniform. He had big brown gentle eyes and I was thinking about him as a cop twisted my arm and said, "Commie slut." I really did believe in that book. But then, I believed in Horton the Elephant and Glinda the Good Witch of the North, too. My view of realpolitik was Dr. Seuss, not Machiavelli.

Then a cop read me my rights, like they do on television, and I said, "I want to see Officer Bear," and a young cop looked at me and grinned and said, "Kind and fair, who keeps us all from harm?"

"That's him."

"Internal Affairs got him for sniffing coke. Busted him back to traffic duty."

"I guess it's not my day," I said.

The wagon took us to prison, a huge gray building that looked like the Château d'If from The Count of Monte Cristo. *As I walked in, wearing handcuffs, I was afraid for the first time. I mean, I am a person who never even had an overdue library book, and I was going to prison. To a place where other people had all the power and I didn't have any at all. And I was scared. Really scared.*

But the worst was the strip search. I had to take all my clothes off and this hard-faced matron stuck her hand up my vagina. She did it really hard, the bitch. I never wanted to kill anybody before, but I wanted to kill her. To have to stand there, naked, and to have her put her hands all over me—in me—it was terrible. I felt so . . . violated. Then I had to get fingerprinted and have a mug shot taken and I kept thinking, Why are they doing this to me, a good citizen, who pays her parking tickets the very same day she gets them?

I was so glad to see that Andrea was going to share my cell. We were stuck in this tiny place, only six feet wide, and it had two bunks with mattresses with yellow stains on them. And no toilet.

"My father is going to be pissed," Andrea said. "He sent me to BU so I should marry a doctor."

"A lawyer is what we need right now," I said.

"My mother will faint. She thinks I am at a prom at Yale."

"They have proms there still?"

"Of course not. But she doesn't know that. She'd never approve of me demonstrating. Her idea of protest is taking a dress back to Loehmann's when it has a spot."

There hadn't been anybody in the cell next to ours, but then the matron brought in a girl who couldn't have been much older than we were, dressed in red sequined shorts and a red halter top, with white high-heeled boots.

"Don't look now," Andrea said, "but I think Ringling Brothers is in town."

I whispered to Andrea, "I don't think she's from the circus. I bet she's a hooker."

"No shit," Andrea said. "I thought it was Princess Grace."

"Be nice, Andrea," I said. "She's a sister." And I turned to the girl, who had this purple eyeshadow on, and I said, "Hi. How are you?"

"I'm in fucking jail, that's how I am."

"Well, other than that."

"OK," said the girl, whose name was Stephi. "What are you two in here for?"

"Demonstrating against the war."

"The war sucks," Stephi said, pulling a thread from her red shorts.

"Right," I said. Then I said, "I think prostitution ought to be legal, don't you?"

"Then I'd have to pay fucking taxes."

"Right. I never thought about that." We were quiet for a minute; then I asked her, "How did you get into hooking?"

82

"Oh, Christ," Andrea said. "She's doing 'This Is Your Life' with a whore!"

"My old man put the moves on me," Stephi said.

"Your father?"

"Yeah, he was a stinking drunk. So was my old lady. I got the hell out at fourteen."

"Aren't you afraid a lot? There's a lot of weird guys out there."

"One guy broke my nose once. That's when I got this." She reached down and pulled a razor blade out of the heel of her boot. "I protect myself."

"It's the patriarchy," I said. "If women had any real power, they wouldn't have to sell their bodies."

"The what?"

"Patriarchy. The system is run by men."

"No shit."

"Yeah, but we are going to tear it down."

"Pardon me if I don't hold my breath, honey."

"It'll take a while. But we can change things."

"I do not believe this," Andrea groaned. "I'm in stir with Gloria Steinem, and she's trying to convert a hooker."

"Oh, Andrea, don't be such a JAP," I said.

Stephi stared at Andrea. "Did she have her eyes done? She doesn't look like a Jap."

"That's Jewish-American princess," I explained.

"I can't stand being in jail," Andrea said. "They took away my mascara!"

"There's probably no nail polish remover either," I said.

"No nail polish remover! Did you say no nail polish remover?" Andrea gripped the bars, the way James Cagney used to do on the "Late Show." "I need my fix of Cutex. I will never get out alive!" she shrieked.

"Quiet down in there!" hollered a voice.

"You two girls are really strange," Stephi said.

We spent the whole night in the cell before we got bailed out. I never felt so smelly and filthy in my whole life. Stephi was still there when we left, but she said she was going to get bailed out soon. She waved goodbye and yelled, "Screw the pat—the patri—"

"The patriarchy," I yelled back.

83

"Yeah. Screw it good."

And we walked out into the sunlight. I don't think I ever really knew, before, what the word "freedom" really meant. And I don't want to go to jail, ever again.

But I will, if I have to.

There are things you just have to do in life. If you break the law for a cause, you have to take the consequences. Thomas Jefferson said, "I have sworn on the altar of God, eternal hostility to all forms of tyranny over the mind of man (and woman—emphasis mine).

If Jefferson were alive today, he would be marching with us. I know he would.

Hell, no, we won't go!

SEVEN

The regular meeting of the Provost's Council brought the usual crowd tramping into the conference room next to Jessie's office: Jake needling Brian; Wendell Phelan needing to be stroked; Liz Hailey and Norman Wineberg; and Mark, observing the proceedings with his usual bemusement. The subject for the day was a review of how Kinsolving was doing in the race for grant money. Not being heavily endowed, Kinsolving had to make increasingly greater efforts to keep up with the larger colleges in the grant sweepstakes. Good things followed the money: prestige, top-notch scholars, shiny new science centers, four-color supplements in the *New York Times,* and a flood of applications. Jessie had hired a staff who did nothing but seek out grant money and offer help to faculty members with proposals. In the old days, Kinsolving had scorned such activity, but the old days—with baby boomers clamoring for admission—were long gone. Some faculty members chafed at the idea of scholarship as horse race, but if that was how the game was to be played, Jessie was determined to play it with

85

the best of them. She asked Liz Hailey what new grant proposals were in the pipeline.

"Dr. Barry from Health Sciences got top ratings in peer review at the National Science Foundation."

"What's his project?"

"A study of the impact of poor nutrition on children from ages one to four."

"That sounds promising."

"Yeah, except they just merged the nutrition budget at NSF with the budget for laser research."

"Lasers?" Brian said. "Isn't that Star Wars?"

"Yeah," Jake mumbled. "Maybe we could get a grant to put death rays in soup kitchens."

"Maybe *we* ought to get in on Star Wars," Norman Wineberg said. "Get some lasers."

"I can't get chalk," Brian complained. "I can't get light bulbs. My classroom is as bright as the Great Dismal Swamp, and he's talking lasers."

"Sorry, Brian, I'll push Buildings and Grounds on that," Jessie said. "Liz, how about the money we've been looking for to expand the Afro program."

"The Ford Foundation did Blacks two years ago. Markle is into illegal aliens."

"Maybe we could find some boat people and give them scholarships," Mark suggested.

"They move too fast," Jake said. "You run after them with financial aid forms and they think you're from immigration."

Jessie sighed. The conversation was getting familiar. "The federal cutbacks have really made the competition tough, especially for liberal arts colleges," she said. "I see BU just got a big grant from DEK. I don't want John Silber leaving us in the dust. I think we're going to have to do more outreach to the high-tech industry. Norman, I wonder if you and Mark and Liz would consider yourselves a committee to work on that. Come up with some proposals."

All three nodded their heads in assent.

"Mark, the ROTC scholarships still look good for next year?"

"Yes, I've heard we're not going to be level-funded. It looks like we're going to get a good hike."

"So we'll have more toy soldiers," Brian snapped. "Wonderful."

"May I remind you, Professor," Mark said, annoyed, "that two of our ROTC students graduated summa last year, and two years ago we had a Rhodes Scholar."

There was a knock, and then the door opened a crack. William Wainscott, assistant to the director of the office of grants and contracts, poked his head in.

"Are you ready for me now?"

"Yes, Bill, come in, please."

Wainscott smiled and walked into the office. He was young and enthusiastic and full of energy, but he hadn't quite gotten the idea yet—having just come to academia from the private sector—that some money was not appropriate for institutions of higher learning. Jessie was certain that, left to his own devices, he would cheerfully accept unmarked bills brought to his office in gym bags by men in dark suits.

"I just got the latest RFP from DOD," Wainscott said. "I think there could be something there for us."

"For God's sake, man, would you say that in English?" Wendell Phelan barely tolerated any form of the English language that postdated the fourteenth century, much less federal jargon.

"He means he has the latest request for proposals from the Department of Defense," Jessie translated.

"Don't we have a lot of acres we're not using, at the conference center in Wayland?" Wainscott asked Jessie.

"At Knotts Hill? Yes, there's quite a lot of land."

"Room for some sheep?"

"Sheep?" Brian asked. "You *did* say sheep? Stupid animals that bleat all the time?"

"Sounds like the freshman class," Jake said.

"Bill," Jessie asked, "why would we be interested in sheep?"

"Animal toxicology. DOD is putting a ton of money into studying the effects of chemicals on mammals."

"Chemicals?" Jessie said, puzzled. "What sort?"

Wainscott looked perplexed. Details were not his forte. "Oh, I don't know. The usual stuff, I guess. Plague, maybe a little recombinant DNA, Agent Orange, nerve gas. They come up with new stuff all the time."

"Uh, Mr. Wainscott," Mark said, "the materials you are talking about are extremely toxic. To experiment with those, you have to have a laboratory that meets the highest NIH safety levels: double airlock doors, special construction, disposal facilities."

"Sure, we could get DOD to fund one at Knotts Hill. It's where the big bucks are. DOD is where it's at, grantwise, these days."

"Right," Jake said. "The National Endowment for the Arts is not going to give us five mil to knock off sheep."

"I—ah—I don't think chemical warfare is exactly the sort of research we want to pursue at Kinsolving," Jessie said tactfully.

Liz Hailey shuddered. "Can you imagine our students getting their hands on that stuff?"

"Especially the sophomores," Brian said. "They'd smoke it."

Jessie laughed. "We had enough trouble with the measles epidemic last year. I don't think the parents could handle a tuition hike *and* the Black death, all in one semester."

Mark chortled and William Wainscott gave him a dark look.

"*You* ought to be interested in DOD funds," he said.

"I am," Mark said. "Maybe we could do a Nuclear Winter proposal. A little dust, a little ice; it's crappy in Wayland in January anyway."

Jessie kicked his good leg under the table. "He's kidding, Bill," she said. "We really do appreciate your efforts."

She could tell that Bill was starting to sulk so she added a few more words of praise; he was only somewhat mollified when Jessie promised to take a close look at the RFP's to see if there would be something more appropriate for Kinsolving scholars.

After the meeting ended and the others had left, Jessie walked up to Mark. "Are we still on for tonight?"

"You bet. By the way—"

"Yes?"

"The army needs to test the new tank-borne nuclear warheads. Could we get a grant to try them out on the Theology building? During lunchtime, so we'd only wipe out the seminar on Luther."

Jessie sighed. "He is a bit overenthusiastic, isn't he."

"Don't laugh. If you asked for a germ warfare center, Cap Weinberger would probably give it to you. With fifty million in cost overruns, you could probably build a whole new campus."

"You disapprove?"

"Of defense contractors getting greedy? I sure as hell do. When they're cutting military pensions and you can't live decently on an enlisted man's pay, you bet I do. Don't get me on my soapbox. Listen, want to come over around seven?"

"Seven would be fine."

After work, Mark went to his favorite market in Chinatown and picked up the makings for dinner. He had spent more time than he cared to admit in the past week poring over his cookbooks. He had learned to cook out of desperation when his marriage broke up. He barely knew how to boil water, and he could hardly afford to eat out all the time. He tackled the task in his usual thorough manner. Anything worth doing was worth doing well. Chinese cooking appealed to him. He liked slicing up the vegetables and the meats and the condiments, pushing them into neat little piles with the edge of his knife, adding them to the wok at precisely the right time. There was an almost military precision to it, and it gave him a great sense of satisfaction. He had become very good at it.

When Jessie arrived she looked around the apartment in surprise and said, "Mark, this is lovely. You have wonderful pieces of art."

"You were expecting the Twenty-fourth Regimental Armory?"

"Oh, maybe a few bandoliers draped across the couch."

He laughed. "We're having orange-flavored beef, rice Szechuan, and Hunan lamb. OK?"

"OK? My God, it's fantastic! You make me feel so inferior. I can't cook at all."

"Nothing?"

"Well, not exactly nothing. I have a couple of party things I can make that won't make people want to barf, but that's it."

"I really like cooking Chinese. Do you know there are more than five thousand dishes in Chinese cuisine?"

"I never knew about Chinese cooking until I was nineteen and my friend Andrea Margolis took me out to eat. At home we had something called chop suey once in a while. It was hamburger with some bean sprouts thrown in. My mother was not a great cook either. Eating is not big with Irish Catholics."

"I wonder why that is?"

"I suppose it's hard to develop a haute cuisine when all you've got is five million potatoes rotting under the ground."

89

He laughed. "You have an Irish face, you know that? I knew you were Irish first time I saw you. I bet you never tan."

"No, I just turn red and peel. And get freckles." She sighed. "I always wanted to be one of the California golden girls. No luck."

"No, being pale is more mysterious. Can you imagine Anna Karenina with a tan? Or Cathy Earnshaw?"

"Heathcliff, pass me the Coppertone?"

"Right. People with tans can't be tragic."

"I think you are something of a romantic, Major."

He laughed. "My mother was a schoolteacher. I read all her books. I used to think I was a deprived child because I didn't have any fog-drenched moors. That was where *everything* happened."

"Not many of those in southern Maryland."

"No. Just scrub pine, salt water, and a lot of chickens." He laughed. "I used to imagine a great old Gothic manor house where the henhouse was. Funny stuff, for a country boy."

"You're just full of surprises."

"No, it's just that you civilians think all soldiers are illiterates, barely able to read the M-16 manual."

"I suppose that's right. In high school, any girl who went out with a soldier was automatically considered a slut."

"Your reputation is in jeopardy, then."

"I don't think women have reputations anymore. They went out with garter belts."

"Damn. And I *liked* garter belts. Hey, you want to watch the great chef in action?"

"I'd love to."

She watched him as he prepared the condiments, making admiring comments all the while, and he was aware of the fact that he was showing off shamelessly, explaining every step in the preparation of the meal with a flourish. But she seemed to enjoy it, and he served the meal and poured the wine, and a tape of Cole Porter played on the stereo. He didn't think his country bluegrass was exactly the stuff for the occasion. He had been worried that there might be long, awkward silences during the meal, and the music would help with that, but she was very easy to talk to, she laughed at his jokes, and gave as good as she got when he slipped in a dig at academics, feminists, or civilians. He relaxed and found he was enjoying himself more than he had in a very long time. After dinner, they sat in the living room and he poured brandy.

They had not, he noticed, talked at all about Vietnam. They had skirted the subject, delicately.

"Mark," she asked him, "what do you plan to do with your doctorate, when it's finished?"

"I've only got a few more years to go till I get my twenty in. There's a book I want to write, and I figure with my army pension, and maybe teaching a couple of courses someplace, I could do it financially."

"What's the book about?"

"A grunt's history of—the war. You know, through most of history we hear only from the generals. Caesar. Guderian. I want to tell the story of Vietnam from the point of view of the men who fought there."

"Sounds like an interesting idea. Have you done any work on it?"

"Yeah. I started taping stuff when I was in the VA hospital. I didn't have any idea for the book then, I just knew I wanted to do it. I have hours of tape. The book will be partly an oral history. Just think if we could hear the voices of the men who fought the Civil War. How would that change our view of it? I'd like to produce a tape library to go along with the book."

"I'm sure you could get a grant for that. Have you thought about it?"

"I'm not a scholar. I don't have any track record in research. I'm a pretty good writer, I think, but I'm just a soldier. Who would give me money?"

"You'd be surprised. The Rockefeller Foundation, the National Endowment. I can think of a number of places. I'll get Liz to send you some material. She's really up on this stuff."

"I'd really appreciate that."

"Listen, why not do a course here at Kinsolving, based on your idea for the book? It would be a great way to start to use the material."

"It's a different kind of course than most. I'm not sure it could get through the bureaucracy."

"Oh, I don't think you'd have any trouble. Just do a syllabus and submit it to the curriculum committee. We could try it out with a workshop number, and you could go for formal approval after you'd done it for a semester."

"It would be that easy?"

"Yes. The nice thing about Kinsolving is that we're flexible. A lot of university bureaucracies seem to be set up to make sure no new ideas creep in."

"I've noticed that."

"Yes, it's the world seen from the view of elite white males. Who give tenure to people just like themselves. They can't see that Black History or Women's Studies counts at all. Or a course like yours. What do soldiers know?"

"Quite a lot, actually."

"Of course. Academics tend to see the world from a pretty narrow perspective. That's one of the things I don't want. We take risks here. We're pretty venturesome."

"Isn't the danger that you can wind up with a lot of trendy junk courses?"

"Sure. We once had one on bathroom graffiti. But those courses don't last."

"You really do like it here, don't you."

"Yes, I do. I wouldn't be happy at a place like Harvard, that reeks of tradition. Of course, Harvard wouldn't hire anybody like me."

"Because of your radical past?"

"Yeah. They'd see me as a bomb thrower. And an uppity woman. The last one is the big sin, actually."

"I can see you're an uppity woman. Were you ever a bomb thrower?"

"Me? No, I was never in the Weathermen, I didn't groove on violence. Some people did." She laughed. "I did write *Off the Pigs* on the building that had Rotcy in it, though."

"Touching," Mark said. "A little something from Hallmark."

"It's hard to be original with spray paint," she said tartly.

Little warning bells flashed "danger" in Mark's mind. Possibly it was the brandy, but he ignored them. If this was where it was all going to fall apart, so be it.

"I used to hate all you people, when I was in 'Nam. I thought you were a bunch of prissy-assed college kids who were having a great time marching and screwing, while we were slogging in the mud."

"I got five stitches, once, from a cop who agreed with you and took a swing at me. For a lot of us, who were committed, it was real hard work. It wasn't all beer and skittles."

"Some of it was."

"Compared to being in a war, sure. And we *were* arrogant. We

92

thought we had God on our side and everybody who didn't agree with us was just dumb."

"I remember Jane Fonda shaking her ass all over Hanoi. Having dinner with the people who were killing guys like me. That made us feel nobody gave a shit for us."

"That was our biggest mistake, I think. Trying to make a saint out of Ho Chi Minh. I thought it was dumb at the time, but I just went along, because it was for the cause. Dumping on our soldiers wasn't just stupid, it was wrong."

"I was standing in a bus station in Richmond, on my way home from the hospital, and I was in uniform. A kid walked by and called me a baby killer. I wanted to wring his neck. I think I would have, if I'd been as fast on the leg as I am now."

"There were a lot of stupid things done. A lot. But the war ended. It ended because so many people made it clear they just wouldn't support it."

"I suppose."

"Do you think we could have won it?"

"No. Oh, maybe if we'd done things right from the start. If there really had been a decent government to prop up."

"A lot of ifs."

"Yeah. I think the army got suckered."

"Suckered?"

"Yes. Got caught in a situation that's fatal, just *fatal,* for an army in a democratic state. We wound up fighting a war that the people didn't want, that Congress never declared, a politician's war. That ought not to happen again."

"But a lot of military men were raring to go."

"Oh sure. Visions of World War Two were dancing in their heads. War is supposed to be good for the army. Promotions, good budget, good press. But not every war is like that. We rode our own horses over the cliff. I think we're sadder and wiser now. You don't see the brass hats—the smart ones—all hot to trot in Central America."

"You've thought about this a lot."

"Sure."

"I think about that whole time a lot too. I see these kids, our students, and it doesn't seem possible that Vietnam is only a word to them. You know, their eyes glaze over when you mention it. One kid asked me, 'So what was the big deal?' "

"Oh, yeah, that drives me nuts. They think the whole thing is a big bore. They don't have any idea what it was like. And I want them to *know*."

"So do I. It wasn't really that long ago, but so much has changed. And it was so real. So important."

"For us it was. It's funny, you and I would have been on opposite sides of the barricades, throwing rocks at each other. But we understand each other better than people who didn't get involved in it."

"Yes, I talk to people my age, who lived through that time but weren't affected by it, and I don't understand them." She laughed. "After Kent State, we closed down every university in Boston. We were rallying the students, running through the dorms shouting, 'Are you striking? Are you striking?' We ran into one room, and this blond girl was doing her nails, and she looked up at us and said—seriously—'Well, people say I'm attractive, but I really don't think I'm *striking*.' "

He laughed and poured her more brandy. "Yeah, it was strange. In World War Two, everybody's life was disrupted. With 'Nam, it was like a giant hand came down and scooped you up and put you down in this strange land. If you didn't die there, it put you right back where you were. Alone. I went home to visit my dad, and people would say to me, 'Oh, I haven't seen you around. You still in school?' "

"That must have felt strange."

"Yeah. I always thought that for Vietnam vets, it was like Dorothy coming home from Oz. She'd tell people, 'I was in this place where there were Munchkins and talking lions,' and somebody would say to her, 'Oh, I was in Topeka once and it was nice too.' "

Jessie laughed. "I never thought about Dorothy needing a rap group."

"Five'll get you ten that after two weeks back in Kansas, Dorothy was hitting the hard cider and popping Valium."

"Can you see her going to a shrink? She'd babble on about ruby slippers and flying monkeys and he'd say, 'Miss Gale, was your toilet training strict?' "

"Then she finally goes berserk and strangles Toto and they cart her off to the snake pit. Every time she says 'I want to go to Oz!' they say 'Of course, dearie' and give her another needle in the butt."

Jessie laughed. "I am never going to be able to hear 'Somewhere Over the Rainbow' without seeing Dorothy in a strait-jacket."

"Now that I've ruined one children's classic," he said, "would you like to hear 'Rumpelstiltskin'?"

She laughed and shook her head; when she laughed, he noticed, she tossed her head back, and her throat was white and small and very fragile. Her laugh was deep and throaty and a little hoarse, not at all a refined laugh. He liked it very much.

They talked more, and he found himself jumping in to fill any lag in the conversation, so that it would keep going, on and on. It was after one when she finally glanced at her watch and said, "Oh, Mark, look at what time it's getting to be."

"I'll walk you home," he said.

"Oh, that's not necessary."

"I know. I want to."

At her front step, she turned and said, "Thank you for a lovely evening," and her breath was fragrant with the orange brandy. "I really did enjoy it."

"Well, we can do it again. Soon."

"I'd like that."

They stood still, facing each other, and neither moved, as if they were both reluctant to disrupt the pleasant lassitude of the moment. Then, impulsively, she leaned up and kissed him gently on the mouth, and her lips were warm and sweet, as they had been in his reveries. They tasted of Cointreau, not grapes, but that was all right too.

"Good night, Mark," she said.

"Good night, Jess."

She went in and he walked down Marlborough Street, toward his apartment. He was going to fall in love with her, he was sure of that. Going to? He laughed. *Oh, you poor fool, this can't ever work.* She could have her pick of men; he saw them: tall, with skin like porcelain and slightly receding hairlines, wearing tweed jackets with leather elbow patches and chatting about Proust. Not one of them had ever seen cow flop or stuck his hand under a hen's fanny for breakfast. He was a one-legged farm boy among the Harvards, and they intimidated him, although he would never admit that to anybody. Their nasal tones and broad *a*'s had the sound of money and family, generations back. Boston was where the Lodges spoke only to the Cabots and the Cabots spoke only to God. Hardly the same as the Del-Mar-Va peninsula, that sandy corner of three states which had produced, as far as he knew, only one famous American, Frank Perdue. So what if Boston had given the world the Tea Party and the Shot Heard Round the World and the Pops; Del-Mar-Va had its slice of Americana too, the Oven Stuffer Roaster.

He sighed as he walked to his door and opened it. *Don't be an asshole, Claymore, you are out of your league.*

It had been a nice dinner, she was friendly and warm—just like she would have been with any member of the faculty. There was a touch of fall in the air, just the sort of night to bring back all the sweet memories of youth. The kiss was brandy and the night and that was it. All of it.

Well, he wouldn't think any more about it. He had a lot of work to do tomorrow, he was tired, and he needed a good night's sleep. Without it, he was a mess. He didn't want Jessie McGrath tramping around in his dreams, he would simply banish her, with her white dress and pale shoulders and warm, soft lips. Jessie McGrath would not occupy his thoughts. Not tonight, not tomorrow. He would just put her out of his mind. Completely.

He wondered if she liked Peking duck.

FROM JESSIE'S DIARY
(SOPHOMORE YEAR)

Dear Diary: Well, we all filed into group today in Talia's room, clutching our hand mirrors. Andrea wasn't going to go, but I made her do it.

"I don't want to look at my crotch," she said. "I don't want to look at anyone's crotch. Why are we doing this?"

"So we won't hate our genitals," I said. "Talia is right. Women have been taught to hate their sexual organs."

"I don't hate mine," Andrea said. "I just don't want to spend the day looking at it. It is not Gone With the Wind.*"*

"Scarlett O'Hara probably hated her vagina too," I said.

"Jessie, the Yankees were invading, her plantation was burning, and she was eating fucking roots to survive. I don't think she was worrying about her vagina."

"Well, I think this is a good thing we are doing."

"Can you imagine what my parents would say if I wrote to them, 'Hi. I am having fun at college. We all took off our panties today and looked at our vaginas. Love, your daughter, Andrea.'"

97

"It's not like it's a course, Andrea."

"Yeah, what would they call it? Pee-Pee Showing 101? Christ, Jess, I did this when I was six."

"When you are six, you don't hate your genitals. It's only when you grow up that you do. Andrea, I saw a men's room once that had a drawing on the wall of a vagina with a spider crawling out of it."

Andrea looked at me as if I were a stupid child. She does that a lot. "That's just male fear of female power, Jess. Some men dream about vaginas with teeth in them."

"They do?" I said.

"Yeah. Good thing it's only a dream. My parents would have made me wear braces there, too."

"That's gross, Andrea."

"Ma, I had a great checkup. Only two cavities with Crest."

"You are not taking this in the right spirit," I said, trying to be serious. We all filed into Talia's room, and Talia gave us a little lecture about how our vaginas were beautiful flowers, with pink petals, and she said we ought to take pictures of them and hang them on our walls. Talia said she was going to do that.

"Talia," Andrea said, "what are you going to do when your parents come to visit?"

"I am not going to take it down," Talia said. "I am proud of it."

"See, Mom and Dad," Andrea said, "here's my Jane Fonda poster and my picture of Ho Chi Minh and right in the middle, there, that's my vagina."

"Andrea, this is no time for levity," Talia said, glowering.

So we all dutifully looked at each other's vaginas and we oh-ed and ah-ed like we were opening shower presents. Talia said we should decide what sort of flowers we looked like, and I decided I was a rose, sort of pale pink and deep red. Talia knew she was a hyacinth. Andrea said she was a man-eating Venus flytrap.

"You are determined not to take this seriously, aren't you, Andrea," Talia said severely.

"Talia, we are fighting for our rights. We are trying to wrestle power away from the patriarchy. We are trying to elect women to Congress, we are trying to end centuries of discrimination. I do not *think that looking at our vaginas with little hand mirrors is our top priority here."*

I said, "Sexual politics is important too, Andrea. I like thinking of myself as a rose. In school, the nuns said we shouldn't ever look at ourselves down there. It made me feel dirty."

"Jess, if it makes you feel good to be a flower, that's fine. Grow a whole fucking bouquet between your legs. But I'd rather work on an equal rights amendment."

We all argued about that for an hour. Nobody changed their minds about anything. Talia was still determined to do her labia majora up in Kodacolor, and Andrea swore that never would she do a self-portrait of her crotch. But we all agreed it was a good discussion and that it was OK for feminists to disagree.

Andrea was still harrumphing when we got back to our room.

"Jess, men don't put pictures of their penises over their beds," she said.

"Sure they do. Airplanes, cars, trains. Phallic symbols."

"But men are even more hung up over their genitals than we are about ours. I mean, you know how they obsess about size."

"Oh, yeah, Ronald always goes on about it. He measures himself to see if he's growing."

"Is he?"

"No, but he's perfectly fine. I used to tell him that human beings are not supposed to be hung like horses."

"Did that help?" Andrea asked.

"No. For two more inches, he'd gladly live in a stable and eat oats."

"Ira thinks he's long enough, but not wide enough. He drinks some kind of fish juice from Japan that's supposed to make his penis fatter."

"Does it?"

"No," Andrea said, "but ten minutes after he drinks it, he wants to pee on Pearl Harbor."

We both broke up and rolled on the bed, cackling. Sexual politics can be a hoot, sometimes.

But Dear Diary, I do think I am a rose. I do, I really do. A lovely, soft, pink-and-red-and-glowing American Beauty rose.

EIGHT

"I'm thinking of throwing myself at Mark," Jessie said. "What do you think, Grace?"

Jessie's roommate looked up from the book of poetry she was reading. "Are you serious?"

"Oh, yeah. He turns me on."

"Jessie, he's got one leg!"

"So what?"

"Oh, Jessie, I know it's wrong, but I couldn't look at that—thing."

"You thought he had a nice ass, before."

"I know. It's just me. But I'm not you. Are you getting vibes?"

"Yes. Oh, I know he's interested, but I wonder if he'd ever make the first move. Sexually, I mean. There's his leg. And I'm his boss, really."

"A wonder he isn't totally immobilized, much less thinking about making a first move."

"You're right."

"I never thought sleeping with soldiers would be your thing."

"Grace, this is hardly like going down to the Greyhound Bus terminal and picking up some guy in khaki."

"I thought you liked intellectual men."

"See what a snob you are? You think that just because Mark is in the army, he's some kind of Neanderthal."

"Neanderthals can be fun, now and then. But you're right, I did stereotype him. Well, if it isn't macho chic, what is it that you see in him?"

"Aside from the nice ass?"

"Right."

"Mark knows who I am, and he likes me anyway."

"What do you mean?"

"He knows I'm smart. He knows I have a big job. It doesn't seem to intimidate him."

"It did with Herb."

"I never used to admit it to myself, but I was always trying to downplay what I did. As if, when I did well, it would diminish *him*, somehow. And that's crazy. I was turning myself into a pretzel."

"You think you were the only one? I used to be into that."

"Were you?"

"Sure. I used to dress like a hooker so nobody would notice my mind. I'm the only holder of the Landseer Prize for Scholarly Excellence who picked up the little Revere bowl in fishnet tights and cleavage."

"Why do we do this, Grace?"

"We're a transitional generation, my dear. Our mothers were the Feminine Mystique. We're Superwoman. And it's a wonder we're not all basket cases. But it's going to be so much easier for our daughters. They'll have us as role models. It won't seem so impossible for women to do things."

"But Grace, we have to find some decent men before we can have daughters!"

"*There's* the catch."

"You know, with Herb I always had the feeling that if I let him know what I was *really* like, he'd leave me. I don't think men live in constant fear that they're going to be left."

"Because men have power, Jess. They're raised to believe that what they do is OK. You're not afraid somebody is going to leave you if you think what you're doing is right."

101

"But *we* always need someone to tell us we're OK. We see ourselves in the mirror of how somebody else sees us."

"And why shouldn't that make us anxious? We have no control over that. It can change at any time."

"*I* didn't change, but the way Herb felt about me did."

"You were changing. You grew, Jess. And he couldn't take it. But that was his problem, not yours."

"It sure as hell turned into my problem."

"You couldn't have stayed with him. You'd have wound up a cripple from trying to twist yourself out of shape to please him."

"Is that our choice? To shrivel and be loved or be alone?"

"You're playing that tune again. Sometimes it is. But not always. I think men are changing too, finding out they don't need women to be crippled for them to be whole."

"I don't ever want to be the way I was with Herb, ever again. On a tightrope, afraid of being left. You know, it was worse, really, worrying about it than when it happened."

"Now *my* pattern, Jess, is different from yours. When men get too close, *I* leave. Before they can do it to me."

"We're quite a pair. You head for the hills, I turn into Jell-O."

"Yeah, but we don't have hand-me-down lives."

"Who said life was easy? Didn't somebody tell us that?"

"I don't know. Dr. Joyce Brothers, maybe?"

Jessie went upstairs to get ready for dinner with Mark. She had not been at all coy about saying yes every time he had asked her over for dinner. Not only was he fun to be with, but his food was fantastic. Just thinking about his Peking duck could make her salivate on cue. Tonight he was doing chicken in plum sauce; she might just sleep with him for the plum sauce alone, never mind the nice ass. Last time they had talked about skiing, and when he discovered she loved to ski too, he had suggested that as soon as there was a good snowfall they should head for the mountains. He said that last year he had rented a place at Gunstock for the season with another guy, but the guy had left town and it was too expensive for him to go it alone—which led her to suggest they might go in together on it. He was very careful to let her know he was not suggesting anything carnal. "We could each use it, any time we wanted to," he said. "The place has a couple of bedrooms."

She dug into her makeup kit, took out a lipstick, and started to put it on. Ugh, purple. Where in hell did she get purple lipstick? She had, she thought, become rather too indifferent about cosmetics since Herb left, grabbing whatever she could find on the bargain counter. Wearing the same shade of lipstick as Boy George was not merely indifferent, it was a breach of taste. She wiped off the purple and tried a washed-out but suitable red. She did her nails, a sure sign that something big was up. She remembered doing her nails the night of the senior prom, waving them about in the air so they wouldn't stain her pink tulle gown. Then nail polish went out of fashion as Protest came in. Did Emma Goldman or Elizabeth Cady Stanton wear Pretty Pink on their nails? On the barricades, did you care about Palmolive hands while a cop bounced a nightstick off your head? She hadn't done her nails in years, and it made her feel giddy with anticipation, as if she were a mere girl again. She wondered if he had had a senior prom. She pictured him, tall and slender, a lock of his dark hair escaping from the Vitalis to tumble across his forehead. He wore a tuxedo with a plaid cummerbund and tie, and the girl with him wore a white dress with ruffles. Her name was Mary Sue. She realized, with a stab of regret, that in her mind's eye he had two legs then.

When she arrived at his apartment, he greeted her at the door, and his face was wreathed in a big grin. It was so nice, she thought, to feel welcomed. Herb had always seemed faintly annoyed when she walked in, the expression on his face the same as when he had been bitten by a mosquito: distracted. The chicken in plum sauce was heavenly, just as she had expected, and when she finished one helping he urged her to have more.

"If you keep feeding me like this, I am going to be fat as a pig."

"Come on, you could use a little more meat on your bones."

"I'm always on a diet. My former husband liked skinny women."

"Ugh. Not us farm boys. A woman needs a little heft if she's going to drive a tractor and keep a man warm in the old double bed at night."

Jessie laughed and took a second helping. "Cheryl Tiegs is not your type?"

"Another twenty-five pounds and she'd be right nice. I see her on TV and I want to make her eat a big bowl of oatmeal."

"This is sure better than oatmeal."

103

"After this there's Black Forest cake. From that place in Cambridge."

"Oh, Mark, this is sinful."

They finished the cake and moved into the living room for brandy. "How long have you been divorced, Jess?" Mark said to her.

"Almost two years." She sighed.

"Bad scene?"

"You could say that. I found him screwing a student on the breakfast table. In the scrambled eggs."

He chuckled and said, "Sorry. But that must have looked real funny."

"Oh, it did. I was very rational about it all. I picked up a dish towel and started whipping the scrambled eggs off their asses." She grinned. "The poor girl was terrified. She ran down the hall screaming."

He laughed. "I can just picture it."

She started to laugh too as she told Mark about the lovers. "But I didn't see the humor at the time," she admitted ruefully.

"That did it? Finished the marriage?"

"Oh, that had fallen apart a long time before. I was just slow catching on."

Mark took a sip of brandy. "My marriage just sort of ran down, like a musical toy."

"A friendly divorce?"

"Not really. Gerry—my wife—well, she married a guy with two legs, and she couldn't handle the whole scene. She was just a kid when we were married."

"Is that an excuse?"

"She did try. She hung in for five years. And I was a lot different from the kid she'd married, I guess. But it was the leg that really did it. She could never look at it. I kept a blanket over it, all the time."

"Always? Even when—" She stopped, realizing the delicacy of what she was asking.

"Yeah, especially then. There isn't a section in *The Joy of Sex* called 'Stumps.' I looked. The last one is S and M." He paused and said, "A little gimp humor."

"Oh, Mark, for chrissake, you're not a gimp. My God, you even ski."

"I know. Supergimp. Invent a new sport, and I'm there. Want to see me breakdance?"

"Still proving something?"

"Sure."

"When do you stop?"

He shrugged. "Who knows? Maybe never." He shook his head. "I didn't mean to get into this."

"Why not? I had the feeling we could talk about anything."

"It's not very original, Jessie, but . . . I don't want pity: take a disabled vet to lunch."

"Good Lord, I don't pity you. Is that what you think?"

"It's what happens to me. I meet someone I like, and then I see it. The pity."

"And if you do, or think you do, what then? You split?"

"I won't be a charity case, Jess."

"Well, you've got the wrong idea where I'm concerned."

"Do I?"

"I'm not quite sure how to say this, but—"

"Just be blunt. It's OK."

"I want to go to bed with you. You turn me on."

Mark blinked. "Well, that's blunt, all right."

"You said I should be. Are you embarrassed?"

"No."

"You can say no politely, you know. You can have a headache. It's OK."

"I don't have a headache."

"So?"

"I want you to see it, Jess."

"Your leg?'

"Yes. It's ugly. To some people. Not to me. I'm used to it."

"All right. Let me see it."

He motioned her to follow him into the bedroom. Standing, he unbuckled his pants and let them fall to the floor and stepped out of them. The leg was plastic, very pink.

She looked at it.

"Well?" he said.

She shrugged. "It's OK. Looks—utilitarian."

"OK. Step two. "He unbuckled the leg and rested it against the bed. His thigh ended halfway down, abruptly. It looked unusual but not repulsive to her. In fact, it was not as bad as she had imagined it would be.

105

"That's it," he said.

"OK."

"Are you still interested? It's OK if you're not. I'd prefer to know, instead of playing games."

She grinned and started to unbutton her blouse. "I love show-and-tell. My turn." In fact, she did rather like showing off her breasts; she was proud of them. A man had once called them elegant: gently sloping globes with prominent and well-shaped red-brown nipples. She thought it rather a shame she hadn't been alive in the decadent days of the French court when women wore beautiful gowns that bared their entire chests to the elements. She was certain she would have wound up as number one courtesan to the king. He would have whispered to a courtier, "Who is *she*? The one with the *elegant* boobs. I must have her."

She unhooked her bra, slowly, and dropped it on the bed. She looked at him and noticed a gratifying bulge under his Jockey shorts.

"There's something *really* interesting," she said, staring boldly at his crotch. "Can I see that too?"

"If you're good," he said, with a grin.

"I will be very, very good," she said.

They lay together on the bed, and he began to touch her, his fingers gentle, skilled, his lips and tongue probing. That was a surprise. She had thought he might be rough or even clumsy.

"Mark—" she said, but he put his fingers to her lips.

"Let me please you. I want to do it."

It was a new idea for Jessie, letting a man please her. She had always thought that was *her* job, and she had gone about it studiously, reading all the manuals, learning the names of the anatomical parts you were supposed to press or squeeze or tickle. It was rather complicated. Herb had been a connoisseur of technique—hers—and he had issued directions *in medias res* like a drum and bugle corps director with a megaphone: No, more to the right; yes, that's it, up a little; oh, good, Jess, that's fine. That's good. Ow! Not too hard, for chrissake, Jess, it's not a lump of hamburger. . . . Yes, that's right, now up a little, more, more . . . no, don't *pinch!* She was so intent on following directions that she often completely forgot about her own orgasm. (Could a person chew gum and have an orgasm at the same time?) This did not seem to bother Herb.

She found herself, suddenly, moaning softly, bathed in a

warm sea of sensation, the pleasure lapping at her gently, and it was unbearably lovely. Guilt, of course, flickered.

"Mark, is this good for you?"

"Wonderful. It feels so good, doing this to you."

"What can I do for you?"

"What do you want to do?"

She ran her fingers across the hard muscles of his chest and then found, to her surprise, that she was kissing the softness of his nipples, moving her lips across the stiff hairs of his chest, putting her tongue in his mouth, all no-nos with Herb. Sex, for Herb, belonged in one place on his body and he would brook no diversionary action.

Mark sighed as she touched him and said, "Oh, yes, please, please." She moved her hands to the joining of his legs and he moaned as she grasped him. It was a few minutes before she realized that she was touching him for her pleasure as well as his. She had been so busy following directions with Herb that she had not noticed how lovely it was to touch a man there, to feel the ridges and the fullness and the hardness, the different textures of flesh beneath her fingers when she was not having to do the sex manual drill, hup-two-three. Then things got rather energetic, by mutual consent, a few reciprocal nips here and there, and then she was beneath Mark and his whole weight plunged into her. She felt like a jungle cat in heat, desperate for the driving force of mating, and she gave out a high, lusty wail of pleasure and surrender.

Afterward, he held her close against his chest, and she nestled against him, sweaty, her body streaked with fluids, his and hers. Herb always wanted her to take a shower, right after. Cuddling had to wait until her body was cleansed and powdered. Afterglow, for Herb, had to smell like Arpège bath talc, not, for God's sake, of sweat.

"Oh, Jess," he said, "no one has loved me like that for so long."

She touched his lips. "It was wonderful. Just so good."

"I'm glad."

"Was I—raucous?"

He laughed. "I love loud, lewd women."

"You were not exactly quiet yourself, Major."

"Yep, we sounded like a couple of hogs, just a-rutting away."

"Oh, that's gross!"

107

"No, it's not. Hogs are nice animals. A little surly sometimes, though."

She snuggled close to him. His arms around her felt strong and sheltering, an oak. How lovely it was to feel his arms. She had slept alone for so long she had gotten used to cold sheets on the other side of the bed. She rested her head against his chest and said, "I've been so alone, Mark."

"So have I, Jess. Oh, God, I've been so lonely. I never thought you'd want me."

"I wanted you so. I did."

He touched the little white scar under her chin and said, "Will you stay with me, Jess? I want you to be here when I wake up."

"Oh, yes, I'll stay."

"An empty bed's a terrible thing," he said. "So goddam cold and lonely. But you're here. I can't believe it."

"Believe it."

"Don't go away, I couldn't bear it," he said.

She nestled closer to him. "I won't go away. Go to sleep. I'll be here, love. I won't go away."

"Good," he said, and he fell asleep holding her in his arms.

NINE

Jessie knew it was going to be a bad day when her first appointment was with a delegation from the student government, asking to drop the English Lit requirement.

"How will knowing about some dumb white whale help me in marketing?" asked Tami, a sophomore.

"Yeah, it's not exactly *Jaws*," said Richard, a senior.

"The *Inferno*, what a drag," said Ian, another senior. Jessie had a mental image of Ian rolling the collected works of Shakespeare, Marlowe, and Dante up a hill for all eternity, wearing his L. L. Bean pants and his digital Seiko. It was the first time she smiled all day.

They went away still burdened by the great voices of literature. The kids knew all about Apple, IBM, and Wang, Jessie thought, but you got a blank stare if you mentioned Chaucer, Milton, or Emily Brontë. They thought maybe they were minor characters on "The Colbys."

And then there was the phone call from Andrea.

109

At first Jessie thought Andrea was calling from Los Angeles, where she had been working on a big contract for her consulting firm, something to do with aerospace. But it turned out she was calling from Belmont.

"I'm killing myself," she said.

"What?"

"Ira has left me for a stewardess. She's twenty-four and she flies for Piedmont. He was fucking her in motel rooms in Cincinnati, between trips for both of them. My God, Cincinnati! I'm killing myself!"

"Andrea, do you mean you wouldn't kill yourself if he was doing it someplace nice, like New Orleans?"

"My life is over, and she's making jokes."

"Andrea, you're not serious."

"Yes I am."

"When did Ira go?"

"The son-of-a-bitch left me a note. I found it when I got home. She gives him joy, he says. The son-of-a-bitch, I'll give him *tsuris*."

"Not if you're dead, you won't."

"He'll be guilty for the rest of his fucking life. Jews know about guilt. Not a day won't go by that it won't twist in his gut. I sent the kids to my mother and gave the maid the day off."

That was when Jessie really started to worry.

"Andrea, get hold of yourself. You can't kill yourself in the middle of a job. It's unprofessional. You think they'll ever hire another woman if you kill yourself?"

"I finished the job yesterday and now I'm doing this. I only called you because I don't want to be decomposed when they find me. I hate dust balls."

"Andrea, this is a put-on, right? You don't mean it."

"Yes I do, Jess."

"Andrea, think of the kids!"

"The kids will be better off without me. They'll have a new mommy. She can take them free to Hawaii six times a year. They don't need me."

"Don't do anything, Andrea! I'm coming right over!"

Jessie was cursing Andrea up one side and down the other as she did seventy up Storrow Drive. She had had to cancel a meeting with the deans she had put off once before, and that meant she owed them a few chits she didn't want to owe. She

110

planned to belt Andrea right in the mouth once she got there, but the front door to the house was open and that was a very bad sign. Andrea had a phobia about safety; she had locks on the doors and windows that the Third Army couldn't get through. Jessie dashed in and found her sprawled on the couch, semiconscious. She slapped her friend's face, yelling, "Andrea, talk to me!" and then she dragged her into the bathroom and made her throw up. A handful of cylindrical yellow pills came right up, many of them still whole, so Jessie knew Andrea hadn't taken them very long ago. Andrea looked very pale, kneeling on the floor by the toilet. She put her head down on the rim and moaned. Jessie had vomit on her new eighty-five-dollar tweed skirt. She scrubbed at the stain with a washcloth and did not feel great waves of sympathy for Andrea at that moment.

"What in hell did you take?" she demanded.

"Ohhhhhhhh!"

"Andrea, answer me!"

"Penicillin, I think. Ohh!"

"Penicillin? You tried to kill yourself with penicillin?"

"Ohhh! It was all we had. Ira has this *thing* about not keeping pills in the house."

Jessie helped her up and took her into the bedroom. Andrea was still pretty shaky and sat down on the edge of the bed. Her hands were trembling, her face was the color of paste, and Jessie forgot about being mad at her.

"I fucked it up, didn't I?" she said.

"Andrea, you are not only *not* dead, you won't get a cold for six months." Jessie was trying to get her to laugh and got a wan grin. That was a start.

"Ohhh, my stomach hurts."

"Andrea," Jessie asked, "did you know? About the stewardess?"

"Oh, I knew Ira was going through a midlife thing. He was moody, he was reading Elisabeth Kübler-Ross, and he took up Nautilus. He was classic, right out of *Passages.*"

"And he just left? Just like that?"

"Yes. Her name is Debbi. Can you *see* her at faculty parties at MIT? 'Coffee, tea, or milk?' is not exactly scintillating small talk in a room full of Nobels."

"Oh, Andrea, I'm so sorry."

"I behaved like a jerk, didn't I."

111

"You're entitled. Remember how I behaved when I found Herb and his little screwee?"

"I feel so bad, Jessie. I feel like . . . nothing."

"I know. I've been there. Look, Andrea, you're a consultant with one of the biggest firms in town, you make a hundred thou a year, you're a terrific mother, you're a terrific person!"

"If I'm so terrific, why did Ira leave me?"

"Because he's almost forty years old and he panicked. He wants to be seventeen again, with everything ahead of him. That's why."

"But he's throwing it all away. We had a good life—OK, so it wasn't exactly a grand passion, but it was good—we have great kids. He's throwing all that away for a fuck in a hotel room in Cincinnati?"

"I never said this, Andrea, but I never did think Ira was what you'd call stable. He has shifty eyes."

"*I* always thought Herb was an egotistical nerd."

I sighed. "I guess we were both right."

"Men are shits."

"Yeah."

"Oh, Jessie, it hurts so goddam much."

"Yeah, it does."

"Do you get over it?"

"Eventually. You'll get to liking yourself again, Andrea. Really you will."

"If Ira can fuck around, so can I. I've had a few fantasies myself."

"Don't do anything rash, Andrea."

"As in herpes?"

"Get laid if you want to, but that's not going to do it."

"Can you think of anything better?"

"Work. It's what did it for me. People know you're good. They say so. It's something you can control. Work is real, Andrea. It makes you feel good. Competent."

"Shit. You sound like a shrink on 'Donahue.' "

"I know. Trite but true."

"I think I'll try fucking." Jessie knew how she felt. At first you just want to get even, fuck everything in trousers, because it's like love is a softball game and it's the ninth inning and you are seven runs behind and have to tie the score. But it doesn't work that way.

112

"Suit yourself, Andrea. But promise me you won't try to kill yourself again."

"I won't. I guess I didn't really want to."

"Call me any time, day or night. I'll be there, Andrea. I'm your best friend."

"Oh, Jess, did we make this mess?"

"Not us, Andrea. It's the old Chinese curse, remember?"

"May you live in interesting times?"

"That's the one."

TEN

Diane Feldman tossed a steak on the grill. "Medium rare, right, Mark?"

"Oh, yeah. Everything smells great."

"We love the indoor barbecue. Eliot had it installed because he didn't want to wait till summer to barbecue steaks. It's not fancy, but it's fun."

"Since when have I been fancy?"

Eliot walked into the room, carrying a drink with his prosthetic hand. "The potatoes are almost done. How are the steaks coming?"

"Twenty minutes. I just put them on. Why don't you and Mark relax in the den. You two haven't had much time to talk this weekend. The kids haven't let Mark alone."

Eliot Feldman had kept the promise he had made in the VA hospital. He made a million dollars, and not by the time he was thirty-five. He did it at thirty-three, by starting a high-tech firm in his garage in a small house in Arlington, Virginia, with his wife as his partner. Within a few years, Feld-Tech had become a major contractor for the federal government in microcomputer systems. The VA often trotted him out, these days, as an example of what a handicapped vet could do. (No mention was made of go-go dancers.) He and Diane had two children, twelve-year-old Sara and ten-year-old Adam. They also had a big house in McLean, his-and-her BMW's, and a house in Aruba; Eliot had been on the cover of *Business Week*. Eliot traveled to Boston often for his company and dropped in on Mark whenever he could. Mark would often hop a MATS transport to spend a weekend with Eliot and Diane. Their friendship, the special bond of survivors, had endured since hospital days.

Mark followed Eliot into the den and watched him flop down on the couch and stick his long legs out on the ottoman. Eliot held his drink easily, with the metallic hand. The left hand was a plastic replica of a real hand, but the right one was for use, not for show.

"Hell, it's really good to see you, Redneck. It's been a while."

"Yeah. How's it going?"

"I'm thinking of starting a new company."

"Another one? Holy shit, Hebe, you want to be Howard Hughes?"

"It's not fun like it was. Things are getting routine at work."

"What do you want to get into?"

"I'm looking around. Maybe publishing. That's something I've never done."

"Do you know anything about it?"

"No. That's what makes it fun."

"What kind of publishing?"

"High tech. And maybe porn. That sells a lot these days. We'll have the microchip of the month. Stories about how to have oral sex with your Apple PC."

"There's a thought."

"Software. The future is software, Redneck."

"You really are thinking about publishing?"

"Yeah, I've got a magazine dummy all set to go. *Tech World.* It's going to be slick and readable. It'll cover a lot of the new stuff in the field, but we'll also have politics, arts, other stuff. Something people will pick up and read."

"Isn't it risky, starting a magazine?"

"Sure. That's the whole point. It's exciting. A real challenge."

115

"I give you credit, Hebe. You're not like a lot of guys; once they got out of 'Nam, that was it for taking risks."

"It's the name of the game, for me. You sit still, you stagnate."

"Have you been watching all the stuff on TV lately?"

"No, I don't want to watch that shit. Who cares if it's ten years this, fifteen years that? Ancient history."

"It seems funny, watching it. I see it on TV, and it seems like yesterday."

"I don't want to live in the past. That's a closed book. It happened. It's over."

"Do you ever get flashbacks?"

"No. I never do."

"I do. I still get 'em. It's the damnedest thing. They only last—I guess it's just a few seconds, but it's like a time machine. I go back. I'm there. Really. It's all the same. The way the jungle smelled, remember, sort of sweet and damp, as if everything was on the edge of going rotten but it hadn't, yet. The way you could feel the air. It was heavy, almost alive. It's like that when I'm back there. So real."

"I dream, sometimes. Not about the crash—I didn't wake up until six days later, in the hospital. About . . . other things. I dream a lot. But no flashbacks."

"I dream too. Guys I knew. Crazy stuff, all jumbled up. The flashbacks are different. It's just like it was."

"Hell, the subconscious loves to play tricks. But it's not real; dream stuff. You can keep the lid on."

"Yeah, I do."

"Some guys, I see them at the VA, they're stuck in the past. Always talking about how it was. That's no good. You just have to move on. That's why I don't watch the TV shit. Water over the dam."

"Right. Yeah, you're right. Water over the dam. Hey, when are you getting to Boston next?"

"End of the month, I think."

"There's somebody I want you to meet."

"Female type?"

"Yeah."

"About time. Awhile back, I thought you were getting something together with that chick—what was her name?—Jill."

"No, that didn't pan out."

"This is the first time you've asked me to meet somebody. Must be serious."

"Yeah, well, I think it is. She's the provost of the college."

"No shit. I didn't think you went in for brainy broads, Redneck."

"Neither did I."

"What's she like?"

"Classy. Good sense of humor. Pretty. Too good for me, probably."

"No broad is too good for a member of the Gimp Tabernacle Choir."

"I took the leg off and she didn't bat an eyelash. No lights out or anything. First time. How many women could do that?"

"Not many. A special one, Redneck."

"Like Diane."

Eliot nodded. "It's funny, though, now that I'm this big-shot corporate type, how some women come on to me. Like the arms don't matter."

"You got three million dollars, Hebe. With some women, you wouldn't need a head."

Diane walked into the room and announced, "Steaks are done. Mark, would you mind pouring the wine?"

The dinner was good and the company, as usual, was warm and accepting—almost like family, Mark thought. It was the only place he got that feeling. After dinner, Eliot left to get ice cream for everybody, and Mark helped Diane clear away the dishes.

"I have a friend I was going to fix you up with, Mark, but Eliot said you have a girlfriend."

"Yeah, I do."

"I knew a good-looking guy like you wouldn't be on the market for long."

"Go ahead, build my ego. I love it."

"I'm so glad you were able to come down, Mark. Eliot's always so up when you come."

"That sounds like he's been down."

"Oh, he doesn't show it much. Not at work, anyhow. But he's been so—restless lately. Jumpy. Bored with work."

"He told me about the new magazine."

"Yes, he's pushing ahead. People are saying it's such a risk, but he doesn't want to hear that."

"He likes the challenge."

"Yes, that's why I'm keeping quiet. Maybe it will make things better. Maybe it's just what he needs."

"That doesn't sound like you. Eliot always said you were the smarts of the outfit."

"Every time I say anything about this, he says I'm putting him down. So I'm going to let him go ahead and see how it works out. I just don't want him getting in over his head."

"He'll be OK. You'll probably have to tie him down to keep him from making another million."

"I hope you're right."

"Of course I am. Remember what I said when you guys were still in that garage?"

She smiled. "You never had any doubts, did you."

"Hell, no. I'd seen Eliot in action. The VA didn't have a chance. Neither did high tech. And he had you. I knew you guys would make it fine."

"We did OK, didn't we? I think those were the happiest days, when we were out in that damn garage every night till midnight. The best days of all."

Eliot came back, put the ice cream in the kitchen, and called out to the kids. There was no answer.

"Are those kids deaf?" he said.

"They've probably got the stereo on."

Eliot went to the bottom of the stairs. "Kids! Ice cream. You were the ones that wanted this!"

A door slammed and Sara came running down the stairs, followed by Adam. She had a Walkman attached to her head.

She ran straight for Eliot, saying, "Dad, it's *my* Walkman! Make Adam stop!"

As Mark watched, Eliot froze. He stood still as a statue, staring as his daughter ran toward him.

"You said I could borrow it!" Adam wailed. "Indian giver!"

Eliot stood still, staring. Then, suddenly, he grabbed his daughter by the shoulder and shook her, roughly.

"Sara! Damn it, go away! Go away, goddam it!"

The two children stopped, and their giggles faded.

"Daddy—"

"You heard me. You *heard* me!"

"Eliot," Diane said.

"Dad, we were only fooling around," Sara said.

"They didn't mean anything, Eliot," Diane said gently.

118

Eliot exhaled, slowly. Mark noticed that a small vein over his temple was throbbing.

"Daddy, why do you always get so mad?" Adam said.

"Kids, just take it easy, huh?" Eliot said. "We have company."

"Uncle Mark isn't company," Adam said.

"Yeah, I guess you're right about that. OK, guys, but just keep it down to a dull roar, OK?"

"Can we have ice cream?" Adam asked.

"Did you get Butter Walnut?" Sara asked.

"Yes and yes," he said.

"Do you like Butter Walnut, Uncle Mark?" Adam asked.

"It's my favorite."

"Me too. I like it when you come to visit."

Eliot laughed and nodded at his son. "You're not the only one," he said. And they went into the dining room to polish off the Butter Walnut.

ELEVEN

Jessie was humming as she poured her morning cup of coffee. Grace looked up from her bagel and said, "God, you're disgusting in the morning, now you're in love."

"Is it that obvious?"

"You hum, you sing, you're more tuneful than Muzak. That's depressing to those of us not in your condition."

"Oh, Grace, you're right. I'm in stage one of a love affair. He says something dreadfully banal and I think it's brilliant."

"You want to be in bed night and day."

"I buy him presents. He brings me flowers."

"You never forget to shave your legs or wear eyeliner."

"I wear sheer nightgowns I dredged up from my honeymoon, not my comfy flannel ones. I even washed a pair of his socks."

"You're a goner for sure."

"Grace, if he asked me to run away with him to herd goats out in Utah and live in a tent and eat goat cheese, I think I'd just say, 'Yes, dear.' I'm turning to Jell-O again."

"It's just stage one."

"But I've been here before, Grace. Several times. I would have done the goat cheese bit for Herb, too. I don't think my judgment is very good when I'm like this."

"It passes."

"Last time I was married before it did. Grace, I think I am not being smart."

"So tell him to get lost."

"I'd rather slit my throat."

"Has he *asked* you to go to Utah?"

"No."

"Has he asked you to do *anything* you don't want to do?"

"No."

"Do you have multiple orgasms?"

"Yes."

"Jessie, you don't seem to have a problem."

"I know. It's just that I—oh, I don't want to get hurt again. I don't want to crumble. Turn myself into a doormat. It's so easy for me to do."

"Jess, it is possible for a man and a woman to live together without one of them being a jelly doughnut. It's not an either-or thing. And people change, Jess. They learn, and so can you."

"Just keep saying that, Grace," Jessie said, and she gulped down her cup of coffee and hurried off to the office. It was going to be a bitch of a day: a meeting with the head of Buildings and Grounds to chew out his ass because maintenance was so lousy, a conference on the candidates coming up for tenure this year, and a pile of paperwork that was starting to climb to the light fixtures. She had barely begun to tackle it when Liz Hailey came in, wearing a face that spoke of trouble.

"Don't tell me: another crisis," Jessie said.

"I have just heard a story that makes me shudder if it's true."

"Tell me it doesn't involve cocaine. Tell me that the clinic has not diagnosed the flu as something terminal again."

"Neither of the above."

"How bad can it be?"

"It's Chip Byron."

"Chip? Arthur Byron's son?"

"Yes indeed. The heir apparent to the chairman of our esteemed Board of Trustees."

"Chip's a nice kid. He worked for me last year."

121

"He has found something more lucrative than filing, Jess."

"What?"

"I have heard that Chip Byron is the Golden Cucumber."

"The what?"

"A male stripper at a club out on Route One."

"Chip? A stripper?"

"Yes. He's doing a land-office business. The highlight of his act—if it is him—is that he flips his jockstrap and his penis is painted gold."

"Oh, good God!"

"Precisely."

"J. Arthur Byron is on the boards of eight Fortune Five Hundred companies. And *I* talked him into sending Chip to Kinsolving."

"Where he has unfortunately picked up some skills not listed in the catalog."

"Oh, Liz, if this is true, his father will kill me. And we're just about to get a huge grant for the new science center from one of Byron's companies."

"This could screw up the deal. If it is Chip, of course. I just heard it secondhand from the students."

"I better check it out. What's the name of the club?"

"Adam-Twelve. It's out in Saugus. Very popular with bored housewives. But I hear a lot of couples go too. That's weird. Jessie, would you take your lover to a male strip club?"

Jessie sighed. "In this case, Liz, I think that's exactly what I'm going to do."

And so, at eight-thirty that night, Mark Claymore found himself driving his van through the Callahan tunnel, heading for Route 1. Jessie was beside him, wearing a pair of very large, very dark sunglasses.

"I used to think higher education was a dull field," he said.

"Are you kidding? First of all there's five thousand students, all with raging hormones and great gaps in their good sense—"

"And a faculty that's exactly the same."

"Right. This job is *never* dull."

"Jess, what are you going to do if it does turn out to be Byron's son?"

"Talk to him. Make him understand how this could hurt Kinsolving. A male stripper, for God's sake."

"A few years ago you were burning your bra. Now you're uptight over a jockstrap."

"A *sequined* jockstrap. And he takes it off. Besides, Mark, that's just sexist propaganda. We didn't burn bras."

"You didn't?"

"No. A group of women were protesting at the Miss America pageant. They threw a couple of bras in a trash can. See how history gets distorted?"

"Next you'll tell me George Washington didn't throw a silver dollar across the Rappahannock."

"No. He threw a bra across."

"George Washington was into cross-dressing?"

"Yeah, that's why Valley Forge was such a bitch. Crotchless panties are real chilly."

Mark laughed. "Oh, Jess, I love your mouth. You're fast, you know that? I love a woman with a sense of humor. And she skis, too."

"Not as well as you do."

"Well, I'm obsessive about it."

"Anybody who goes down a hill called Jaws of Death has to be obsessive."

"Next time, you'll try it."

"I will not. It's supposed to be a sport, Mark, not suicide."

"The best part was in the ski lodge."

"I'll buy that."

"Sure, I'll take Deep Throat over Jaws of Death any day."

"Pervert," she said.

"Me? Who is the person dragging me out to see men take off their clothes?"

"Don't remind me."

"I saw my first stripper at the county fair in Ocean City. Lulu Belle and Her Talented Titties."

"Oh, God!"

"She was gorgeous. Tipped the scale at one eighty-five. She was real good, too; she could make one tassel go left and the other go right."

"The degrading things that women have to do."

"Beats sloppin' hogs. And she made a hundred fifty a week easy. I tell you, it was real excitin'. Jess, if you could pick up a couple of tassels—"

"Mark, I have had men tell me weird fantasies, but this one takes the cake."

"Acting out your fantasies is healthy, if you're not an ax murderer or anything."

Jessie laughed. "You do not know to whom you speak. I was expelled from Miss Marie's School of Tap and Jazz for terminal uncoordination. I couldn't get the shuffle step. And you're talking tassels?"

"She did a number with pinwheels, too. Just put them on with flesh-colored tape. For a buck you could blow and make them go round. No touching, though. One guy tried and Lulu knocked him cold. She had a better right cross than Floyd Patterson. Weighed about the same, too."

"Pinwheels I could do. I would make a fool out of myself with tassels."

"Are you serious?'

"Sure. I'm not a prude, Mark. I bet it would be fun."

"Oh, my God, can we turn around?"

"No, we have important business."

"Pinwheels. Jess, I'm as horny as a goat."

"Well, just get yourself un-horny right now. I may need you to help me with Chip."

"How?"

"Maybe you could talk sense to him. After all, you *are* an officer."

"Oh, sure. 'Hey, kid, you don't want to hang out in this place, with ladies stuffing dollar bills in your jock. Join the army and have real fun. Camp out in a field with five hundred guys and a can of Spam.' "

"I was thinking about what they used to do in the war of 1812. Just grab people and make them serve on ships."

"I don't think that the Secretary of the Navy wants the Golden Cucumber doing his act on the *JFK*."

"Better his problem than mine. Oh, look, Mark, this must be it. Adam-Twelve."

They pulled into the parking lot of a gaudy building with a façade shaped like a huge apple, painted red and outlined with neon. They got out of the van and walked into the club, where one of the warm-up acts had just concluded. The interior was a modern well-decorated room, with plush theater seats surrounding a stage with a parquet floor in the middle of the room. The club was packed, with a decidedly middle-class clientele. There were groups of women, obviously housewives on a girls' night out, and well-dressed couples dotted throughout the predominantly female crowd. It had more the air of a shopping mall than of the old smoke-filled burly house. Jessie and Mark took a seat in one of the back rows and Jessie hunched down in her seat and looked around at the crowd.

"Look at these people, Mark. They look so ordinary. Middle-American housewives."

"Beats Monday night football. Dan Marino doesn't take his pants off."

"Maybe it won't be Chip. Can you imagine the *Herald* getting hold of this? Remember what they called that doctor who got accused of rape?"

"Rape Doc. Then there was Pot Cop, the captain who got caught with the grass."

"I wonder what they would call Chip if they got this story."

"Cock Kid. There's a snappy headline, Jess: Cock Kid Makes Dean's List."

"Oh, God." Jessie groaned. "Mark, this would be ver-ry funny if we didn't stand to lose five million dollars if this thing gets out. We just have to talk Chip out of this craziness. Our whole science center may be hanging by a jockstrap."

Just then an announcer, wearing a tux, stepped to the stage, took a hand mike, and said, "And now the event you have all been waiting for. Our featured performer who drives the ladies wild!"

The man, Jessie thought, had precisely the same pitch as a TV game show host, working up the crowd for the cameras.

"Come on, folks, let's have a big hand for the sensation of the North Shore, in the flesh—and I do mean flesh—ladies and gentlemen, the Golden Cucumber!"

The band burst into a zippy melody and the crowd applauded wildly as a young man trotted onstage, wearing a green form-fitting body suit and a green sequined mask. He began to dance, sensuously, moving his body to the now insinuating rhythm. The crowd cheered its encouragement, good-naturedly.

"Is it him?" Mark whispered to Jessie.

"I don't know. I can't tell with that damn mask. It sure looks a lot like him."

"How well do you know him?"

"He worked for me all last semester."

Onstage, the dancer stripped off his jacket to reveal a bare well-muscled chest. The women in the audience whistled, cheered, and howled. Mark said to Jessie, "Well?"

"He was filing! He never took his clothes off."

The dancer, bumping and grinding, slowly peeled off his trousers, until the only clothing he wore was a green sequined jockstrap. He faced one side of the audience, then the other, for a series of pelvic thrusts. The audience adored it.

"That's quite a cucumber he's got there," Mark said.

"Women aren't hung up about size," Jessie said sternly. "Men just think they are."

"Oh? And just what is it women like, Professor?"

"Sensitivity, consideration—"

Just then a member of the audience, overcome with emotion, dashed onto the stage, fell to her knees, and tucked a bill inside the dancer's jock, feeling the muscles of his stomach as she did so. Two other women followed suit.

"Oh, my God!" Jessie said. "I don't believe these women!"

"Sensitivity, consideration—"

"Oh, shut up, Mark," Jessie said.

The noise had risen to a crescendo, with the music blaring, and the women in the audience, obviously having a grand time, whooped and hollered like a band of Comanches. The dancer let his hands fall to his jockstrap and then took them away again. The audience howled its approval. Then he brought his hands to his green-sequined mask and flipped it off—a harbinger of things to come.

"Oh, Lord, it's him," Jessie groaned. "It's Chip."

Another woman leaped up out of the crowd, ran to the dancer, tucked a folded bill in his jock, and kissed the dancer full on the mouth. He grinned and did another bump and grind and let his hands again rest on the jockstrap. This time he kept them there as he gyrated, and then he snapped the jockstrap teasingly. The crowd loved it. He kept on teasing them, tugging just a bit on the strap and then letting it slide back to its accustomed place. The crowd began to chant, "Take it off! Take it off! Take it off!"

As the chanting of the crowd rose to fever pitch, the dancer put both his hands on his jockstrap, gave one energetic bump and grind as the drums rolled, and then with a swift motion, yanked the strap away from his genitals. The exposed member, admirable in configuration, was indeed painted a shiny golden hue. It glinted in the spotlight.

"Oh, my God, he did it!" Jessie said, stunned.

"And you had him *filing?*" Mark said, above the roar.

Just then, the sound of a whistle split the air, and from the two side entrances men in blue ran down the aisles toward the stage. Jessie stared at them uncomprehendingly for a minute.

"Mark, is this part of the act?"

"Jessie, this is a raid! Let's get the hell out of here."

Two policemen ran up to the stage and threw a towel around the startled Chip Byron and started to lead him away, as the crowd screamed in protest.

"They can't arrest him!" Jessie said.

"They just did."

"I've got to stop this," Jessie said. She leaped up from her seat and plunged into the churning mass of bodies in front of her, elbowing her way toward the exit where the policemen were leading the dancer out the door.

"Jessie, dammit, wait a minute," Mark called out. He jumped up to go after her, but he had a hard time making any headway through the crowd. He thought, for a minute, that he was going to be knocked off his feet as people began to panic. He saw Jessie disappear out the entrance where the two policemen had led Chip Byron, so he turned around to head for the nearest exit.

Jessie, meanwhile, emerged from the rear door just in time to see Chip being led toward a waiting paddy wagon. The *Herald* headline flashed before her eyes: COCK KID IN SLAMMER. The vision drained her of any caution she might have possessed. She rushed up to the policeman who had Chip by the arm and said, "Officer, you can't arrest him. He didn't break the law."

Chip looked at Jessie, astonished. "Professor McGrath, what are you doing here?"

"Why are you arresting this young man?" Jessie demanded. Such was the tone of authority that she had worked on for the past few years that it brought the officer up short.

"Answer me, please!" she demanded.

"Lewd and lascivious behavior, public exhibitionism, endangering public morality—"

"He was just dancing," Jessie said. "Since when is that against the law?"

The policeman didn't answer but started again to lead Chip to the wagon. Jessie planted herself firmly in front of him. "Look at those signs, all up and down this road. *Live Nudes. Nude Dancers.* You let women dance in the nude all the time. This is unequal treatment under the law!"

"Ma'am, please step aside," said the policeman nervously.

"Young man, you just stop this nonsense right now!" Jessie said, using the tone she took with sophomores caught with pot in their rooms. "You will be sued for false arrest!"

"Lady," the policeman said, "you are interfering with an arrest."

"I am *in loco parentis* for this young man, and I demand that he be released in my custody," Jessie said. At that moment, Mark rounded the back corner of the building and took in the whole scene.

"Jessie, what the hell—"

"Release that young man this instant," Jessie said. "I am the provost of Kinsolving College, and this is one of my students."

"If you don't get out of my way, lady, I'll run you in too," the young cop said.

"Don't you threaten me," Jessie said, not moving.

"Jessie—" Mark said, but the policeman, his patience finally snapping, turned to an older cop beside him.

"What do I do with her?"

"Take her in."

The cop grabbed Jessie's arm to pull her out of the way, roughly. Mark grabbed his hand and yanked it from Jessie's arm. "Take it easy, bud!"

"Oh, for Christ's sake, another one," said the older cop. "Jesus Christ, what a night. Arrest him too."

"You can't arrest him," Jessie said, now so angry as to be almost incoherent. "He's a—Vietnam veteran!"

"So am I, lady," said the cop. "Now, folks, I am going to read you your rights, so you just stand there nice and quiet. I don't want any trouble. 'You have the right to remain silent—'"

"What outfit?" Mark asked.

"Marines. Khe San. 'You have the right to consult an attorney—' Where were you?"

"Mekong Delta. Infantry."

128

" 'Anything you say can be used against you in a court of law—' You guys took a lot of shit."

"You weren't exactly on a picnic."

Chip, who had been watching the whole scene incredulously, grinned and said to Jessie, "Professor McGrath, the catalog was right. The faculty does take a personal interest in the students."

The policeman finished reading Mark and Jessie their rights and said to Mark, "Sorry, buddy, I got a job to do."

"That's OK," Mark said.

"How did you get involved with this crazy broad?" he asked, looking at Jessie, who glared at him.

"She's my boss," Mark said.

"Jeez, what kind of a funny farm do you work at?"

"Sometimes I wonder," he said.

The three of them were herded into the paddy wagon, where they sat side by side, under the watchful eye of the young policeman.

"I am going to have one hell of a time explaining this to my CO," Mark said.

"Chip," Jessie said, "what on earth impelled you to take a job like this?"

"I've had a lot of dance training, you know. I thought it would be a good way to make some money."

"But painting your—uh, I mean, *painting* it gold?"

"That was my idea, not the club's. I thought it would be a great finish. It's just body paint; it's not harmful."

"Chip, we are all going to jail because of your great idea."

"I'm sorry, Professor McGrath. I never thought I'd get arrested. I mean, what's the big deal? It's only a penis."

"It's sort of against the law to whip it out in public, Chip," Mark said.

"It's not like I'm a pervert, exposing myself in alleys. I'm an artist."

Mark shook his head. "Chip, a green-sequined jockstrap and a painted prick are not everybody's idea of art."

"We live in an increasingly repressive society," Chip said darkly. "The lights of artistic freedom are going out across the land."

Jessie sighed. Philosophically she agreed, of course, but at the moment the particular lights that she saw dimming were those of the new five-million-dollar science center.

"Chip, don't you think you ought to hang up your jockstrap? At least until you graduate?"

"But I'm a star. Besides, I make nine hundred a week, plus tips. And I don't think I ought to just knuckle under to the repressive power of the state. This is a moral question."

Jessie sighed again. "Well, I guess your father will hear about this pretty fast."

"About me being the Golden Cucumber?"

"Yes."

"Oh, he knows."

"He does?"

"Sure."

"What does he think?"

"He says it shows real initiative. It's the first time since I had a paper route that I've made any real money. Besides, my grandmother was in vaudeville, so this is really natural for me."

"Your grandmother? Your father's mother?"

"Yes. My dad was practically born in a trunk. My grandmother had an act with her brother, called Rose and Jack. He juggled and she danced and told jokes. She retired from the stage when my dad was school age, but she taught him all her routines. He's pretty good, actually."

Jessie began to laugh. "Oh, Lord, he knows. We're going to the slammer for nothing. Oh, that is funny!"

Chip, Jessie, and Mark were taken immediately before a judge, who was used to being summoned at odd hours in similar cases, especially since a local rep had begun his campaign against Filth in Suburbia. The local police, stung by charges of being soft on slime, had picked up their surveillance of the clubs.

"Your honor," Jessie said, "Chip isn't a criminal, he's a college student. He's working his way through college. He has to repay a loan from his father."

"Professor McGrath, doesn't your school have work-study?"

"It doesn't pay the same, sir."

"Young man, are you aware of the laws of the Commonwealth against indecent exposure?"

"I didn't think it was indecent, your honor. It was painted, it wasn't just hanging out there. The natives in East Basutoland paint their penises in earth colors to give homage to the fertility

130

gods. Then they dance. It is really a very historic tradition, sir."

"Mr. Byron, in Massachusetts we prefer our fertility rites to be somewhat less spectacular."

"I didn't know I was breaking the law, sir. I wouldn't have done it if I had."

"Major, may I ask what your role is in all of this? You weren't on maneuvers, I presume."

"No, sir. I'm the head of ROTC at Kinsolving."

"The New Army has gotten a bit out of hand."

"He just came along to help me," Jessie said. "We were going to try to convince Chip that his act was not in the best interests of the college."

"I should say not. Young man, since this is your first offense, I'm going to let you off with a warning. But in the future, during any and all performances, you will keep your private parts covered by a substance more substantial than paint. Is that clear?"

"But sir—"

"Chip!" Jessie said.

"Yes, sir."

Mark and Jessie gave Chip a ride back to his dorm. By the time they got there, the Golden Cucumber had worked out a new finale for his act. He would wear a form-fitting sheath of gold latex, which would display anatomical contour but would keep the flesh completely covered, as the law decreed. He might even, he said, have it adorned with multicolor spangles to catch the spotlight. "Illusion is as good as reality for an artist. Besides, I might get them to put more money in my jock if I glitter."

When they arrived back at Mark's apartment, Jessie made herself a drink. "I need this," she said.

"You don't have to worry about that kid. He picks up three hundred a night in his jockstrap, he's paying his tuition, and he's buying a Thunderbird. He may own the goddam school by graduation."

"I think I am having an attack of penis envy. He slaps on some gold paint and he makes three times what I make in a week."

"Oh, you have nicer things," Mark said, running a finger gently across her breasts.

"Nobody gives me three hundred bucks a night for them."

131

"If you could do tassels, you could get thirty bucks a night easy." She punched him in the ribs and he said, "Hitting a man with two Purple Hearts. What kind of a patriot are you?" Then he pulled her close and she felt the familiar wave of desire rising inside her. All he had to do was touch her, it seemed, and she was lost.

"Jess," he said, "life with you is not going to be dull."

"I was pretty dumb tonight, wasn't I? I nearly got us both in a cell block. I should know better than to argue with cops."

"I thought you were terrific. Stupid, but terrific."

"The Joan of Arc of the Jockstrap, that's me."

"I always wanted to go to bed with Joan of Arc. Steel undies turn me on."

"Sure, you could Scotch-tape the pinwheels to the armor plate."

He laughed and kissed her and said, "Enough talk. Time for bed."

Bed, as always, was lovely with Mark. When she felt his deep thrusting inside her, she felt a wonderful, glorious power in her femaleness, capturing him, holding him, giving pleasure. Why did people say that women were passive when they could encompass a man this way? And who was *had,* the woman or the man? Both, perhaps, in the best sense of the word. Triumph and surrender, tasting both, intermingled.

Later, she put her head against his chest and felt his heart beating; wonderful thing, a heart. It kept pumping away quietly, sending the blood coursing through your body, and you just took it for granted. She listened, for the moment content.

"Jess?" he said.

"Yes?"

"Marry me."

"I don't even know your middle name."

"It's Clifford. After my grandfather. Mark Clifford Claymore."

"Sounds presidential."

"Don't change the subject. Do you love me?"

"You know I do."

"I love you. I don't want to lose you."

"There's no danger of that."

"I'm serious, Jess."

"I know."

"I'm so far behind. It's like Vietnam swallowed up a chunk of my life, not just while I was there but everything that came after. The guys who didn't go, I see them in the distance, far ahead of me."

"You're catching up, Mark. And you know a lot of things they don't."

"Oh, yeah. I know about flashbacks. And nightmares. I know life is too damn short to waste it. Any of it."

"Mark, we have time. All the time we need."

"Do we, Jess? When I was on the airplane, flying back from 'Nam, I felt death right next to me. Breathing on me, it was so close. I'll never be afraid of it, ever again, but I know it's there. Breathing."

She touched his face, traced the line of his nose, ran her finger across the gentle swells of his lips. She felt a throb of regret for the things that had been taken from him—his youth, his leg, the sense that life just stretched on, a rolling landscape that met the horizon at some far meridian. She had been afraid, herself, but she had never heard death breathing. She wanted to say to him, My love, I'll marry you, because that would have helped to quiet the sound of death's rhythmic breath. But she couldn't say it. Not yet.

"I'm here, Mark. I'll be here tomorrow. And the next day. That's enough for tonight, isn't it?"

"For tonight, yes, but—"

She put her finger on his lips. "Later. We'll talk later."

"I love you, Jess. I swear to God I do."

"I love you, Mark. I promise you, I do."

"Good," he said. "That's good."

He was asleep long before she was. She lay still, staring up into the blackness, hearing, now, her own heart beating. A stab of panic clutched at her. Why was she here, in this strange room, with this strange man, whom she loved but did not really know? Why did she feel as if she were losing control of things? Why did love have such tiny sharp teeth at its edges? Was *Jessie* such a small, pale moon that she would simply be extinguished by the heat of any male sun?

She looked at Mark, at his dark curly hair against the pillow, at the breath fluttering through his lips in the depth of sleep. He

133

seemed impossibly vulnerable. How could there be menace in him? She felt suspended, in bed beside him, not able to leave or fully to stay.

"I do love you," she whispered. "I want to cry when I think of how much you've been hurt. I don't want anyone to hurt you, ever again. God knows, I don't want to hurt you.

"But why am I so afraid?"

TWELVE

Jessie was supposed to be studying the trustees' report, but the words just blurred together. She was worrying about Andrea. Andrea had gone on a sexual toot, true to her promise, after Ira moved out. Jessie figured this would pass; it was just a phase. It did. Only now there was Tex.

Tex was living with Andrea and the kids. He was a rodeo rider. Jessie was not sure what he rode, precisely, except that it was certain to be big and mean and undoubtedly stupid. Andrea had picked him up at a bar one night, and he moved in the next day. And it was Jessie who was getting the phone calls.

First it was Andrea's mother, calling to ask if Tex was Jewish. She sounded as if she was about to be hysterical, so Jessie told her he probably was. She said she *personally* didn't know any Jews named Tex, but then, she was from Brockton. In San Antonio, the name Tex was probably as big at Bar Mitzvahs as Benjamin or Sol.

Then Ira called, and he was, in a word, shit-faced. Jessie was in the middle of the first round of budget talks with the deans, and Ira was screaming at her on the phone because his children were living with a cowboy. She got annoyed.

"Ira," she said, "you might have thought of this before you ran off with a stewardess."

"Flight attendant," he said. "They don't call them stewardesses anymore. Jessie, my kids are in the same house as some drunken rodeo rider. He's probably a pervert."

"He's not a drunk, as far as I know. What makes you think he's a pervert?"

"He's a *cowboy*, for Christ's sake. I thought Andrea had better taste. I thought she'd at least take up with somebody who'd be intellectually stimulating for the kids."

"What is your girlfriend going to teach them, Ira? How to buckle their seat belts? You're the one who made this mess."

"You're her friend, Jess," he said pleadingly. "Can't you talk to her?"

"Ira, she's a grown woman. And I've met Tex and he seems to be perfectly nice."

"Jessie, the man gets thrown on his head from cows."

"I don't think they're cows. Bulls or something."

"What kind of an influence is a—a cretin like that on two nice Jewish children? One who is going to be Bas Mitzvahed in two years?"

Jessie was beginning to lose her patience at that point.

"Andrea's changed the caterer, Ira. No chopped liver. Tex-Mex and barbecued ribs at the temple."

"Dammit, Jess, this is serious! I am really concerned."

"Ira, don't you give me that crap. You walked out on your wife and you deserted your children. Suddenly you're Abraham the Patriarch?"

"You don't understand what I went through."

"I certainly don't. If you have problems with your wife, you talk to her. Just leave me out of it."

She didn't tell him she had already tried to talk Andrea out of her Tex fixation, even before she had met her friend's new lover. She thought that Andrea was just using Tex, because without a man around twenty-four hours a day, Andrea had this strange notion that she would disappear. Maybe Andrea was just doing it to aggravate Ira, because she knew that an MIT professor of astrophysics was guaranteed to go right out of his tree with a cowboy sleeping in his Magic Fingers bed. But after she met Tex, Jessie started worrying about him too. He really did seem to be head over heels in love with Andrea. He had an offer to join a new rodeo, but he turned it down to stay with her. Now he was doing odd jobs around Belmont and Cambridge to pick up a few dollars. Before she met Tex and discovered how sweet a man he was, Jessie thought Andrea was quite out of her mind. She dragged Andrea off to the Harvest for a good heart-to-heart.

"Andrea, what in hell do you think you are doing?"

"I can handle my own life, thank you."

"You meet him one night, and he is living with you the next day. That is not exactly mature behavior."

"I liked him. I'm fed up with all these intellectuals around here with egos the size of Harvard Yard. Tex is—uncomplicated."

"What does that mean?"

"He likes to eat, drink, sleep, and screw. And get thrown off of bulls, when there are any around."

"This is not a relationship you are describing, Andrea. This is Tarzan of the Apes."

"Actually, he's very sweet, Jess. Wait till you meet him. He's repaired the back stairs and paneled the bathroom. Ira never did anything around the house. The man helped put up the space shuttle, and he couldn't put together a three-piece barbecue grill made in Taiwan."

"Andrea, your mother keeps calling me. She is very upset."

"Yeah, she keeps telling me she will not set foot in my house as long as Roy Rogers is in it. I tell her to come on over, she'll love Trigger, he counts to ten with his hoof."

"Be nice to her, Andrea, so she'll stop calling me."

"Nice to her! Jess, she took Ira's side. Said it was *my* fault. I said to her, 'Ma, he ran off with a stewardess and deserted his children.' And she said if I'd stayed home and didn't work Ira wouldn't have left. Jess, this is the woman who spent so many hours in shopping malls her children had to look at Polaroids to remember what she looked like. Like hell I'll be nice to her!"

"What do your kids think about Tex?" Jessie asked her.

"They like him. He's going to roast a steer in the back yard, if the snow holds off. He's digging the pit right now. You put the whole steer in the coals. The kids are excited."

"They certainly didn't get that with Ira."

"No. And Tex is teaching them Navajo and he's going to

137

teach them to ride. Ira's idea of a fun day was to make them visit the wind tunnel at MIT. With no wind in it, yet."

"Andrea, are things OK? Really?"

"Yeah, I'm OK, Jessie. I really am. I wanted to kill Ira for a while, but I don't now. I sort of wonder how I spent all those years with him. Maybe because we were both so busy we didn't have to bother with each other."

"What if he gets over this Debbi thing and wants to come back?"

"Tell you the truth, I don't think there's much to come back to. I think we lost our way a long time ago—and just didn't notice."

It had not turned out, Jessie mused, like she and Andrea had expected. At their age, their parents had been settled in with marriages, kids, homes, mortgages. But now Andrea was living with a cowboy and Jessie was divorced and scared to death of making another commitment. They were a strange generation. Maybe it was because there were so many of them: baby boomers. By their sheer numbers, they overwhelmed society. Their music, their clothes, their life-styles, their causes held the nation in thrall. Who could blame them if they believed their own prophecies? She remembered how fervently she believed that they were going to change the world, believed it as she had believed the words in the little green Baltimore catechism in fifth grade.

And now, where did they belong? The settled pattern of their parents' lives did not seem to apply. But the craziness, the good old dope-smoking, screwing, do-your-own thing mania of the sixties seemed a bit arcane for people pushing forty. The old rules were gone, and the new ones—there were so many new ones. It was as if Moses had come down from the mountain with God's Commandments on two tablets and said, "Pick one from column A, two from column B."

They called her generation narcissistic, the Me Generation, but Jessie didn't think that was quite it. All the old institutions had lost their authority. The parish priest had run off to get married, the schools didn't teach kids to read, a president had to say, "I am not a crook." No wonder they looked inward. Inventing yourself was not easy. Grace Darlington was right; they did not have hand-me-down lives. And there was freedom in that.

I wouldn't want one of those, Jessie thought.

But the designer labels sure could be a bitch.

THIRTEEN

The heat was almost a living thing; it pressed against you, with arms like the tentacles of a maddened octopus, squeezing, drawing the breath out of you. This terrain was low and swampy, not like the higher grasslands. It was a jungle that turned the predator into prey. The dense foliage was cover for an enemy that belonged to the shadows. He remembered how, in the summer dusk when he was a kid, he used to see phantoms weaving in and out of the trees, how he would view them from the safety of the porch, where they would not dare to venture. Here, the ghosts were real. Deadly.

He walked along, sweating, wanting nothing more than that the day would end, that the red sun would swell and fatten, turning pink-orange and dropping behind the line of the distant hills, and the night would come and they could stop walking. They had come in by chopper, daylight soldiers who dropped into this world from huge steel birds and would vanish the same way. They were like the gods of the old myths, dropped from the sky. Unlike the gods, they could die.

139

"Christ, it must be a hundred and ten degrees," said Nichols, next to him. Nichols was a green lieutenant, another farm boy, from Pennsylvania. They had become friends.

"Damn fucking near," Mark said.

"There's a quarry not far from my house," Nichols said. They were resting beside a trail, their shirts soaked through with sweat. "No bottom, not that anybody ever found. You dive down, it just gets colder and colder."

"Sounds nice."

"I think about that and it makes me cooler. Mentally, I make myself cool. You can raise or lower your body temperature with your mind, you know."

"Maybe I'll try it."

"Just think. You're going down, and the water is getting a dark green, and the water is real cold. Feel it against your skin."

"Yeah. It does work. Cold. Real cold."

Nichols sighed. "You think there's any fucking VC for a hundred miles?"

"Could be. No sign, though."

"Yeah, just another crazy Boy Scout hike."

Then they were walking again, Mark's eyes straining to pierce the veil of green around him. Suddenly he picked up on something, an out-of-placeness. What? Quiet. The natural noises of the bush were too still. He was about to say to Nichols, "Careful," when there was a burst of automatic weapon fire and he dove for the cover of the dirt. Nichols went down right beside him.

"Fucking sniper," he said to Nichols, but there was no reply. He turned to look, and Nichols had no face. A huge gaping maw of flesh hung where his features used to be. He was swimming, in clear, cold water, moving along slowly, his face a death's-head grin, and behind the sockets of his eyes there was a bright, terrible, empty blue. . . .

He woke up screaming. Nichols had no face. But it was cool, not hot. Why was it cool?

"Mark, what is it, what's the matter?"

He sat up, dazed, not knowing where he was. He expected the jungle and the heat, a living thing, but his hands felt something cool. Sheets. Jessie was next to him, not Nichols with no face. Part of his consciousness was back in the jungle, another part in a bedroom. His bedroom?

"Jessie?" he said.

140

"It was a nightmare, Mark. It's not real."

"He hasn't got any face left."

"It's all right. You're not there, Mark. You're here."

The jungle began to fade. The feel of it, the smell of it, drifted away. He was in a bedroom in Boston, his body soaked with sweat.

"Tell me about it," she said. "Let me help."

He told her about Nichols and about the cool, deep quarry. "I saw him swimming at the bottom of the quarry. He was grinning at me but he didn't have a face. But he had—oh, Jesus, Jessie, he had this awful grin. And the eyes. I can't describe the eyes."

She wiped his forehead gently, and she said, "You're OK. It was just a dream."

"The dreams are so real, Jess. Realer than life. Everything is so bright and clear in them. They're so—real."

"They're phantoms, Mark. They can't hurt you."

He was shaking. He tried to will his body to stop shaking, but it wouldn't obey him. She stroked his hair.

"I'm here," she said.

"One reason I wanted to go, Jess, was to find out what it was like. The big secret. War. Killing people. It was like some big fraternity you wanted to belong to."

"And now you do."

"Shit, yes. It's a fraternity you don't get out of. It's always there, in your dreams, waiting. That's what they don't tell you."

"The dreams will go away, in time."

He shook his head. "I got hardened, Jess, in 'Nam. I could look at corpses and not bat an eyelash. I could make jokes beside them. My waking mind drained all the terror out, like juice out of an orange. But it all drains into your dreams. Terror juice. Things are always terrible there, Jess. Raw. New. Clear. Every detail so clear, just so goddam *clear*."

"I wish I could make them go away."

"So do I. Hold me, Jess. It's better when you hold me."

"I'm here, Mark. Oh, love, I'm here."

"Don't leave me, Jess."

"I won't. I'm here, love."

When he went back to sleep, the dreams did not return. He slept as if he had been drugged, in a deep dreamless silence. When he awoke, the sun was streaming in through the window. Jessie was up; he could smell the coffee brewing. The daylight was

141

safe. It was as if the nights were a twilight zone, a strange country where memory, fantasy, and nightmare intermingled in a half-lit world of dreams. He ran through the nights for the safety of the daylight, and when he got there it all seemed unreal. Had it happened? The sun outside glinted on a sheen of frost across the branches of a nearby tree. It was a winter day in Boston and he was safe. He always had been. Had the night happened at all?

He walked into the kitchen, kissed Jessie on the back of the neck, and said, "Sorry about last night. I didn't mean to scare you."

"I'm glad I was there."

"I get them now and then. In the morning, I hardly remember. It's no sweat."

"Waking up screaming is hardly no sweat, Mark."

"It's OK. I can handle it. I'm not ready for the funny farm or anything."

"Did you ever have any therapy? After Vietnam?"

"Therapy? No, my head was on straight."

"Never really talked to anyone? About what happened?"

"They weren't things I wanted to remember, especially."

"I think it's worse when you bury things."

"I don't need any amateur psychoanalysis, thanks."

"I'm just saying there's some heavy stuff there. I don't think you've dealt with it."

"Psychobabble."

"No, it isn't."

"Goddammit, Jess, don't patronize me!" He slammed his fist down on the table, hard. The coffee cup jumped and landed on the floor with a loud crash. He blinked, looking at it.

"Sorry," he said.

"There's a lot of anger in you, Mark. You control it, but it scares me."

"Jess, that's behind me. Sure, 'Nam was a head trip, but I want it back there, where it is, in the past."

"Will it stay there?"

"If I make it stay there."

"I don't think you have that much control over it."

"Jess, can we not talk about this?"

"That's no way to solve things."

"You have your way, I have mine."

She nodded. "OK. You're saying that it's your life and I should butt out."

"No, I didn't mean that." He reached out to touch her hair. "I love you. I don't want you to butt out. It's just that—let me work on this my own way, OK?"

"OK, Mark. Who am I to lecture, anyhow? I have enough hang-ups of my own, God knows. I'm good at giving advice, but not at taking it."

He cleaned up the mess from the broken coffee cup. "Do you have to leave today?"

"Yes. I have meetings with alumni groups in Washington and New York. But I'll be back on Wednesday."

"I miss you. I hate it when you're away, even for a day."

"Don't you think I'd rather be here? But it's my job, Mark."

"I know. I'm not trying to say you shouldn't go. Just that I'll miss you."

"I'll miss you too."

He walked along Beacon Street to his office, feeling jittery and out of sorts. What in the hell was happening to him? Christ, it had been fourteen years ago. He'd had another flashback last week, and the nightmares were coming with more frequency. It was all the goddam anniversaries. Every day there was a new magazine cover, a TV special, another rehash of the war. Why couldn't they just let it be, let the old ghosts lie quiet in the mists of the jungles and the swamps? Why dredge it all up, one more time?

Was Jessie right? he wondered. The tar pit had always been there, at the edge of his consciousness. He had been careful to walk around it. Would it always be there, waiting for him, as bottomless as the quarry Nichols used to dive into? Could he run away from it forever? What did he feel about Vietnam? Christ, who knew? Who the fuck knew? Who wanted to?

No, he could control it. He had, for fourteen years. He had come home, adjusted to being without a leg, lived through the wreck of his marriage without cracking up, got his Master's, nearly his PhD, did his job well. He was a model vet, one of the lucky ones. You just had to slog on. Dwelling on the past was unhealthy.

Once you wandered into the tar pit, would you ever come out again?

He spent his time that day coordinating plans for a week of

winter survival training in Maine for ROTC members and other students who wanted to sign up. He would go along, as an observer and instructor. He wasn't able to take part in the most strenuous activities, but he liked the challenge of living outdoors for a week, showing the students how the land could feed them, even in winter, if they knew where to look. He was fairly mobile on cross-country skis, even though the motion he had worked out was hardly the graceful glide of a two-legged man. It would be good to get out into the woods, away from the radio and the TV, out of his own head.

That evening, when he was in the middle of dinner, the phone rang and a familiar voice came on the line.

"Guess who the fuck this is?"

"Some asshole without any arms."

"I run marathons, sucker. Tried that lately?"

"Eliot, where the fuck are you?"

"At Logan. I got four hours between flights. I'm coming over."

"I'll be here."

When the bell rang, Eliot breezed in and said, "Where the fuck's the booze? I have had one *shitty* day. I spent two fucking hours in Atlanta waiting for Eastern to get its ass in gear."

"Christ, Eliot, look at that tan. You look so fucking healthy, who'd guess you were a gimp?"

"You look pretty good yourself, Redneck. Kicked sand in the face of any ninety-eight-pound weaklings lately? Or do you just stick the leg in the picnic basket when you go to the beach?"

Mark cackled and said, "Oh, Christ, it's good to see you!" and he poured Eliot a Scotch on the rocks.

"Make it a double," Eliot said.

They relaxed in the living room.

"Hey, Mark, you'll never guess who I met when I was in Vegas for the aerospace convention," Eliot said.

"Who?"

"Sarah Jane Gridley. She's working at Caesar's Palace. As a dealer."

"No kidding."

"Yeah. She used to be a showgirl, but now she has a couple of kids and makes more money dealing. Her husband works the bar."

"So she made it. Hot damn!"

"Yeah, she seems real happy. Christ, I hope she deals better than she dances."

"What do you hear from Spic?"

"This you will never believe. Spic is going to run for Congress."

"You're shitting me."

"No. You know he was head of Veterans' Affairs down in Jersey. He got a lot of good press, so he plans to run for the House in the fall."

"Christ, can you see him hot-wiring cars in the House garage?"

"Yeah, he says somebody leaked his juvenile record to the papers. God knows who did it. He's got an ad ready. 'Keep your car *safe*. Send Julio Colon to Congress.' "

"Hey, Ward L-Fifteen is flying high."

"I saw Spade and Pimp when I was in Dee-troit. They're still in business together, doing OK. You heard about Mick?"

"No. What happened?"

"Died a couple of weeks ago. Liver infection. I guess they never did get his insides back quite right."

"Oh, Jesus, I didn't know."

"I saw him last year when I went through San Diego. He didn't look great then. One infection after another, I guess. Had a nice wife and a kid."

"Christ, that sucks."

"Well, he had fourteen years. That's better than the guys who didn't make it. Give me another one of these, Redneck."

Mark poured Eliot another double and did the same for himself. "We are going to get plowed. What about your plane?"

"Oh, screw my plane. Let's get wasted."

They brought each other up to date, and then for old times' sake did a few Goldies, including a slightly slurred rendition of "My Funny Valentine":

Is your figure less than Greek
Since they caught you up Shit's Creek—

They laughed and drank and drank and laughed some more. Then they were quiet for a bit and Eliot said, "Redneck, me and Diane are separated."

"What? When did this happen?"

"Last month."

"What's the drill? I thought you two really had it together."

"I thought so too. It's not her, it's me."

"You walked out?"

"No. She tossed me out."

"Why?"

"I had this thing going, with a chippy. And I was boozing." He shrugged. "I don't know why I did it. My head's screwed up, Redneck."

"We're all a little messed up, Hebe. Why don't you patch things up? Diane is a dynamite woman."

"I know. But I—this is going to sound weird—I have trouble looking at my own daughter. My kid, I love her, and—Jesus Christ, my head is screwed up."

"Why? What the fuck is going on, Eliot?"

"I never told you, did I? Shit, I never told anybody."

"Told me what?"

"About what happened."

"In 'Nam?"

"Yeah."

"You never told me."

Eliot was quiet for a minute, staring at his hands.

"Tell me, Hebe," Mark said.

Eliot sat for what seemed a long time, silent, staring. Finally, he spoke.

"We went into a village. It had been real hairy, our guys had gotten the shit kicked out of them. The village was supposed to be VC. Five guys went into a hooch, and there was this woman there. I told them not to do it, but it didn't do any good. I didn't go in, but I heard them. They were giving her a good going over, and she was screaming. There were VC all around, and I was scared shitless. I figured either the VC would get me or we'd all be court-martialed, me for just standing there. Then something comes running at me, this black figure—it was getting dark and I just—the damn gun went off so fast. I did it by reflex. It was a kid, about twelve, my daughter's age. Running to help her mother. She was a beautiful kid. My bullet got her in the throat. She just looked at me with these big eyes, as she bled to death. I tried to stop the blood, but it just kept coming and coming. She never said a word, just looked at me. She bled to death in my arms. I see those eyes when I look at my kid, Redneck. And I'm so fucking

146

afraid. Afraid something's going to happen to her, because of what I did."

"Eliot, it was an accident. It's not like you did it in cold blood."

"No, I panicked. I didn't have to shoot. It could have been one of our guys. I panicked. And I killed a child."

"It was a war, Eliot. Things happen in wars. Shit, this isn't like My Lai; Christ, lots of crazy things happened. That shouldn't have happened. If it hadn't been dark, if—oh, hell, a dozen things."

"I could have stopped it. I could have told those guys to get the hell out of the hooch. I always wondered how people in Germany could have just stood around, and shit, there I was, just standing there."

"One of those crazy sons-of-bitches could have blown your head off too. I've seen guys when they get like that. Crazy for revenge. They could have wasted you, and who the fuck would know? Another VC casualty."

"It all makes sense when you say it. But I know what I feel. My kid, she's so beautiful, she has long dark hair and eyes like the kid I shot. And something's going to happen to her. Something awful. I know."

"That's why you left?"

"Yeah, that's really it. See, if I'm gone, maybe it won't happen."

"Eliot, that is nuts."

"Of course it's nuts. I know that. But when I'm at home, I panic. I look for kidnappers. Big trucks. Airplanes falling out of the sky."

"The answer isn't just to run out."

"I love her so fucking much, Redneck. I'm out of my head from worrying. I'm no good when I'm there. I'm not much good when I'm not there either."

"Eliot, get some help. Talk to somebody."

"A shrink? Talk about my toilet training?"

"Talk to Diane."

"I don't want to put this on Diane. It's my problem. I got to work it out somehow."

"Christ, I said that this morning. To Jessie."

"Give me another double Scotch."

"Yeah, I'll have one too."

"You ever think, Redneck, what your life would be like if you hadn't gone to 'Nam?"

"I'd have been a running back for the Miami Dolphins."

"I'd never have been a millionaire. Getting creamed over there made me ambitious."

"That is one fucking hard way to get ambition, Hebe."

"Yeah, I wouldn't have made the bucks. But my head wouldn't have been fucked up either. But you don't get to choose your hand. You play the one you get." He chuckled. "No pun intended."

"But you don't get flashbacks? Never get them?"

"No, I just get this crazy feeling, like this cold hand squeezing my windpipe, when I look at my kid."

"We got screwed, didn't we? I see guys my age, walking down the street, nice suits, two legs, and I want to ask them, Did you go? Where the fuck were you? Sometimes I get so pissed I want to go up and punch them out."

"Nobody gives a shit, Redneck. Nobody wants to think about us. They just want to forget it. Kids in school today, Vietnam is ancient history for them. We're as real to them as some old guy in a Civil War uniform. We're the past, Redneck."

"Jeez, there's a cheerful thought."

"Yeah, come on, let's get wasted. We might as well," Eliot said.

"Fucking A," Mark said, pouring himself another Scotch.

FROM JESSIE'S DIARY
(JUNIOR YEAR, 1970)

Dear Diary: I liberated the men's dining room at Locke-Ober's restaurant today.

Well, not just me. It was the fiftieth anniversary of women's suffrage, and there was this big march through the city and we were all feeling great and we wanted to do something symbolic. So a bunch of us started over to Locke-Ober's, where they don't let women in the downstairs dining room.

Why make a big deal about lunch, you ask? Well, in the South they didn't let Blacks into the white lunch counters or white toilets, and the real issues weren't eating or peeing. It was keeping them out of the white world. It was keeping them out of power.

And that's what men's dining rooms are all about: power. You know what goes on at the lunch tables? Business. People are cutting deals, making alliances, greasing the wheels. I bet more business gets done at lunch than the whole rest of the day. So by keeping us out of the dining rooms and the Jaycees and the Rotarys, they cut us out of power.

Well, people were pretty surprised when we marched in, but there were reporters along, so they let us sit down. I was at a table with Andrea and Talia. All these guys in their three-piece suits were giving us the fish eye, like they'd just been invaded by Martians. 'Course, we were dressed in jeans and boots, which you don't see a lot of in Locke-Ober's.

"Look at those guys," Andrea said. "Practically holding their noses."

"If we said we wanted to go to bed with them, they'd hustle their asses over here," I said. "If we're good enough to screw, we're good enough to eat their goddam lunch."

"Right on," said Andrea, and we picked up the menus.

"Christ, look at the prices," Andrea said. "How much money do you have?"

I reached in my pocket and pulled out wadded-up bills and change. "Three dollars and thirty cents," I said. "How about you?"

Andrea had a buck fifty, but she found another two dollars folded up in her blusher case. Mad money. Talia had two dollars in change. She was flushed with the elation of victory.

"A historic triumph over the patriarchy!" she exclaimed.

"Talia, it is not going to be much of a triumph if we can't pay for lunch," Andrea said.

"Come on, there must be something we can afford," I said, and we pored over the menu.

"A club sandwich," Andrea said. "We can split it."

The waiter came over and gave us an icy look of disdain. "Are you ready to order, ladies?" he said.

"We'd like the Turkey Club," Andrea said.

"And three plates," I added.

"And a ginger ale. Three straws," Talia said.

The waiter sneered as he wrote it down. "Will that be all?"

"You don't have any Dom Perignon 1928, do you? That was a very good year," Andrea said.

"No madam." He looked at Andrea with new respect.

"Jeez, and this was supposed to be a fancy place. Well, we'll stick with ginger ale."

"Andrea," I whispered, "what if they'd had it?"

150

"We'd punt," Andrea said. "But I will not be patronized by a snot-nosed waiter."

A reporter from the Globe came over. "Well, girls, now that you're here, what do you have to say?"

"We are not girls," Talia said icily. "Girls is a word coined by the minions of the patriarchy to keep female members of the human species subdued, powerless, and subject to an authoritarian regime of sexual politics."

Talia is very smart and a good radical, but every time she opens her mouth she sounds like a mimeograph machine in a basement in Cambridge.

"I've been waiting for years to eat here," Andrea said, "but when I got here, I couldn't find anything I liked."

"You stole that line from Dick Gregory," the reporter said. Andrea pouted.

"It took us two hundred years to get the vote," I said, "and now we're going after the three-martini lunch."

He wrote that down, and I beamed. OK, maybe it wasn't "Give Me Liberty or Give Me Death" but it was snappy. One thing I've learned from the movement, if you want to be a revolutionary, you have to be quotable. Treatises aren't any good these days. What you really want is a thirty-second bite on the six o'clock news.

The waiter brought the club sandwich and Talia said, "The masses of women are moving inexorably toward destiny. We cannot be stopped."

"This turkey is from a roll," Andrea said, chewing. "Six-fifty for a club sandwich, and it's from a fucking roll." She looked around the room at the paneled walls and the sparkling linen. "Goyim don't know how to eat," she said.

"I wonder when they bring in the police dogs and the hoses," I said.

"Are you kidding?" Andrea said, her mouth crammed full of turkey. "And get water stains on the linen? They just smile nice and polite, up here, while they cut your balls off." She grinned. "Figure of speech."

Most of the diners just tried to pretend we didn't exist, which was hard, with the TV lights and all, but one young guy, dressed in a three-piece suit like the rest of them, walked over to us and said,

"Power to the people!" and gave the Black Power salute. Me, Talia, and Andrea gave it right back.

"Right on, brother!" I said, as I waved my fist in the air, and guys choked on their Parker House rolls all over the room. It is a moment I will never forget: the day we did the Black Power salute in the men's dining room at Locke-Ober's.

It's funny, but as we were marching along today, we would call out to women on the street and ask them to join us, and some did, but others were scared, you could see it in their eyes. Scared to celebrate the year we finally got the vote. Some people say we are trying to break down the structures that protect women. I have the funny feeling we are being protected, all right—from money, from power, and from the great adventure of trying to run the world.

But I do think I understand why women are afraid. If you're a woman and you don't have skills you can market for much dough and you're alone, the world can be a hell of a scary place. But gambling on a man to protect you, does that pay off? I see a lot of widows waiting on tables, and divorcées checking out stuff at the supermarket, and old ladies with everything they own in a shopping bag. It's true, most women are one man away from welfare. Even if a man wants to take care of you, what happens if he gets sick? Or dies? Or gets laid off? Dear Diary, it seems to me that if you can't take care of yourself economically, some day you are going to be a victim. And I won't be that. Not ever.

I think, Dear Diary, that when women stay home and let men be in charge of everything they get a view of the world like the one in the fun-house mirror. They see men as much bigger than they are. They think men have some magic powers that enable them to run the world. But they don't. Men aren't any smarter than we are. That's the big secret we haven't been let in on. There aren't any magic powers. You get by on luck and sweat and smarts and hustle and luck. And who you know.

Dear Diary, I make a promise to you and to myself: I will never hide from life. Edith Hamilton said that men are not made for safe havens. Well, women aren't either. There are people who want to put fences around us, who want to say there are things we can't do, because we're women. Because we should want to be "protected."

But I won't let them do it to me. Oh Dear Diary, whether it's a lunchroom or whether it's the world, nobody can say to me, "Keep out." I don't know what's going to happen to me in life. Sometimes I'm scared, I admit that. I wonder if I can really do all the things I want to do.

But I will try. No matter what happens, nobody will ever be able to say, "She didn't try."

Nobody.

FOURTEEN

Mark piled fresh strawberries on his plate and looked around at the well-dressed young men and women milling around in the banquet room of the Copley Plaza. Jake had invited Mark and Jessie—gratis—to one of his success brunches, and they were too intrigued to refuse.

"Look at these people, Jess. Do they strike you as movers and shakers?"

"If they were, they wouldn't be paying fifty bucks a head to be here."

"This is quite a crowd. Does he get this many people every time he does this?"

"I guess success is a hot commodity these days."

"I think if leprosy suddenly became chic," Mark said, "Jake would be peddling leper colonies in Maui."

"Condos. Unclean Acres. 'Rot away with the kind of people who can afford the very best.'"

Mark chuckled and Jessie crunched a strawberry with her

teeth. "You know, I was terrified of leprosy when I was a kid," she said.

"You were?"

"Yes. We read the Bible all the time in school, and I used to have awful dreams about turning yellow and walking around with a bell on my neck. It was stupid, I guess. There weren't many lepers in Brockton."

"Poor Jess."

"I thought I'd get it at the movies. From the seats. I always wore my raincoat, even when it was ninety degrees. I'd spread it across the seat."

"Why the movies?"

"I don't know. Kids get some funny ideas. I mean, they didn't go to movies a lot in the New Testament. They must have picked up leprosy somewhere else."

"I can just picture you. I bet you had braces and knobby knees."

"I did. And my raincoat was brown corduroy, and it was really ugly. But I loved it, because the rain would go right through it, but the leprosy wouldn't."

Jake breezed over, resplendent in a three-piece suit and a silk tie from Louie's. On his arm was a young blond woman wearing a dress-for-success suit and a tie that matched Jake's. He introduced the young woman as his associate, Melanie, and asked, "Having a good time, folks?"

"We're talking about leprosy," Mark said.

Jake made a face. "At my success brunch?"

"It's the new Yuppie disease, Jake," Jessie said. "Herpes is passé."

"Business seems to be booming, Jake," Mark said.

Jake beamed. "Nearly three hundred people."

"Success is what *everybody's* into!" Melanie burbled.

"Is it?" Mark said.

"Yes. I used to be very big on causes, like Jake. I was arrested at Seabrook. But I think I'm still helping humanity, setting up brunches. Helping people reach their potential is very satisfying," Melanie said.

"It must be," Jessie said politely.

"Oh, yes, I'm a people person, so a people job is good for me." She turned to Mark. "What business are you in?"

"The army," he said.

Melanie smiled. "Oh, that's a people business too."

"Yes," Mark said. "We kill them."

"Oh, Jake, he does have such a sense of humor, doesn't he!"

"He's a laff riot," Jakes said. "Funnier than General Sherman."

"Oh, is he your general, Mark?" Melanie asked.

"Uh—no."

"Sherman burned Atlanta, Melanie," Jake told her.

"Well, *that* wasn't a very funny thing to do," she said.

Jake and Melanie drifted off, and Mark poured Jessie a glass of champagne and took a Bloody Mary for himself from the waiter. As he turned around, Mark saw, by the entrance, an incongrous figure, given this particular gathering. It was Brian, wearing his ponytail, his jeans, and a necklace of handmade bells from Samoa. Brian looked around at the scene and blinked several times, as if he couldn't quite believe what he saw.

A young man in an expensive gray suit standing behind Mark turned to an equally well-groomed companion and said, "Where did *he* come from? The cast of *Hair*?"

"Nobody told him the Age of Aquarius dawned twenty years ago," the second man said, with a sneer.

Mark watched Brian looking around and said to Jessie, "He looks lost, doesn't he."

"Yes, let's go talk to him. The other people in this place are acting like those bells he's wearing are chiming out, *Unclean!*"

They walked over to Brian, who was muttering to himself as he scanned the crowd. "Look at this! Look at it."

"Hi, Brian," Jessie said.

"Bourgeois materialistic decadence," he said.

Jessie nodded. "We were going to make a revolution," she said.

"Twenty years ago these people would have been in the streets," Brian said. "Now they're in the fucking Copley Plaza."

"Yeah," Jessie said, munching another strawberry. "Who would have believed it, Jake Siegel a success guru."

"Twenty years ago Jake would have said people like this ought to be lined up against the wall and shot." Brian sighed. "Now he's giving them brunch."

Jessie nodded, sighing also. "Up against the wall, motherfuckers."

"Folks, I'm sorry to spoil all this nostalgia," Mark said, "but I think I'd prefer fresh strawberries to hot lead."

Brian glowered at him. "*You* were a mercenary."

"Watch your mouth, Brian. I went where my country told me to go."

"Where we had no business being."

"Believe me, I'd just as soon have passed. But I saw a lot of brave men die there. They died for their country."

"To save San Diego from the Reds?"

"For whatever reason. Because you didn't like the war, you just want to forget them. Who gives a shit?"

"I fought too," Brian said. "I fought against the war. I went to jail and got my teeth kicked in. Who thanks me for that? Who remembers?" He swept his hand across the room. "I try to tell them, the kids, what it was like, that we had a dream we could make things better. That we really could give peace a chance. And we did good things, for a while. We ended a war, and things got better for poor people and Blacks and women. For a while. And we cared, dammit, we did care. I try to tell them that, about the passion, and they just sit there and stare at me, as if I'm speaking Greek. The passion! Oh, God, I wish I had the words to make them understand what it was like—" He stopped suddenly, aware that he was talking too loud and that people had turned and were staring at him. He looked down at his shoes, unshined, unfashionable.

"Brian, can I get you some champagne?" Jessie said gently.

"No. I think I'll go home. Smoke some dope. Forget that a right-wing movie actor is president."

"Things will get better, Brian."

"Will they?" he said. "I don't know. I just don't know."

Later, back in Mark's apartment, Mark put logs in the fireplace and they both sat in front of the fire quietly. Then Mark said, "I don't know who's better off, Jess. Jake, who's sold out to the brunch bunch, or Brian, who's stuck in the past."

"I guess I'd vote for Brian, if that's the choice. He's right about one thing; we did care. I can't imagine being alive without being able to be passionate about something real. Besides success. I think it must be awful to be young today."

"Not so bad. They don't have a war to go off to."

"No. Not yet."

"It was really strange to see all those people today, all hyped

157

up about success. Makes me laugh. A guy on my ward died a few weeks ago. I just heard. Shit, I can remember when my idea of success meant making it through the fucking day alive."

"Oh, I understand some of it. But not all. It's so—self-centered now. I want to count for something, because for so long women have been invisible. I want to be one of the people who makes things go. I think I might even want to go into politics someday. Run for office."

He whistled. "You *are* ambitious."

"Well, some people from the Women's Political Caucus talked to me about it. Down the road, someday. But I hope I'm not like so many men. I want to have power to do something constructive with it. Not just groove on having it. But maybe they all start out like me."

He laughed. "I used to dream of being a famous writer. Not that I ever did anything about it. But the war made a lot of things seem—oh, I don't know—trivial. I do want to write my book. All those voices need to be heard. But I haven't got your drive, Jess."

"Herb didn't either. After a while, he hated me for it."

"I won't."

"Are you sure? Men say that—Herb did—but do they mean it? In their heart of hearts, don't they want a sweet little helpmate who'll stay back in their shadow?"

"I don't think so. I had a wife like that. I think we might have broken up eventually, even if it hadn't been for the war. Gerry always needed more from me than I could give. I couldn't give her the life she wanted to have. Made me feel pretty crummy. You don't make me feel that way."

"I kept trying to shrink myself, with Herb. Like Alice in Wonderland. He couldn't bear to see me the way I really was."

"Jess, I don't need you to be a midget for me. I did not fall in love with a fucking Munchkin."

"I do love you, Mark Clifford Claymore."

"Do you?"

"Yes."

"Can you prove it?"

"Persuade me."

"How's that?"

"Oh. Oh, my! Oh, my God!"

"I love doing this to you. Taking off your clothes, real slow and sexy. Oh, that's lovely. Lovely."

"Now let *me* undress you."

"Jess—"

"I've never done it. I want to."

He stood still, suddenly trembling, as she gently undressed him. No woman had ever done this for him before. He stood before her, feeling more naked than he had ever felt in his life before. And more vulnerable.

"You're beautiful," she said. "Your body is beautiful." She moved to him and put both her hands on his erect penis. "I love to touch you. Your cock is beautiful. I love to look at you."

"Love me, Jessie," he said. "Please love me."

"I will," she said.

Afterward, in the bed, he said to her, "You heal me, Jess. I'm whole when I'm with you. I never wanted to undress in front of a woman. I was afraid she'd find me—ugly. I wanted to do it in the dark all the time. You make me like my body. Do you know what that does for me?"

"I think so. And you let me stand up straight. I feel—cared for, with you. But I don't have to be *little*—like a child—to get cared for. And that's something new. Oh, Mark, can it be as good as we think it is?"

"Yes," he said, "it can."

But later, much later, as she slept the sleep of the just beside him, he sat up, staring into the darkness.

Can it be as good as we think it is?

"Yes," he said. "Yes, it can." But as he said it, he saw, in his mind's eye, the body of Nichols swimming through the clear water, seeming to mock them—seeming to mock love and life and hope itself—with his missing face and terrible blue empty eyes.

"Go away," Mark said to him, but he only swam closer, grinning his death's-head grin.

"Go away, damn you!" Mark said, inside his mind, and Nichols turned, very slowly, and started to swim away, until he disappeared into some murky fastness.

Mark moved close to Jessie and put his arms around her. She sighed and did not wake. The feel of her in his arms was wonderful. There was nothing but the darkness and the sound of her breathing. Nichols had gone away.

But he would be back.

FROM JESSIE'S DIARY
(JUNIOR YEAR)

Dear Diary: My mother died today.

The words look funny on the page. Not my *mother. It can't be true. But it is.*

She was only sick for two months. When she went in for the operation, I was sure it would be OK. I mean, people's mothers aren't supposed to die. Not till they're old.

We took her in the morning of the operation. She wasn't even in the hospital before that, she felt pretty good. She played the piano the night before, I heard her. Nothing somber—sort of up-tempo stuff, not ragtime or anything, something classical I didn't recognize, but it was high and light. It sounded like birds chirping or water running.

My dad and I drove her to the hospital. It was so early in the morning that the sky was still dark and a full moon rode high and bright over our heads. I remember thinking that the mountains looked like blue veins, stretching across the surface of the moon. It is still as clear as a snapshot in my mind, that bright, shining,

160

blue-veined moon, over the roof of our house. It was luminous and lovely, hanging up there, just out of reach. My mother looked at it and smiled. "It's beautiful," she said. "A good sign. Full of promise."

Three hours later the doctors told us. They just sewed her up. There was too much of it. And I thought of an odd thing: Romeo saying, "Swear not by the moon, the inconstant moon." And I hated it, the lying, treacherous, beautiful moon. How could it be so beautiful on the day my mother discovered she was going to die?

She wanted to be a concert pianist, you know. But when she married my dad, she gave up her dream. She still played, of course. Her grand piano was in the living room the whole time I was growing up. It was beautiful, all polished wood; the only time my mother got really mad at me for anything in the house was when I put wet things on the piano. She kept the top covered with a Spanish throw with long black fringe with embroidered red roses on it, and sometimes, when my mother wasn't looking, I used to take it and drape it around me and pretend I was a princess. It was the most beautiful thing I ever saw.

My mother played in public now and then—reluctantly, because she said she was rusty. She played at a PTA concert at the high school and at a parish musicale to benefit the missions. She was nervous the day before; she would go around the house dusting and tidying things that didn't need to be dusted or tidied, and smoking a lot. But she was always wonderful. People would come up afterward and tell her how talented she was.

She was pretty happy, all in all. She loved my dad and he loved her. But he got to try out what he wanted to be and she didn't. I wonder if she would have been happy as a concert pianist. When I was a kid, I built up this elaborate fantasy in my mind about how it would be if she played a solo with a big symphony orchestra. The details are still cataloged in my mind like on file cards. I think of her, wearing a blue taffeta dress, her hair pulled back in a French braid like she used to wear it sometimes when she got dressed up. The taffeta dress has an A-line skirt, and the fabric is the color of washable blue ink, the kind the nuns made us use. She is sitting in a metal chair backstage, smoking nervously, tapping her feet up and down. She does not know what I know—that she will be wonderful.

161

I think that's how I will always remember her, even though it never really happened. It was how she would have wanted it to happen, and I think she will be pleased.

She always pushed me to do things. Other girls' mothers wanted to keep them close, but my mother was always hurling me out into the world. I didn't want to skate on the pond near our house when I was six and had a new pair of skates. I remember standing there, clutching her hand and saying, "I can't do it," and she said, "Of course you can. You can do anything."

And it was like the voice of God, saying, "You can do anything." So I skated. And it was easy. I think I will hear that voice inside my head for the rest of my life, and I guess it is the best present a mother can give her daughter. She wanted me to be fearless, maybe because she hadn't been. "Find out what you can do," she told me. "You have to know." And I know there was a sadness in her, because she never did. When she'd get that faraway look in her eyes I knew she was someplace else, lost in the web of music she had created in her mind. She was very special because she could do that. Oh, she hadn't really been a concert pianist, but I had no doubt that she could have been, and it made her special. It made me special too. Now and then she would play at other people's houses and the people all sat very quiet, not speaking. My mother had the power to do that. It was something.

It's funny, other people's mothers were always worried about doing the right thing—not right like in the Bible, but the correct thing—having manners and wearing what everybody else wore and all that stuff. My mother just didn't seem to notice all that. Other people's mothers were really shocked when their children went on antiwar marches or yelled rude things about the president. I could never figure that out. They didn't seem to get so upset by the idea that lots of kids were going to get shipped off to get slaughtered, but they got ripshit *when their kids were rude to a public official. But my mother wasn't like that. She even went on a couple of marches with us, and once she yelled "Pigs!" at the cops. My father turned green when he heard that. But I think she had a grand time.*

My mother had this voice—it was musical. She said hello on the telephone like you were about to tell her something wonderful and exciting. I liked to call her from school when I was down and things

162

were rotten, because just hearing her "Hello" perked me up. It made me feel that the world was wonderful and exciting too. The worst time was the day I realized I would never hear that sound, never again in my whole life, never hear her say hello that way again. It was the most awful moment of my life.

After she died, Andrea went with me out to the cemetery to pick out the headstone. My father was a wreck, he didn't want to do it. I said I would. I really knew my childhood was over, that day. But it's funny, Andrea and I got to giggling a little as we drove out there. It's like after so much tension, something happens, and you feel giddy, with release.

I said to Andrea, "I guess I'll get something tasteful. My mother will kill me if I get something crappy." And we both giggled, of course, at that.

"If my mother died," Andrea said, "I would get a big Bloomingdale's credit card to put on her grave. It would make her feel at home."

"Oh, Andrea," I said.

"Jessie, the woman has spent so many hours there they've named a cash register after her. My grandfather gave a whole operating room at the Jewish Memorial Hospital. My mother hates hospitals, except for the gift shop, so we have the Margolis Memorial cash register, right between Career Women and Designers."

"Is she still pissed at you?" I asked her. Mrs. Margolis was very upset that Andrea was in the antiwar movement.

"She prays, every night, that I will get hit by a club at one of the marches. Nothing really messy, though, so I will look incredibly beautiful when they bring me in on a stretcher to Beth Israel. The doctor on duty will fall madly in love with me. He'll be Jewish, of course."

"He'll fall in love with you while you're unconscious?" I asked.

"He can perform lewd perversions on me in the OR while I'm out cold, as long as he's Jewish and the ring is at least three karats."

"What if they take you to Boston City and the doctor groping you is Irish?"

"You would not believe the size of the malpractice suit."

"Our mothers really got stuck, didn't they," I said to Andrea. "Stay home, make babies, and let men run the world."

163

"Why do you think my mother shops all the time? It gives her something to do. But how can I say that to her? She'd only say, 'You're book-smart, but you don't know life.'"

"As if she does."

"Right. You know, under the designer junk she wears, I think there is a smart person there. But she's afraid of everything. 'What will people say?' That's her favorite line. She kowtows to my father, but she says the meanest things about him to her friends. To his face, though, she treats him like he's a genius."

"Is he?" I asked.

"He sells shmattes, we are not talking Bernard Baruch here. Christ, I don't want to be anything like her."

"My mother wanted to be a pianist. I wish she had tried. She just gave it up, like there was no way she could be a mother and a pianist too. I'm going to try whatever it is I want to be. I'd rather fall on my face than not know."

"You know what my nightmare is? That I'm going to wake up one day and be her," Andrea said. "I'll have this overwhelming urge to run to Bloomingdale's and buy a Bill Blass and marry a doctor who gave to the Nixon campaign. If that ever happens, I'll slit my throat with the sharp edge of my Diner's Club card."

"We won't cop out, Andrea. We'll set the world on its ear."

"Will we, Jess? Will we really?"

"Of course we will. We can do anything."

"How do you know?" she asked me.

"My mother said so."

FIFTEEN

"Ira is on a campaign," Andrea said, "to get Tex out of the house. I am really pissed."

They were eating lunch, as usual, at the Harvest in Harvard Square. Jessie took a forkful of chicken salad with walnuts. "Ira always was sort of self-righteous, Andrea. What's he doing now?"

"He's got my mother on his side. Can you believe it? My mother, Ira, and his little fly-girl. Groucho, Harpo, and Shiksa."

"Gunfight at the OK Corral?"

"Yeah. And I do not intend to lose. Ira has some nerve. He and Tinker Bell are shacked up at her place at Harbor Towers. An efficiency. He wants the kids to visit and sleep in sleeping bags on the floor. I said no way are they camping out in Adultery Acres. Rachel will not get her bird-watching badge by spotting Tinker Bell in bed with her dad."

"So you and Tex are settling in?"

"Yeah. He's thinking of starting a catering business. Doing Tex-Mex for Yuppies. I'm putting up the front money."

165

"Does Ira know that?"

"No, and he'll have a fit. All of a sudden he has become food conscious. Keeps telling me that tacos are *trayf*. I said, 'What does she feed them, Ira, cellophane sandwiches left over from the Toledo run?' "

"This sounds like it could get messy, Andrea."

"I'm willing to be civilized, and I am the injured party."

"How is Tex taking all this?"

"He's been very good about it. And he's so excited about the business. I think it could do real well. People are fed up with quiche and cutesy."

"I never cook when we eat in. Mark is such a wonderful cook, and I'm awful."

"You're telling me? I used to coat my stomach with Pepto-Bismol when you invited us to dinner."

"Herb wanted me to be a gourmet cook. Another one of my failures, as far as he was concerned."

"I learned to cook Jewish for Ira. When we were married, all I could cook was chicken à l'orange."

"I remember that. You threw chicken in a pot with orange juice and boiled it until it was the consistency of tar."

"We were out stopping the war, Jess. Who had time to cook? But I really worked hard at it, after we got married. When I think of the hours I slaved over Jennie Grossinger's cookbook for that ungrateful crud."

"You learned good."

"You think *she's* going to learn to do noodle kugel? All he cares is that her thighs don't look like pudding."

"Andrea, they wanted us to be liberated flower children, screwing at the drop of a hat, but also their mothers, cooking and cleaning and making everything nice. It's hard to be the Sensuous Woman *and* Betty Crocker."

"Jess, imagine if I'd just been a housewife. I'd have been shattered. You were right, it was my work that saved me. At work I'm a valuable person. That's what kept me from going under."

"Yeah, it's *interesting* out there. That's the big secret about work, Andrea. You get to do interesting things."

"You know, I've been thinking: What if Ira and the kids were my whole life? Even if he hadn't left? My kids will be leaving the nest in not too many years, and I'd look in the mirror and I wouldn't see this fresh-faced twenty-year-old girl. Things would

166

be ending. But here I am at thirty-five, and I'm just starting to reach my potential in my field. The best times are ahead, for me. It was really awful, when the kids were babies, to juggle everything, but it paid off."

"Yeah, when you've got work you love, not being young anymore is OK. You have other things. Better things, really."

"You know," Andrea said, "at first I just grabbed onto Tex because he was there, and he was a man. But he takes care of me in a lot of ways that Ira didn't. I have fun with him. We don't discuss the latest Supreme Court decisions, but I can do that at work. And the kids adore him."

"Sounds like you plan to make this homestead arrangement permanent."

"I was always worried about finding the *appropriate* kind of man. One who was ambitious, upwardly mobile. Who could make money. But *I* make money. *I'm* upwardly mobile. Why can't I have a man who likes to fix porches and roast bulls?"

"It seems like you do."

"Right. And I am not going to let Ira and my mother spoil it for me."

"Listen, Mark would love to do his Peking duck for you and Tex. Mark loves to show off his talents as a chef. And the duck is so good it melts in your mouth."

"Now who's settling in?"

"Well, we're taking it day by day."

"If you let him get away, Jess, you're crazy. He's adorable and he cooks Chinese. You do not pick up guys like that in the five-and-dime."

"Yeah, it all does seem too good to be true."

"Don't look a gift horse in the mouth."

"Believe me, Andrea, I'm trying not to. I'm trying."

The following Saturday, Andrea and Tex were invited to Mark's apartment to sample his special Peking duck. Jessie spent the day shopping, fretting, and dusting. She was still staying half the time at her apartment, half the time at Mark's, so while she had something of a proprietary feeling about his place, it wasn't hers, and she didn't feel she could rearrange the furniture or start acting like the mistress of the manor. But she didn't want to feel useless either, so she fussed.

167

"For God's sake, Jess, you've dusted that chair eight times," Mark said. "I think it's clean."

"This is the first time we've entertained together, do you realize that? Oh, I hope Tex will feel comfortable. Ira has been such a shit about him. I want to let Tex know that *we* don't feel that way."

"Ira sounds like a real asshole."

"Oh, he's absolutely brilliant. Started at MIT when he was fifteen. But you're right, basically he's an asshole. He's so self-important. Ira has the answers to everything, whether he knows anything about a subject or not. I never really liked him, but I had to put up with him, because Andrea's my best friend."

"How long have you two known each other?"

"She was assigned as my roommate freshman year in college. We went to jail together. We go back a long way. Oh, I hope you like Tex. He's a very sweet man. He just looks a little strange at first, with the silver belt and the jeans."

"I met Texans in 'Nam. A lot of mouth, but mostly they'll stick by you. Good guys to have by your side when things get hairy."

Tex and Andrea arrived at eight, Tex in his best jeans and his silver belt. He was a large man, built like the bulls he used to ride, and a luxuriant handlebar mustache gave him a Teddy Roosevelt appearance. The first few minutes were a bit awkward, with Andrea talking too fast, the way she did when she was nervous, and Tex hitching up his pants too often. But Tex and Mark hit it off, especially when Mark got Tex talking about his rodeo days. Tex had come to realize that rodeos were thought of as quaint but slightly déclassé in the environs of Harvard Square, and he tended to keep his mouth shut around people who might poke fun.

"It must be rough work, doing rodeos," Mark said, pouring Tex a bourbon on the rocks.

"Oh, yeah, you get busted up a lot. I broke my collarbone six times. Lots of busted ribs. Bull stepped on my foot once. Broke all my toes."

"Good money?"

"Not bad, but when you figure in all the risks you take, all the injuries, it's not so great. And I wasn't good with money. I been doin' this since I was nineteen, and hell, when I was a kid, I'd run right through it. Booze, gambling, women. It's OK when you're a kid, but I figure I'm getting long in the tooth for that stuff. I didn't want to end up as a broke-down old cowpoke. Hanging round, doin' odd jobs. Time for me to branch out."

"Tex was National Calf Roping champion in 1974," Andrea said. "He has a big trophy."

"You must have been really good," Jessie said.

"Oh, yeah, ropin' was my best event. But people like the broncs best. More exciting than watching a guy hog-tie a dogie. More talent to ropin', though."

"How do you like Boston, now that you've been here awhile?" Jessie asked.

"It's right nice. Except for the wet cold. I come from Montana, where it gets cold as a witch's tit—excuse me, ladies— but it's a dry cold. Here, my nose gets runny all the time."

"You should try skiing," Jessie said. "I used to hate the winter until I learned to ski. Andrea, you and Tex ought to come up to Gunstock with Mark and me."

"Are you out of your mind? Me, on skis?"

"You don't have to actually ski. You can sit in the hot tub and then wear great-looking après-ski stuff while you drink in the lodge. Mark and I rented a place for the season."

"Tex," Andrea said, "I think I'd like that."

"Hell, I'll try it," Tex said.

"Mark's a terrific skier. He can give you lessons."

"Except I only know how to ski on one leg."

"That's OK," Tex said. "I'll just rent one ski. It'll be cheaper."

Mark went into the kitchen to check on the duck, then came back and poured another round of drinks. As he was handing Tex the bourbon, the doorbell rang. He looked at Jessie. "Were you expecting anyone?"

"No, were you?"

He shook his head. "Probably the paper boy."

"I'll get it," Jessie said. She got up, went to the door, opened it. There stood Ira, his hair wet and askew from the wet snow that was falling, his eyes glassy. He weaved a bit as he stood in the doorway.

"Ira, what—"

He marched right past her into the living room. Raising his hand like Uncle Sam saying "I Want You," and pointing his index finger directly at Tex.

"I came to see *him*."

"Ira, we are having a dinner party here," Andrea said. "Have you lost all your marbles?"

"I did not want to do this in front of the children, Andrea," he said, speaking very precisely, the way people do when they have had too much to drink and do not want anyone to notice. "Andrea, this man is not going back to my house."

"How did you know I was here?" Andrea asked him.

"Your mother told me."

"I am going to tear that woman's tongue out," Andrea said.

Mark looked at Jessie and Jessie shrugged. Ira repeated, "That man is not going back to my house."

"Your house? I paid for half of that house, Ira. If you remember."

Tex stood up and said, "Mister, I am just going to ask you politely to leave. You're drunk and we're havin' a nice dinner here and you are messin' things up."

"*You!*" Ira's voice rose several octaves. "You are nothing but a—a—goddamned *cowboy!*"

"Watch your mouth. There's ladies present."

"I am going to ask you, in a civilized fashion, sir, to leave my wife and children alone."

"Seems to me, friend, that when you ran out on 'em you gave up the right to say what they ought to do."

"I am still the father of my children," Ira said, weaving a bit. "And I do not think you are the proper role model for them. What kind of man makes a living falling off of cows?"

"Bulls," Jessie said.

"Look, mister, what I do for a living is my business, and you can—"

Ira interrupted. "Andrea, for God's sake, he has a *tattoo* on his wrist. Do you know what kind of people get tattoos? Bikies. Sickies. Perverts!"

"Now you look here, mister, you're a bigot," Tex said, deeply offended. "Lots of nice folks got tattoos."

"It's an American flag, Ira," Andrea snapped. "That's better than having 'I'm Debbie, fly me' stamped on your ass."

"I can't deal with you, Andrea, you're hysterical."

"Ira, I am not hysterical. You are drunk."

Ira turned to Tex. "I am going to appeal to your sense of decency, if you have any. I am going to ask you to move out of my house and stay away from my children."

170

"No, sir, I am not going to do that. I love Andrea, and I'm going to stand by her."

"Then you will have to accept the consequences."

"Ira, just go home," Andrea said.

"I think you ought to do what she says," Mark said. "You've had too much to drink."

"I have a duty, sir, a duty," Ira said gravely. He straightened up, braced his shoulders, and curled his hands into fists. He looked at Tex. "I am going to thrash you to within an inch of your life," he announced.

"Oh, Ira, for God's sake," said Andrea, "you haven't had a fist fight since the sixth grade."

"A lot you know!" Ira sneered. "I was in Golden Gloves."

"Was he?" Mark said to Jessie.

"That's news to me."

"Ira, you were at MIT when you were fifteen," Andrea said. "They don't have Golden Gloves there. Sparring would break all the test tubes."

"Stand up and fight like a man!" Ira barked to Tex, ignoring her.

"Mister, I'm not going to fight with you. You're drunk, and I don't think you've done a whole lot of fighting."

"You coward!" Ira sneered and dropped into a crouch. He motioned to Tex with his hands. "Come at me, come on. Come on!"

"Oh, this is mortifying." Andrea groaned. "Jess, I'm really sorry."

"That's OK."

"Slime," Ira said, advancing on Tex, his dukes still up. Tex backed away. "Pervert!" Ira said, and took a tipsy swing at Tex, missing him by three feet.

"Ira, stop that!" Jessie said.

Ira flailed away again, and Tex kept backing up, saying, "You stop that, now!" but Ira kept advancing, throwing drunken punches, as Tex retreated. Tex was nearly against the wall when Mark stepped up behind Ira, grabbed him with a neat half nelson, and immobilized him. At which point, Ira, unused to both alcohol and throwing haymakers, passed out cold.

"What's that funny smell?" Andrea said. "Is there a fire?"

"Oh, shit," Mark said, holding the slumping Ira, "the *duck!*"

"Oh my God!" Jessie said, and she ran into the kitchen, which

171

was filling up with smoke. She tried to rescue the duck from the oven, but it was spitting fire as she pulled it out, singed beyond repair. She stuck it under the cold water and opened the kitchen window to let out some of the smoke. Then she let the duck sit, smoldering, in the sink while she went back to the living room. Ira was out cold, lying on the floor, and Mark, Andrea, and Tex were standing there, looking at him.

"The duck?" Mark said.

Jessie shook her head.

"Damn."

Tex sighed and looked at Ira. "Fella doesn't hold his liquor very good."

Andrea prodded Ira's inert form with her foot. "He's probably going to win the Nobel Prize this year," she said, "and look at him."

"He passed out at your wedding reception too, as I remember," Jessie said.

"Yeah, the champagne got to him. He never did learn to drink worth shit."

"Well, folks, the duck bought one," Mark said.

"I guess we'd better take him back to Harbor Towers," Andrea said. "Unless you want to keep him, as a rug."

"No, thanks."

Tex picked up Ira and tossed the inert form over his shoulder in a fireman's carry. He shook Mark's hand somberly. "Sure sorry about all of this."

"Take a raincheck, OK?"

"Jessie, I really do apologize," Andrea said. "I don't know what on earth got into him."

"Don't worry about it, Andrea. I'll call you tomorrow."

They trooped out the door and Mark and Jessie looked at each other. She said, "Oh, Mark, our first dinner party!" and then they both cracked up and laughed until they were doubled up with the exertion of laughing.

"Well, Jess, this has been an interesting evening," he said. "Do you have any more friends you want me to meet?"

Jessie sighed. "Astrophysicists don't handle emotion very well."

"Or booze."

"Oh, Mark, I guess we ought to clean up the kitchen."

"No, leave it. I'm starving. Let's go out to Chef Chang and eat, for chrissake. We'll clean up later."

After they ate—neither one ordered the Peking duck—they went back to the apartment to clean up the mess. Pieces of duck were stuck to the pan, and Jessie had to scrub hard to dislodge them. The smell of singed duck still filled the air. Mark made coffee and they both stood in the kitchen quietly, sipping it. Then Mark put his cup down and moved close to Jessie and put his arms around her and kissed the back of her neck.

"Um, I like that," she said.

"Jess, we have to talk."

"Ummm?"

"I want to marry you."

"Oh, Mark, let's talk about that later."

He moved away from her. "That's what you always say. It's always *later*."

"Things are going along just fine. We have each other. Why change things?"

"Jess, we're not a couple of kids shacking up. We're grown-ups. Grown-ups get married, they make commitments."

"We have time. I'm not going anywhere."

"Why is it that every time I mention the word 'marriage,' you fly off like some little bird on the windowsill?"

"Why won't you let things be? Why do you keep pressing me?"

"Dammit, Jess, I want to marry you. I want to have kids. I want to have a real life."

"This isn't real?"

"Yes, of course it is, but I'm going to be forty in a few years. I don't just want to play house."

"What about what *I* want?"

"What are you saying, that I'm OK to shack up with but not OK to marry?"

"You know I'm not saying that."

"What *are* you saying?"

"I have one failed marriage. I want to take it slow, Mark. I couldn't bear to fail again."

"I don't want to rush you to the church, Jess. I just want some sense of—commitment. I don't like the feeling that I'll wake up some morning to find you've packed your skivvies and gone."

"I wouldn't do that."

"All right, let's get engaged. I'll give you a ring; we'll do it up right."

"I don't think people our age get engaged."

"Who cares what other people do?"

"Rings make my fingers itch."

"So I'll give you dog tags. Jess, you're backing away again. Why are you doing that?"

She sighed, took a sip of coffee, and put down the cup. "Because in my whole life I always did what the man wanted me to do. I do this doormat act, and then I'm miserable. I don't want the same old thing again. I did it with Herb, and I didn't like myself."

"Jess, I'm not Herb. I'm not like him. You're not married to him anymore. Forget Herb."

"I don't want you telling me what to do," she said, annoyed.

"I'm not telling you what to do, dammit!" Mark said, his voice rising.

"Yes, you are. You're ordering me around. And you're yelling."

"Jesus Christ!"

"Mark, please try to understand. I can't stand to feel I'm being crowded. I need some space of my own. I need time. That's all I'm asking."

"Jesus, I'm not asking for much. Just some sense of where we're headed. Dammit, I lost so much time. My marriage broke up. I can't—I don't want to just have a fling and then say, 'Hey, one of those things. See you around.' "

"That's not what I want either."

"What's *space*, Jessie? I don't understand that. And I hate those jargon terms. You're thirty-five years old, you're not a kid. If you don't want to commit now, will you ever?"

"Yes, Mark, I'm not just playing. This goes deep with me. Don't you know that?"

"What about a kid, Jess? I'd like to have a kid, before I get much older."

"I—I think I would too. But I don't know if I could . . . manage it all. I love my work. I can't lie to you and say I'd quit my job and stay home when I had a child."

"Who said that? Millions of people work and raise kids. I wouldn't be the kind of guy who'd say it's all your job. I think I'd like doing a lot of it."

174

"Oh, Mark, it all sounds so good. But it's not that simple."

"Jess, what *is* simple? I'm just saying it's possible."

"I just think—Mark, your life has been messed up, and now you want it to be normal. And I understand that, I do. I just don't know if I can give you what you need. I mean, some night you'd want me there, to sit by the fire or to change a diaper, and I'd have to run for a plane. I think you'd hate that. And then I'd feel guilty. Always, with men, when I did the things I needed to do, I felt guilty. I can't live with that."

"Look, Jess, I can't promise to be a saint. Sure, there's going to be times when I'll want you around and the job will take you away. But it's not like you're on the road all the time. I could manage a kid. I'm pretty competent. I've lived alone for a lot of years, I'm pretty self-sufficient."

"A lot of men, when they get married, they don't want to be self-sufficient anymore."

"Jess, you're talking like I'm some—some sort of representative of the whole male sex. 'Men do this. Men do that.' Do I ask you to be my servant? You know me. Why do you think I'm suddenly going to be different? Some kind of Simon Legree?"

"I guess it's not you I'm scared of, it's me. It took me so long to like myself again after Herb left me that I'm scared. What if I fail again? Could I pick myself up a second time?"

"You're not the only one who got kicked around. What do you think it did to me when my wife hated to go to bed with me? Did it out of duty? You think I'm not taking a risk? You think I'm not scared that someday you'll look at me and think, He's only a dumb soldier with one leg?"

"No, Mark, I'd never think that! But I wonder, will you look at me and think, She isn't beautiful, she isn't young. And then you'll just—leave."

"Jess, don't you hear me? Don't you hear what I'm saying? I want you. Not just for now. I want to spend the rest of my life with you. First you're scared if I get too close. Then you're scared I'll leave. *Trust* me. If you love me, trust me."

"You'd really like to get engaged, wouldn't you?"

"Yes. I won't crowd you. We'll marry when you're ready. I just want a commitment."

"You know what I'd like? A gold ring with a piece of jade in it. My grandmother had one, and I always loved it."

"Are you saying yes?"

"Yes. I'm saying yes."

"I'm glad."

"So am I. I do trust you, Mark."

"You can, Jess. I promise."

"Mark—"

"Yes?"

"Take me to bed. Make love to me. And in the morning, make love to me again. I love it when you're inside of me."

"I will," he said.

SIXTEEN

Jessie sat on the bed and stared at her hand. On the ring finger of her left hand she wore a gold ring inset with a pearl and a piece of jade. At her age, a diamond would have been tacky, but this was just right. She wore it proudly, comfortably, with no regrets. Looking at it, she realized that Mark was the first man who had loved her with no strings attached. He said, "I love you. I need you." He did not say I-love-you-sometimes or I-love-you-only-when-I'm-losing-you or I-love-you-when-you're-doing-what-I-want. He was willing to make a commitment, and finally Jessie did not back off. Was she growing up? Wonder of wonders!

She rubbed the ring with her thumb, thinking that the other men she had been involved with had been entwined with her in some strange, destructive dance. Ronald, her first love, had been Dr. Jekyll and Mr. Hyde. He'd be indifferent and mean until she decided she'd had enough, and then he would throw himself at her feet and beg forgiveness and promise to do better. They battered each other emotionally this way. Ronald made the rules, but she played the game. They both grooved on the big emotional scenes. He only loved her when he was losing her, which was about half the time, and so she was either unloved and ignored or desperately needed. She wondered if that experience, so early, got her on a crazy roller coaster, looking for men who could love her sort-of or only-when.

Ronald finally left for another girl. He played the same games with her, and she, poor fool, went right along. Jessie had never believed that Ronald would go, and when he did it left a deep scar. She was *leavable*. For a time, she thought she wore the word emblazoned on her breast, in scarlet letters. After Ronald, there were a couple of young men who might have loved her, but by then she couldn't accept it. She was looking for another roller-coaster ride. That's what attracted her to Jon, who was into sleeping around, talking about it in front of her friends. Jon was certainly a challenge. But even Jessie wasn't masochistic enough to put up with that for long.

And then there was Herb, who seemed so different from Ronald. In fact, they were very much alike, though she couldn't see it at the time. Herb loved her when she was being his ideal woman. The way he would intimidate her by threatening to take love away when she slipped up should have given her a clue, but of course she was too starry-eyed to see clearly. Even when Herb was proclaiming his passion for her, his eyes would be flickering around the room. She was the merchandise he was buying, but even as he wrote the check he was looking for other bargains.

Jessie was always off balance with Herb. She could never fill in all the details of his ideal-woman portrait, even as she diligently painted by the numbers. She was never sure when he would love her and when he wouldn't. She came to believe that love was a dance, one in which the music always changed and she didn't know the steps.

It was different with Mark. Not that he was uncomplicated; he had depths she could not fathom. But where she was concerned, it did seem to be clear and simple. He wanted her, and he didn't play games.

It's very odd, she thought. I don't have to *do* anything to be loved. She still found that a bit difficult to accept. Could someone just love her, plain and simple?

Possibly, what she was experiencing for the first time was grown-up love. Like her parents must have had. You get all your

178

ideas about love from the movies, where it's all passion and crisis and Technicolor bliss. But grown-up love was like the gas burner. You didn't have to keep checking it all the time. It was always there, glowing blue and steady.

She had wanted to do things for Herb, she remembered, but her generosity was driven by the itch of needing his approval. She liked doing things for Mark, just because he was Mark. And when she thought of the pain he'd had, of how much life had hurt him, she wanted to make it all up to him. Love him so much that it would all go away.

But it wouldn't. That was another thing she had learned. She used to think she had to be everything for a man, that if she didn't have some magic power that made everything wonderful—the Good Witch of the North with her magic wand—she had failed as a woman.

But the past was too solid for incantations and spells. And for all its scar tissue, the past had made Mark the man he was. She would not will it away. Two people didn't have to merge with each other, like carnivorous plants. A simple thing to understand. Why the hell had it taken her so long?

Could it be possible that things were coming together for her at last? She was shocked to realize that she had been counting on only one half of her life, the job half. On that side lived a competent, proud, no-nonsense woman. On the other side was the dormouse, tiny, gray, and always scrambling at its master's voice.

She was also surprised to discover that she wanted to have a child with Mark. She had never trusted any man enough for children before. There were times, though, when she looked at him, that she could tell by his eyes that he was someplace lost in time, halfway across the world. There was a world he lived in only in his dreams. She worried about that, but she was sure it would come right, with love and trust. They could handle it.

There had always been something of Irish pessimism in her nature. She tended to agree with Yeats: Things fall apart, the center cannot hold. But perhaps it could.

This was the time when perhaps it could.

SEVENTEEN

Mark made a left turn and drove the van down the winding streets of Chinatown. He was a little anxious about how the night would go. He wanted Eliot to like Jess. He wanted Jess to like Eliot. He had a secret weapon—food. He had planned a special five-course dinner, and the ingredients had to be fresh.

Sitting beside him, Jessie seemed to read his thoughts. "I'm glad I'm finally going to get to meet him," she said.

"You'll like him. You may have to fight to get a word in edgewise, though." He swung the van to curbside, saying, "Hot damn, a spot!"

"No signal. You're getting to be a real Boston driver."

"Yeah, in this town using your signal means you're not macho. Come on."

Jessie was starting to get good at the shopping detail. She had begun to know the names of the exotic ingredients, and even which brand was preferred by the true initiates. In a short time, they had gathered all the supplies they needed, and an elderly woman added up the total on a brown paper bag, then put the groceries in the bag. Jessie and Mark walked toward the door, and as they came out onto the street Mark accidentally bumped into a burly teenager who was hurrying along.

"Excuse me," Mark said.

"Fuck you," the boy snarled.

So quickly that Jessie barely realized it was happening, Mark had dropped the bag and grabbed the kid's jacket, swung him against the wall, and had his hand poised by the boy's windpipe, rigid as a knife blade. Terror flickered in the boy's eyes.

"Mark, no!" she screamed. Mark stood still, frozen. Then he let his hand drop. The boy took off on a dead run, calling out— when he was well out of range—"Mister, you're crazy!"

Mark stood still and took a deep breath. She could see his hand was trembling.

"Come on, let's go," she said.

He stood very still. Then he said, "I'm sorry. For a minute I lost control."

"You would have hurt him."

"No. I would have stopped."

"Are you sure?"

He shrugged. "Over there, you had to react fast. Your life could hang on a sliver of a second. You didn't stop to think. It's second nature."

Jessie found she was shaking. It had all been so fast, and the fear in the boy's eyes had been so naked. Had it really happened?"

"He didn't attack you."

"He was crowding me. I reacted."

His eyes had narrowed; they seemed to be only slits in his face. For the first time, she knew that he could kill. Had killed. She shivered again.

"Mark," she said quietly, "what if someday your control slips, just for an instant?"

"It won't. In 'Nam, he would have been a dead man. I stopped." He reached down and picked up the bag he had dropped.

"You scared me. I—I don't think I know the man I just saw."

"You think it was a fucking picnic, over there? That's who I *was*. And I'm alive. When I first came back from 'Nam, I used to fly off the handle all the time. I chased a guy with a tire iron once because he bumped my fender. It was nuts. But I'm over that."

181

They walked along in silence for a minute. The man she had seen about to choke a kid was not "over it." She didn't know if she should say anything more or just let it go.

"Look," he said, "I know how to work it off now. Smack the punching bag instead of somebody's face. It works for me, Jess. I handle it."

She listened in silence, unconvinced. He seemed aware of her doubts.

"We all find our own ways. Like Eliot. He moves. Uses this incredible energy he has. Builds things. Makes things. He said 'Nam made him ambitious. He's the smartest man I know."

"I guess he is. He's already a millionaire."

"Started out in a fucking garage. He saw the way things were going, made the right moves. In five years the firm went from zip to thirty million."

His face had softened; he was back, now, to the Mark she knew. He liked to talk about Eliot, and she was glad for the change of subject.

"You guys really have stayed close, haven't you?"

"Yeah, we get together a lot. He spends a lot of time in Boston on business, with the high-tech guys out on One twenty-eight."

"You said once that he saved your life. What did you mean by that?"

"When they wheeled me into that hospital, I didn't want to live. A big piece of me was gone. I mean really *gone*. It had just hit me that I had only one fucking leg. I didn't want to deal with all the shit. I wished I'd just died. Eliot spent a lot of time with me. He kidded me. He bullied me. He made me fight back."

"And he was in worse shape than you, really. No arms. God, it's amazing what he's done."

"He was the guy who held the ward together. He was the glue. He whipped us into a real unit, gimps against the world. A lot of us owe Eliot. Spade had tried suicide twice. Tried to hack his throat with a fork in the can, bled all over the fucking place. A tough black street kid with no legs? What the hell did he have to go back to? Except he had an IQ of 140. It was Eliot who convinced him he had a lot of smarts, got him to take his high school equivalency exam. Set it up right in the hospital. Eliot knew how to pull strings to make the damn bureaucracy jump. Just cut through the shit. He taught me a good lesson. A lot of rules are made just to keep the people who have power insulated. And those are the ones you don't pay any attention to."

"Do you think Eliot would like to be Dean of Arts and Sciences? He sounds like just the kind of person to deal with Rip Van Winkle." This was Jessie's pet name for her boss, the president.

"Can you pay him six hundred thou a year?"

She laughed. "How about forty-five and he gets to use the gym free."

He laughed too. "You know, I look at Eliot, at all he's done, and I think, Shit, I can do the things I want to do. They're not very hard, really, compared to what he's done. If he can be a millionaire, I can sure as hell be a writer. Eliot does what he wants. He never lets anything stop him. Funny, we're from such different backgrounds. He's a city kid, from the Bronx, and me, I'm a hick. But, shit, we almost know what we're each going to say before we open our mouths. I guess you only have one friend like that in your life. Guys, anyhow. We don't have friends, a lot."

"He really has put it all together. He's a good father, too, from what you tell me."

"Yeah, he's nuts about the kids. But he—well, he flies off the handle at them sometimes. It's sort of complicated. In Vietnam, kids were sometimes victims, sometimes even enemies. I had a friend who got killed when a ten-year-old boy threw a grenade into his jeep. So Eliot—well, he worries a lot. About what could happen to his kids. Over there, you got used to seeing people die. Kids too. That's hard to handle."

"You're worried about him, aren't you, Mark?"

"I guess I am, a little." They walked up to the van, and he opened the back door and they put the groceries inside. "But one thing I know for sure, Eliot's going to come through OK. The rest of us, the guys on the ward—I wouldn't say that about us. Eliot's the only one I'm sure about. If Eliot can't do it, the rest of us can just hang up our gloves."

At seven-thirty that night Eliot rang the doorbell, and when Mark opened the door—Jessie was in the kitchen making the rice—Eliot sailed in and said, "OK, where is she, where is this creature you've talked my ear off about?"

Jessie walked into the living room and Eliot gave her a big bear hug with his artificial arms and said, "Jessie, he lied, you are

183

not just good-looking, you are *gorgeous!*" It was blarney, of course, but such good-natured blarney that it was infectious. He reminded her of her Uncle Sean, who used to make the old aunts giggle as if they were girls again.

Inside of five minutes, Jessie and Eliot were chatting away as if they had been friends for years. He had a facility, she noticed, for drawing you into his world and making you think you had entered of your own accord. She saw why he was such a good businessman. He could make his agenda *your* agenda, and even if you knew he was doing it, you found it charming. He was restless even when he sat—moving his body, crossing and uncrossing his legs; you had the sense that he was never still. That drive—coupled with his obvious intelligence—had taken him far. No wonder Mark saw him as an inspiration.

"I'm going to keep things stirring," Mark said. "Be right back," and he disappeared into the kitchen. Eliot followed him with his eyes, and Jessie liked the smile on Eliot's face as he watched his friend. Nothing contrived about *that.*

"He's some guy, Jessie."

She smiled too. "I know."

"I worry about him. It really broke him up, when his marriage came apart. I mean, shit, first 'Nam and then his wife leaves him. He was real depressed for a long time. A good woman is what he needs."

"We do have something good, I think."

"Yeah, I can see it. He's nuts about you. I haven't seen him so up in a long time. I guess I just want to say to you—hell, he's my best friend. I don't want to see him get hurt."

"Neither do I, Eliot."

"Good. Sometimes he's—well, he can be moody. But he comes out of it. Just give him time."

"I will."

"He's a gutsy guy. When we were in the hospital, hell, I was scared shitless to think about leaving. I was good at being the cheerful gimp. I could have just hid out. Mark, he knew when it was time to go and he just cut out. Just like that. That made me do it too. So I owe him."

"You've both done a lot for each other."

"Yeah, Mark seems to think it's all one way. That I do stuff for him. He doesn't know how much he does for me. Most of the guys I work with, it's all business. Mark and me—hell, he's the only one I can really talk to."

Mark came into the room and said, "Come and get it," and they dug into Mark's special with an obvious relish and outrageous compliments to the chef, who said modestly, "I am just the best fucking-A Chinese cook west of Peking, that's all there is to it."

During dinner, Eliot asked Jessie about herself, and under his questions and the very nice wine she became quite voluble. The years with Herb had made her reticent to talk about herself. But since Herb was not there with his disapproving frown, she became quite chatty.

"You ran a lobbying group, didn't you?" Eliot asked. "Tough job."

"Oh, yeah, it really was. When I left that job, I had a bad case of burnout. Public-interest lobbying is really a tightrope. The hours are long, and you always wonder where the next dollar is coming from."

"Not like the corporate side," Mark said. "No perks. And you really have to know your stuff."

"We had such a wide range of issues. One day it was plant closings, the next day, utility rates. You had to do your homework. We were always up against companies that had ten lobbyists. We were lucky if there were two of us."

"Did you ever think of going into the corporate side?" Eliot asked. "You could pull down one hell of a salary, with your know-how."

"No. I have this—prejudice, I guess, against the private sector. Comes from my radical days. Education is a good place for me. I can use the management skills I've learned and feel that I'm working for something other than just private profit."

"She's thinking about politics, one day," Mark said.

"Oh, it's just an idea," Jessica said. "But I think I might like it."

"I'll be her campaign manager," Mark said. "I'll use *my* management skills. Drop out of a chopper and march people off to the voting booth. Somebody pulls the wrong lever, I waste him. *I* know about winning hearts and minds."

They all laughed and Jessie said, "Did Mark tell you about how well he's coming on his book?"

"No, he didn't."

"He has some terrific material. You know, he's been doing this interviewing ever since the hospital."

"So you're really going to do it, Redneck?"

"Yep. I have three chapters nearly done and I'm working on a couple of short stories. Jessie's really lighting a fire under me."

"All I did was say 'Go to it!' He took it from there. He's applied for a Rockefeller grant, and I think he has a good chance. He's a wonderful writer. Very crisp and vivid."

"I remember you doing all that taping, on the ward. You still have all that stuff?"

"Yeah. I got a great tape you did. All the guys."

"Everywhere Mark's been, he's taped veterans talking about their experiences. He has more than three hundred tapes."

"Yeah, I'm organizing it all now. My big problem is getting it focused, sorting the material into chapters. My secretary is helping me type the transcripts on the computer. Jessie and I are sorting out the stuff and getting it onto disks for the chapters. I've got so damn much stuff. I know I'll have to cut a lot."

"Do you have a name for the book?"

"How about 'Grunts: A Soldiers' History of Vietnam'?"

"Yeah, I like that," Eliot said. "Jeez, Redneck, you're really taking off like a rocket here."

"I always wanted to write books, when I was a kid. If I can get a publisher for this one, I think I'd have the nerve to try to make a living as a writer. I know a hell of a lot about the military, and there's a couple of other subjects I'd like to take on."

"Yeah? Like what?"

"The New Army. A lot of the stuff you read on it is so damn superficial. I know it from the inside. I can get people to talk."

"He's even got a title," Jessie said. " 'Be All That You Can Be.' "

"I was thinking of trying for an article first," Mark said. "Jessie thinks it could even go to the *Atlantic, The New Yorker*."

Eliot whistled. "God, you'll be one of the literati. Will you even admit you know an old gimp from Virginia?"

"When I'm a famous author, you can forge my signature and peddle it for big bucks." Mark said to Jessie, "He learned to write with his toes in the hospital. He got so good at forging Doc Greeley's signature that we used to get all kinds of crap."

"Remember the time Spade set up the still with the medicinal alcohol?"

"Worst swill I ever had. Oh, Christ, did I get drunk!"

"You forged his signature with your feet?" Jessie said.

"Sure," Mark said. "Show her."

"OK. Write your name, Jessie."

Jessie wrote her name on a piece of paper as Mark slipped off Eliot's shoe and sock.

"Good thing I showered," he said. Mark put the pen between his toes and Eliot studied Jessie's signature for a minute. Then he said, "Watch the master." He proceeded to write, using his big toe for leverage the way a person signing his name uses his thumb. He wrote, in neat block-lettered script, *Jessica McGrath*. Mark handed it to Jessie. It was a near-perfect replica.

"That's absolutely amazing!" Jessie said.

"I sign all my letters that way. I even sketch sometimes. I can write with the arms, a little bit, but they're too clumsy. They're OK for the gross movements, but not for the fine ones."

"Eliot does this trick at a lot of the VA hospitals," Mark said. "How many hospitals have you been to, anyhow?"

"Oh, I don't know, a lot. It really pisses me off, every year they're nibbling away at veterans' services. First the Vet Centers. And look at how long it took to get an Agent Orange settlement. And that's just a drop in the bucket compared to all the problems guys have. A guy comes back from 'Nam, where they dumped this defoliant all over him, and he has four kids, all deformed, and they say, 'Well, you can't *prove* that was it.' Shit."

"Reagan cut back on the centers."

"Yeah, that little rat David Stockman. He kept his ass out of the war by going to divinity school. Then he gets to be a big cheese in the Reagan White House and starts cutting funds for the guys who did go, the prick."

"It's funny," Jessie said, "but we seem to always want to forget the guys who fought the wars, once they're over. When I was a kid, I used to drive with my father past a VA hospital. These old guys were always sitting on the porch, World War One veterans. Nobody ever went to see them. They just sat there, rocking. All alone."

"Yeah, and they were *heroes*," Mark said. "We're just baby killers and psychotics. Think what they'll do to us."

"Put fucking nails in the rocking chairs," Eliot said. "I was at a meeting out in Chicago last week, and when a guy found out I had been in 'Nam, he said, 'Well, you're not like the rest of them.'

I knew exactly what the fuck he meant: Losers, suckers. I set him straight, damn fast."

"It's one of the reasons I want to write," Mark said. "I want it down in black and white, what happened to us. It's harder for them to forget us when it's there. In type."

"Losers and suckers," Eliot said. "Yeah, some of us, maybe. Like in any war. But not most of us. I got so pissed off at that guy. Losers and suckers!"

"That's not us," Mark said.

"No," Jessie said. "It isn't."

"You're fucking right about that, Redneck," Eliot said. "That is not us. Not the gimps from L-Fifteen. We are the best there is. The greatest."

"I'll drink to that," Mark said, lifting his glass.

"So will I," Jessie said.

Eliot raised his glass. "To Mick," he said. "We won't forget him. Gimps are like elephants. They never forget."

And they all drank.

EIGHTEEN

"We've got trouble, right here in River City," Liz Hailey said. Jessie sighed. Running an urban university was like being in a guerrilla war. Somebody was always sniping at you when you least expected it. But that was what the Provost's Council was for, to take the incoming.

"What is it, Liz?"

"The Reverend Mr. Kinsolving Junior is back in town."

There was a collective groan from everyone around the table except Mark.

"Who is he?" Mark asked.

"The Reverend Mr. Kinsolving Senior was head of World Humanists when Kinsolving was founded," Brian Kelly said. "So he became the college's first president."

"His son took over in 1962." Norman Wineberg picked up the story. "But then the counterculture arrived, which changed the life of Mr. Kinsolving Junior."

"To say the least," Jessie added.

189

Jake Siegel said, "He became a disciple of Timothy Leary."

"Tune in, turn on, drop out?" Mark asked. "*That* Timothy Leary? The LSD guy?"

"You got it," Brian said. "Mr. Kinsolving Junior grew a beard and started going to Parents' Nights in flowing robes, stoned out of his gourd and chanting mantras."

"Did he stay president long?"

"The World Humanists are very patient," Jessie explained, "but when Mr. Kinsolving Junior said that Mick Jagger was the Holy Spirit reincarnated, that did it."

"And the Holy Spirit descended upon them," Jake intoned, "and He spake unto them: 'I can't get no *satisfaction*!' "

"What happened to him?"

"He became a guru," Brian said. "He and his band of followers—including the president of the Student Council at the time—went off to Mexico to sniff mushrooms. We haven't heard from him in years."

"You're sure he's back?" Jessie asked Liz.

"I saw him myself, wandering around the trolley tracks. He's got about fifteen people with him, a real ratty bunch. He was preaching something about the end of the world."

"Oh, Lord, the *Herald* will get this for sure!" Jessie moaned.

"Peyote Prexy?" Mark said.

"Acid Academic?" Jake suggested.

"Mushroom Man," said Brian.

"Anybody calls the *Herald* Newsline, they're dead," Liz said.

"Well, he's showed up at a great time." Jessie sighed. "With the fund drive about to kick off. Is there anything we can do?"

"We can have the campus cops keep an eye on him," Liz said, "and the first time he does anything illegal they can pick him up. But there's no law against preaching about Armageddon."

"OK. Tell the cops to watch him real close. If there's any sniffing or snorting, I want him out of here pronto. Now, before we get to the dispute between the sociology department and the psychology department over who gets the new offices, is there any pressing business?"

"Jessie," Jake said, "we have to do something about the bag lady, Edith. She's sleeping in the stacks again."

"I arranged a place for her in a shelter. What happened?"

"Edith didn't like it there," Liz said. "She says the people there are crazy."

"She's right," Brian said. "Where do you think the people go who get dumped from mental institutions?"

"She won't go back to the shelter?"

"No," Liz said. "And I'm afraid if we force her out of the stacks, she'll freeze to death on the street."

"What does she eat?" Jessie asked.

"Who knows?"

"I think the least we can do is let her sleep where it's warm," Jessie said. "Liz, would you get someone to see that she has something to eat?"

"Give her a food service card," Jake said. "If she can survive that, she's one tough broad."

With that issue resolved, they went on to the pitched battle between the psych and soc departments. The two chairmen arrived to hurl epithets at each other. Patiently, Jessie negotiated a compromise that left neither man happy, but at least each side thought the other side hadn't won.

As they walked back across campus, Mark said to Jessie, "You need the wisdom of Solomon."

"And the patience of Job. Academics tend to use a biblical weapon."

"Don't tell me," he said. They recited, in unison, "The jawbone of an ass!"

Then Mark went back to his office, where he had interviews with students for the rest of the afternoon. When those were done, he sat down to wade through more of the endless paperwork. It was warm in the office—a faulty heater—so he took off his sweater and rolled up his sleeves.

He was sweating; rivulets of sweat ran down his face. The sweat soaked his shirt and made his armpits clammy. Wolfson was beside him and he was walking carefully, like stepping on eggs, watching the ground for any irregularities. And then it happened. He was in the air and that was very odd, because the air was not where he was supposed to be. Then he was on the ground, staring up at the blue sky. It occurred to him that he had been damaged. He grabbed for his penis and said "Thank you, God" when he found it was still there. And then he looked at his leg.

"No!" he cried out. "God, no!"

The kaleidoscope turned again and 'Nam vanished, He was in his office, the room was warm, and he was sweating. His secretary came to the door. "Major, did you call me?"

"No. Sorry, I didn't mean to disturb you."

191

His shirt was drenched and his armpits felt clammy. Dammit. *Dammit.* Why was this happening so often? A stab of panic rippled through him. He began to breathe deeply. Control. *Control.* His heart was pounding wildly, thumping inside his chest. He willed it to slow down and went on breathing deeply. Finally, his heart obeyed. His breathing returned to normal.

Why was this happening? Why now, when for the first time in a long while things were really going his way? He was getting it all together, and now *this*? What the fuck was happening? The past seemed to be spinning out of control, into the present.

The tar pit loomed in front of him: dark, murky, bottomless. He willed it out of his mind. It suddenly occurred to him what was going on. For more years than he cared to remember, he had kept a shield around his emotions, like the one that kept the starship *Enterprise* safe on *Star Trek. Full power to the shields, Mr. Scott.* With Jessie, they had evaporated. He let her walk right through them to his heart, touching it in a way no one had since Gerry, in those early days before the war. He thought of Jessie in bed beside him, her breasts gentle against his chest, her long and lovely legs parted to welcome him. He came erect, immediately.

He sat down again in his chair, trying to ignore what was happening between his legs. Then the tar pit returned to his mind, and his erection wilted.

He had a sudden chilling thought. Were all feelings closely tied together, the way muscle and sinew linked each other so that one movement inexorably led to another? If you let one feeling through the shield, were you vulnerable to all of them? *More power, Scotty, the shields are going!* Was the tar pit's sudden nearness the price he paid for loving? And if it was, would he have to wade out into it? Inside it, would the coverings be ripped from the old wounds, the bloody sutures pulled out once again?

The panic returned. He felt the urge to run—if he could run—as far as he could, just run and run until he dropped from exhaustion. He was suddenly terribly and irrationally afraid.

Control! He had to control it.

He began the rhythmic breathing, once again willing his body into submission. Slowly, the panic receded. He would master it. He always had. When he was getting ready to drop out of the chopper to face a faceless enemy, time and time again he had mastered it. In the high grass, where death hid, he had mastered it. He could do it now. But why was it happening so often? Why?

Full power to the shields, Mr. Scott. We can't lose the shields!

He shook off the thought and went back to the paperwork, narrowing his attention to the width of a pencil lead. He had always had a facility for doing this, concentrating so intently that nothing else in the world existed for a time. So focused was he on what he was reading that when the phone rang forty minutes later it startled him. He looked at it for a second, then picked it up. The voice on the other end of the line said, "This is General Westmoreland. We didn't get it right the first time, so I want a few good men to do it again. Re-up time."

"Shee-it, honky, shove yo' re-up right up yo' fuckin' white ass," he said, imitating Spade. Spade had taught him how to sound just like a street dude from Dee-troit.

"Can you get your tail right over to Logan?" Eliot said. "I only got two hours. I'm at the Hilton."

"I'm on my way."

Mark grabbed a cab on Beacon and told the cabbie to avoid the expressway and go through town to the tunnel. He made it to Logan in twenty minutes and took the elevator upstairs to the suite where Eliot was registered.

"You got three rooms? For two hours?" he said.

"Why the fuck not? It's only money. I got some good dope, Redneck."

"You brought it on the plane?"

"Yeah."

"Jeez, that's risky, Hebe."

"Shit, it's only grass. Real good, though. Besides, who would think that a guy with no arms was a dope fiend. Want some?"

"Yeah."

They both lit up and relaxed in the easy chairs.

"This is good stuff," Mark said. "God, I haven't smoked for a long time. The army gets its ass in an uproar over dope. And who knows what the fuck is in the stuff you get on the street."

"I need it. It relaxes me. I got a connection who gets high-class stuff. Coke too."

"You do coke?"

"Sometimes."

"Expensive."

"Yeah. But I need to relax, Redneck. I have to hustle my ass around all the time. The vibes are not great. The big high-tech boom is slowing down, and a lot of companies are going under. I

193

sure as hell am not going to be one of them. My magazine's on hold."

"You were really revved up about that."

"The company is taking all my time. It used to be fun, a game. But it's getting boring. The fun's gone. Now it's work."

"Eliot, what's with you and Diane?"

Eliot took a drag on his joint and shrugged. "We talk. I don't think it's going to work."

"Jeez, Hebe, that is a fucking shame."

"*C'est la guerre.* A lot of things don't work out."

"That doesn't sound like you: Mr. Can-do. Makes everything work."

"Yeah, maybe I'm mellowing out."

"I don't think you're mellow, Hebe."

"I been running for fourteen years, ole buddy. Running to make things make sense."

"What do you mean?"

"Before I went to 'Nam, the world made sense. Things were in the right places. 'Nam turned everything on its ear. Things were—meaningless. Did you feel that?"

"No," Mark said.

"I can't explain it. It wasn't getting my arms shot off. It was— everything. God bought one in 'Nam."

"I didn't think you were religious."

"Me? I didn't even get Bar Mitzvahed. But I think, Redneck, that people have to believe in a world that makes sense or they go crazy."

"Yeah, I'll buy that."

"I came back from 'Nam knowing it didn't. When I saw that twelve-year-old girl bleed to death, I knew no God existed. Who could do that to her? But it wasn't only that. In physics, there's a certain microscopic level below which none of the rules of the universe apply. Not gravity. Not magnetism. 'Nam was like that."

"You've been thinking a lot about this."

"Oh, yeah. Trying to figure it out. After 'Nam, I ran hard, to make the world make sense again. Got married. Had kids. Made a million dollars. But I was still in that world, like in particle physics, where the rules were crazy. I tried to make the world make sense again. Force it to. Macho man. But it doesn't."

"Survival guilt, Eliot. You live, a lot of people die, it doesn't make sense. It's pretty common."

Eliot took another drag and laughed. "Oh, yeah, I know all the names. All the syndromes. From Holocaust to Hiroshima. Read it all. Heard all the shrink talk. Doesn't mean shit. Knowing doesn't change things."

"You got kids that need you. That's something."

"I'm a rotten father, tell you the truth. No patience. My son's not like me, he doesn't want to burn up the track. Shit, he's only ten. But I get on his ass. Dumb. And I'm scared of messing up my daughter's head with my crazy guilt."

"It was an accident, Hebe."

"Yeah, yeah, so what? Doesn't seem to matter that it was an accident. You know, I tried to figure out what it was I was feeling. Couldn't explain it, till I read this."

He pulled out a wrinkled, folded piece of paper from his breast pocket, a page torn out of a book. One passage of a poem was marked in red. Mark looked at it, read it aloud.

Yea, though I walk through the valley of death
I shall fear no evil,
For the valleys are gone
And only death awaits
And *I* am the evil.

"Stan Platke, Specialist Four Rifleman, Fourth Infantry Division. Son-of-a-bitch has it right from the horse's mouth," Eliot said. "Christ, he *knows*. The whole fucking valley's gone. Oh, this is good dope. I'm floating."

Mark hadn't smoked any dope in a long time, and it was starting to affect him. He was drifting. Things seemed just a bit out of focus.

"Shit, Eliot, what's all this *evil* crap? You're a model veteran. The fucking VA says so. Would the fucking VA lie?"

"Yeah, I'm the VA version of a centerfold. Gimp of the Month. 'Eliot plays the guitar and takes classes in ceramics at UCLA. He hasn't got any arms but he has a bubbling personality and he ran the New York City Marathon in three forty-two.'"

"Christ, did you?"

"Yeah."

"You ever tried skiing?"

"No."

195

"So come up next month, we'll go to Gunstock and you'll learn. Jessie and me have a place."

"I hate being cold."

"No, you get real warm, once you get going. Nothing beats gimp skiing, Hebe. You have to watch out for the blind skiers, though. They get in your way, you got to go right over them."

"Can you aim for them?"

"Sure. But the little suckers are clever. They got hearing like you would not *believe*."

Eliot laughed. "Hey, Redneck, walk me to my plane. I got an eight o'clock meeting in the Big Apple tomorrow."

They walked together to the terminal, Mark still feeling a little woozy from the dope. "Hey, buddy, are you going to be OK?" he said to Eliot.

"Yeah, I am, Redneck. Sorry to bend your ear. It's the dope. It makes me morbid."

"Listen, we been through a lot of shit together. You can always talk to me. I know the drill."

"Talking doesn't seem to do much good. I go round and round in circles. What the fuck."

"We all got our ups and downs."

"Jesus H. Christ, that's for sure."

"You'll be on top of the world again, Hebe. Shit, I know you. Listen, you're coming up to ski. I'm making plans."

"That would be a blast, wouldn't it? We'll send old Doc Greeley a photo. Hebe and Redneck, après ski."

"How about the third weekend in February?"

"Lemme look." He took out his calendar. "Yeah, I'm free."

"You and me, on the slopes. I'll stock the hills with blind people, Hebe."

"Hoo-ee! Jean-Claude Feldman is on the slopes." He shook his head and laughed. "Shit, Redneck, you always make me feel better about things. A regular Dr. Feelgood."

"You'll get my bill."

"I'm going to get that magazine off the back burners, too. Why the hell am I dragging my butt? Gimps can do anything!" They walked toward the gate, silent, glad to be together. Then Eliot said, "We've had some times, huh, Redneck? God, the shit we've been through. Those days in the hospital. Christ, they were a bitch, but I think about them a lot. I've never been so close to people, ever. Not even family."

196

"I guess we *were* a weird kind of family. We came back all messed up, no arms, no legs, whatever, and the guys accepted us. We'd never have made it if we didn't have each other."

"Would you think I was nuts if I said that sometimes I want to be back there again? With all the guys?"

"No. I wouldn't think you were nuts."

The announcement of Eliot's flight boomed over the loudspeaker, and Eliot threw his bags on the belt that moved toward the X-ray.

"Upward and onward. See you on the slopes, Redneck. Look out below!"

Eliot left and Mark, his head starting to clear, hailed a cab. Neither he nor Jessie felt like cooking anything, so they decided to try a new Indonesian restaurant they had read about in the *Phoenix*. Mark took his van, and as he was driving down Commonwealth Avenue a woman in a Honda swerved in front of him and cut him out of line. Pulling even with the Honda at the next light, he rolled down the window and yelled, "You stupid idiot, what the fuck do you think you're doing?"

The woman on the passenger side of the car looked at the cold fury in his eyes and her eyes registered a flash of alarm. She looked away. The light turned green and the Honda shot forward, but Mark floored the accelerator on the van and passed the Honda. "Fucker!" he screamed, as he swerved in front of the small car, cutting it off and narrowly missing a collision.

"Mark!" Jessie called out.

He sped ahead to the next light and jammed on the brakes. Jessie had to brace herself to avoid being thrown against the windshield. Mark was gripping the wheel, tightly, and his breath was coming in deep, jagged gasps.

"Mark, calm down!"

"I'm all right."

"You nearly hit that car."

"She cut me off. Fucker."

They drove in silence for a while and then she said, "What was that all about?"

"I'm sorry. I lost my temper."

"You did more than that. You were out of control."

"I was pissed. I'm sorry, OK?"

"It scares me, Mark, that anger."

"Look, Jess, I'm sorry. I had a hard day, that's all. I blew off some steam."

"Would you rather go home? There's stuff in the fridge."

"No, I'd rather eat out. I'll be OK."

He was distracted all through dinner. Jessie had to repeat several things she said, and he apologized. Back at the apartment, he read a chapter for his Asian history course and Jessie worked on papers she had brought home. They spent many evenings this way, but tonight the quiet between them was uneasy. He knew he had upset her, and later he made love to her with a special tenderness, to make up for having frightened her. She fell asleep in his arms, content. But he lay awake, staring at the ceiling, and Nichols swam by again, his empty blue eyes as cold as death. More phantoms came—the first VC he had ever killed, the man whose jugular was cut by shrapnel, who bled like a geyser, and the man who had died next to him, trying to hold his intestines in with his own hands. They floated through his mind as they had once come only in his dreams. It was as if the lid to Pandora's box had been lifted, and all the ghosts set free.

She stirred in her sleep and he kissed the top of her head, gently. She sighed and was still. He had said to her, "You heal me, Jess," but what if that was not true? What if she was the key that unlocked the box that held the phantoms, the one that had been sealed shut all these years? What if there was a Hobson's choice he had to make: to love, and to lose control, or to run, and keep it?

He felt the panic clawing at him again. He batted it down resolutely. It was all right. He would handle it. He had done it so many times before: pound the punching bag, strain at the weights, wrestle with the devil that wanted his hands to shake and his heart to pound. He could win at it. He could keep in control.

He had to.

NINETEEN

"Mark, there's a couple of good movies at the Nickelodeon," Jessie said. "Want to go?"

Mark looked up from the book he was reading. "No, I have a couple of chapters to finish. And I want to do more work on my Vietnam course."

"You've really been grinding away. A break might do you good."

"I really have to keep at it. Why don't you go?"

"No. I'll stay in too. I have some reading to get done."

Annoyance flickered across his face. "You can go if you want."

"I hate going to the movies alone. Leprosy has to be shared if it's going to be any fun."

He frowned and looked down at his book.

"Mark, that was a joke."

"I don't know why you can't go to the movies without me."

"I can go, of course. It's just not fun to go to the movies alone and watch the students necking."

"Call Andrea. She likes movies."

"You've been saying that a lot lately: 'Call Andrea.' I get the distinct impression that you want to be left alone."

"Oh, for God's sake, Jess."

"OK, OK, I'll go to the damn movies alone."

She drove to the Nickelodeon, feeling martyred, and splurged on a dollar bucket of hot buttered popcorn, which assuaged her injured feelings slightly. By the time the movie ended she had decided she was just being a jerk. He was working hard, he was tired; why did she make a big deal out of a stupid movie? She decided to go home and apologize and make up in the most enjoyable way she could think of. But when she got back, the light was out in the bedroom and he was sleeping. He had been going to bed early a lot lately. Did he make sure to go to bed early tonight so that he wouldn't be up when she got home? What about all that work he said he had to do? What was happening here? Suddenly he seemed to have pulled back from her, as if he were a turtle who, alarmed, drew all his visible parts—all his *vulnerable* parts—back inside his shell. What was he doing? Had she done anything to anger him? She tried to think of things she had said or done and couldn't figure it out. What was happening? And why?

When she awoke the next morning, he was already showered and dressed. She said to him, "Mark, we have to talk."

"I have to be in early," he said.

"Mark, you're running away from me. What is it? Are you having more flashbacks?"

"It's just something I have to work out. I'll be OK."

"Mark, talk to me. Don't shut me out."

"Look, I just need a little time."

"Isn't that *my* line? Mark, you wanted me to stay over more often, so I changed my schedule, and now you don't even want to be in the same room with me. What have I done? Are you angry at me? What's going on?"

"Christ, can't you get off my back?"

"I just want you not to shut me out."

"I'm not," he said, but he was backing up as he said it. "Look, I'll be OK. Trust me. I just have some stuff to work out.

"Mark, wait—"

"Jess, I'll see you later," he said, and he almost ran out the door.

The cold February air hit him in the face as he went down the steps and walked, fast, along Marlborough Street. He tried to gulp down the panic as he walked. It came so often, now. Out of the blue.

He hadn't been asleep when Jessie came in from the movies, he only feigned sleep. When he felt the warmth of her body next to his in the bed, he wanted to reach out to her, but he was afraid that the panic might come again. He lay still and waited until her breathing became deep and even. Then he sat up and looked at her. She was turned away from him, and all he could see of her was her tangled dark curls against the pillow. He seemed to be looking at someone he didn't know. Love and lust deserted him. What the hell was this strange woman doing in his bed?

He got up, very quietly so as not to wake her, and used the crutch he kept by the bed to go into the living room. He sat down on a chair, feeling the cold sweat on his forehead. It was all falling apart, the control it had taken him fourteen years to build. It was going. He felt nauseous, as if he were on a high ledge, looking down. He gripped the side of the chair and took a deep breath.

It was going, and it was her fault. No, that wasn't fair. Or was it? She had made the first move. She had said, "I want to go to bed with you." What kind of a woman did that? It was her fault.

He shook his head. What kind of crazy thoughts were these. This was *Jessie,* the woman he loved. And he was the one who pushed her to take the ring. What was happening to him? Was he going crazy? Why the panic, ambushing him from behind unexpected corners, and the anger, spurting out with no specific target? Was he going nuts? Could it be the war? Hell, the damn war ended more than a decade ago. What was going on?

He hobbled back into the bedroom. Jessie had turned, and her face was toward him now, and a lock of hair fell across her forehead. She made a small snuffling sound in her sleep. She looked like a little girl, sleeping.

A wave of tenderness for her washed over him, and he wanted to take her in his arms and hold her and say, Jess, I'm sorry. I'm so sorry. I love you, God knows I do. But she was sleeping so soundly he didn't want to wake her, so he climbed back in bed, and finally he too fell asleep. In the morning he awoke early and felt good, refreshed. Everything, he thought, was going to be fine. He had been through moody spells before, long ones, and they had passed.

He was making coffee when the panic hit again. Then she was awake and questioning him and he couldn't answer her questions, so he hurried out the door.

The cold air and the walking blew the anxiety away. He was glad to be on his way to work, where he just had to think, he didn't have to feel. He realized, with a twinge of guilt, that tonight was Jessie's night to stay in her own apartment and he was relieved. He wouldn't have to face her questions tonight. He could be alone. It was easier to stay in control, alone.

He worked with prodigious energy all through the day—the panic rarely came at work—and then he walked home again, planning to finish a book he had been assigned for his seminar and to review the material he was getting together for the Vietnam course, which had been approved by the curriculum committee.

He walked into the apartment, pulled out some cold chicken and a beer, and flopped down in front of the TV set. It all felt very familiar. This was what his life had been like before Jessie. He had forgotten how lonely it was. He thought of how a few short months ago he had sat in the same chair and fantasized about her, wearing a long white dress and kissing him, her mouth sweet and smelling of grapes.

The real Jess was not ethereal at all; there were prickly edges to her, and a depth of passion he had not expected. Real, she was much better than a fantasy could ever be. Why was he behaving so badly to her? He had never been the kind of guy who got an emotional bang out of giving a woman a rough time. He had been so damn forgiving with Gerry, who didn't want him; why was he acting like this with Jess, who gave him only love? Why was his head messed up? What was going on?

He gnawed on a chicken leg, watched the local sports, and then switched the channel to the "CBS Evening News." Dan Rather told about a kidnapping in Lebanon and a bombing in the Persian Gulf. Then he said, "There was a tragic ending to a success story in Washington today. From the nation's capital, here is our report."

A picture of Eliot, facing the camera and smiling, flashed on the screen. Mark stared. What was Eliot doing on TV?

"Eliot Feldman was president of Feld-Tech, the business he

started in his garage, and a self-made millionaire," said the reporter's voice, as Eliot smiled out into Mark's living room. "And he was a Vietnam veteran who lost both arms in a helicopter crash in the Mekong Delta. Today he was found dead in his office, a suicide note by his side, by shocked employees."

"No," Mark said. "No." He shook his head.

"Eliot Feldman had been estranged from his family for several months, but employees said he showed no signs of being despondent. He left a note to his wife, the contents of which have not been divulged. But there is a sadly ironic twist to this story of a man who overcame such tremendous odds. Eliot Feldman was cited as Vet of the Year by the Disabled American Veterans in 1980. He worked tirelessly to set up job programs for vets and to visit hospitals to encourage other handicapped veterans. After he lost his arms, Eliot Feldman learned to use his toes the way many people use their fingers. He could sign his name perfectly with his toes—a skill he used to show off to his employees.

"Yesterday, sometime in the afternoon, Eliot Feldman, who was thirty-seven last month, walked into his office and locked the door."

The camera panned to the door of Eliot's office and moved through it.

"He sat down at his desk, and then he apparently removed his shoes and socks. Sitting at his desk, police say, he must have picked up his service revolver with his feet and aimed it at his chest. He pulled the trigger with his toes. His aim was perfect. He died instantly, it is believed, from a bullet in the heart."

The camera moved to a close up of the desk chair, where a dark stain of blood was clearly visible against the nubby bright blue fabric.

"The Veterans Administration released this statement to the press just minutes ago. 'Eliot Feldman was an inspiration to handicapped veterans everywhere. His loss saddens us. He will be missed.' "

And then Dan Rather introduced a feature about a herd of elk who were being saved from starvation by schoolchildren in Montana.

Mark sat still, staring at the elk moving across the screen, wondering if he had been hallucinating. Eliot dead? Impossible. Not possible. That would mean he couldn't come skiing.

He aimed the channel gun at the set and switched to ABC.

203

Peter Jennings was saying, "And, from Washington, the tragic story of one Vietnam veteran who was a hero to so many vets." And there was Eliot, this time accepting the DAV award, smiling and nodding and looking at the camera. Mark fired the gun again and the image disappeared.

He got up, grabbed his car keys from the table, and pulled on his parka. Just as he reached the door, the phone rang. It would be Jessie; she always watched the ABC news. He didn't answer the phone but walked out to his van, started it, and drove off. He had no idea where he was going.

He drove down Beacon Street, barely seeing the buildings and the other cars as they slipped by the windows.

"Aw, Hebe, why? Oh, Jesus, why?"

He shook his head. He tried to figure out what he was feeling, but he could not. He felt numb, as if he had been dipped in ice water. Just numb.

He drove aimlessly: Commonwealth Avenue, through Kenmore, up Storrow, by the Hatch Shell. Eliot was dead. He said it out loud to make it seem real. It didn't. He thought of the videotape, moving through the door. He saw Eliot, picking up the gun, turning it around, aiming.

"Sweet Jesus! Don't. Don't!" He realized he had said it out loud. He didn't want to imagine the rest, but he did. He felt the shock of the bullet, saw the blood pumping out. *Don't let it hurt him. God, don't let it!*

For all the valleys are gone
And *I* am the evil.

"Dammit, Eliot, why didn't you call me? Why didn't you pick up the phone instead of the goddam gun? I would have come. Shit, Hebe, we could have worked it out, you and I. It couldn't have been that bad. It couldn't have been!"

But it could have.

He drove. Soldiers Field Road, Greenough Boulevard, back again toward Memorial Drive. Finally he pulled the van up on Memorial Drive, beside the river. He sat there, his hands gripping the wheel, watching the lights of Boston dance icily on the dark surface of the river. The pinpoints of light reminded him of the tiny world where none of the rules applied. Not gravity. Not magnetism. Nothing.

He felt as cold as the river itself. He wanted to feel something besides the numbness. Eliot was dead. He sat there, staring at the water, wanting to feel.

Damn you, cry!

He sat still and tried to cry for his best friend, dead by his own hand. No, foot. Oh, Eliot would get a kick out of that one. Dead by his own foot. He would write a Goldie about that one. What rhymes with foot? Damn. Oh, damn! *Hebe.*

But he still couldn't cry, and the numbness was as deep as the river, so he drove the van back home and went into his apartment. He was only there a few minutes when the phone rang. It was Jessie.

"Mark! Mark, did you see the news tonight?"

"I saw it," he said.

"Oh, Mark. Oh, God, it's so awful."

"Yes. It's awful."

"Oh, Mark, I'm so sorry."

"So am I."

"Why, Mark? God, of all people. Eliot seemed—he had it all together, I thought. Why now?"

"Ghosts."

"Ghosts? What do you mean?"

"You people who weren't there, you think it's so easy. That it's all in the past. 'Forget it.' You wouldn't say that if you'd been there."

"Mark, I don't say—"

"One thing Eliot didn't put in his bio. It didn't get read out at the VA dinners. He shot a little girl. In the throat. She bled to death."

"Oh, Jesus!"

"He thought she was VC. But she was just a little kid. Easy mistake to make, over there. You'd have called him a baby killer. 'Hey, hey, LBJ, how many kids did you kill today?' "

"I never—"

"You weren't *there.* Nobody knows who wasn't there. We're the only ones who know. Not you people."

"Mark, I'm not 'you people.' I'm Jessie!"

"He thought his wife would call him a killer. You think that's crazy? Maybe it is. He was in that world, the little one. Where nothing makes sense."

"I'm coming over."

205

"I don't want you to come over."

"Mark, I want to be with you."

"Jess, I—don't come."

"Mark, please let me come."

"No, don't."

At the other end of the line, Jess felt the chill in his voice. It was cold and dry.

"Mark, they said the funeral's on Saturday. My secretary can get us plane tickets."

"I'm not going."

"What?"

"I said I'm not going."

"But Mark—"

"I can't go. He'd understand."

"Mark—"

"I'm going to go away for a couple of days."

"Go away? Where?"

"I don't know. I just need a few days."

"Mark, let me help."

"You can't. No one can."

"I'm coming over."

"I won't be here. I'll call you when I get back."

"I'll go with you. I'll take time off."

"No."

"Mark, don't push me away. Please!"

"I have to go now."

"Mark, don't go. If you go now, I know you won't be back. Don't run from me." There was silence at the other end of the line. "Mark? Are you there?"

"I'll call you when I get back. Goodbye." The line went dead.

Jessie stood, the receiver in her hand, until the phone began to whine. She wanted to throw on her coat, run out the door, and go to him. But he would be gone before she got there. He traveled light. He didn't want her. She had never felt so useless in her whole life. He didn't want her.

Jess, don't come.

Well, it was not exactly new, a man not wanting her. She should be used to it by now.

She read for a while, until the letters swam before her eyes. She lay in bed and tried to sleep, but sleep would not come. She got up and went to the bathroom and took a sleeping pill, something she rarely did. It put her in a drugged, troubled sleep.

The next day she went to her office and arranged to have a large bouquet of flowers sent to the funeral home in Mark's name. And another on behalf of herself and Kinsolving College. She read the stories in the *Times* and in the *Globe*, over and over again. She tried to concentrate on work but found it impossible, so on impulse she picked up the telephone and made a call. Two hours later she was at the Jamaica Plain VA hospital, talking to Dr. John Dunning, a man in his early thirties, a psychiatrist. He nodded soberly as she told her story.

"The flashbacks seem to be happening a lot. He seems nervous. And angry. He'll blow up at nothing."

"He saw a lot of combat?"

"Yes. Awful things. His friends getting their faces shot off. Holding their intestines in with their hands. He says it's all very clear in the nightmares."

"PTSD. Post-traumatic stress disorder," the doctor said. "Delayed stress. We see a lot of it."

"But it was fourteen years ago," Jessie said.

"There are World War Two vets who are affected twenty-five years after a traumatic event. You know, only recently has PTSD been recognized as a legitimate disorder. A lot of Vietnam vets experience it."

"What are their symptoms, doctor?"

"Often the person reexperiences the event, in flashbacks, in nightmares. There's rage, apparently senseless. Anxiety, depression. Some vets get suicidal."

"Having a hard time getting close to someone?"

"Yes, that's very common. We see vets who get into relationships, then make sure that they fail. They're afraid of losing more than they already have. When they get too close to someone, the danger signals flash. They back off."

"He was the one who wanted to get engaged. Wanted a commitment from me. Now he seems to be pushing me away."

"He has lost a lot, from what you tell me. Leg blown off, marriage failed, now his best friend commits suicide. I think he's absolutely terrified of going through the pain of loss again. He probably doesn't understand the reason for all this."

"He never wants to talk much about Vietnam. He thinks he can keep it buried."

"He can't. He saw terrible things, felt a lot of pain. Who wants

207

to dwell on that? But they're in there. He has to accept that. He has to say, 'This happened to me.' Then he can start healing."

"But he's done so well. Nearly has his doctorate, he's working on a book. He's held it all together."

"That's how he's coped. He's just denied the problems and charged straight ahead. That only works as long as you can pretend the past didn't happen. You know, some of the smarter and more sophisticated vets seem to handle the stress fine at first. They can quote you chapter and verse on the technical terms. But they're held together with spit and baling wire. They're really not coping, just avoiding. And everybody is astonished when they come apart. They don't think it's about Vietnam. But it is."

"And he's running away from me to avoid the past?"

"Yes. It's probably part of his pattern. I would bet he's done it before."

"Doctor, I—well, I don't take rejection very well either. Sometimes I think spit and baling wire is what I use too."

"You really care for him?"

"Yes. I do. He's a gentle, caring man. Very special."

"You'll have to be patient with him. If you think he's worth it."

"Oh, yes, he's worth it. But I can't live at the end of a yo-yo. What's the chance that he can come out of this? Over the long haul? Can he ever really love anyone, without running away?"

"I don't know. A lot of vets do learn to. But he has to decide he wants to confront this, head on. You can't make him do it." He paused. "Most of the time, PTSD can be as hard on the woman who's involved with the vet as it is on the guy himself. You see him screwed up, and you feel helpless."

"We have something so good. Something that could last. It's crazy for him to want to just run away."

"The reaction to delayed stress isn't a rational one. It's about feelings. Things that are hard to face."

"He doesn't want to feel all those things again."

"Of course he doesn't. But he can't get away from them."

"But maybe he can dodge them for a while. By pulling away from me. I *make* him feel."

"Yes. And that's dangerous. At least he sees it as dangerous."

"I love him, doctor. He has a special sensitivity, a special tenderness, that I think is rare."

"Yes, I hear that a lot from women who are involved with

Vietnam vets. But along with the sensitivity, there can be other things. Anger. Restlessness. A sense that they can't hold things together. A tendency to give, then pull back."

She listened, trying to let the words sink in. She hadn't really said it to herself. Not yet. She'd danced around it in the past twenty-four hours, but she had never let the words take form. The pain was bad, but she forced the words out.

"I'm going to lose him. I ought to be prepared. Is that what you're saying?"

"I don't know. There's a lot he hasn't come to terms with. But remember, you can't change him if *he* doesn't want to change. Don't kid yourself about that." He paused. "A lot of bright women do."

"I can imagine," she said. "Bright women do some very stupid things." She sighed. "Take it from one who knows."

TWENTY

Jessie shivered from the cold as an officer in full-dress uniform removed the flag from Eliot's casket, folded it crisply into a triangle, and handed it to Diane Feldman. A large number of people, many of them from Eliot's company, she guessed, stood among the tombstones at Arlington National Cemetery to bid their last farewells. Mark was not among them; he was mourning in his own way.

As the bugler played "Taps," Jessie realized that Vietnam had claimed another victim, and it was more than a decade since the guns fell silent. She remembered what Dr. Dunning had said about the vets. "We sent them off to fight in a strange land where it was hard to tell your friends from your enemies. We sent them off for only a year, so they had no time to develop any sense of being part of a cause; the only thing that mattered was surviving. We brought them home, if they came home, suddenly, to a country that didn't want to hear about their war. We blamed *them* because it was a dirty war, and we were disgusted with them

210

because it was a lost war. We isolated them and stigmatized them, cut their benefits and let them scrounge for jobs where they could find them. What the war didn't do to them, we did."

She looked at Eliot's little girl, standing stone-still beside her mother, her face a tiny frozen mask, her eyes shuttered. Would the sound of a gunshot echo forever through her life, as the same sound had haunted her father? She wondered if Eliot had really died in Vietnam that day, when the little girl bled to death in his arms and life's hope drained away with it. Should the date on the tombstone in Arlington that would soon be in place bear a date fourteen years earlier?

Eliot's son stood at attention, trying to mimic images he had seen of bravery. But his lips trembled. The children were casualties too. They seemed so small and alone that Jessie wanted to weep for them. How would they ever understand?

She was not sure that Mark would appreciate her coming to the service, and to the gravesite after. But she was glad she had come. It made her feel even more strongly that she had been right to march. How many more graves would there be, if they hadn't marched and yelled, Hell, no! How many more children with shuttered eyes?

It was the image of war that would stay with her for a long time, she thought: two children at a grave, so terribly alone. It was what women saw of war. They never got the glory or the camaraderie, none of the "good stuff" that made the bards sing of arms and men. Women just got to stand in graveyards. Maybe war would never end until women ended it. It was an idea that went back to ancient Greece. Maybe now that war was so terrible, it could finally happen. They would stand up and say, "Enough." Enough of graveyards. Enough of dying. Maybe they were the only ones who could do it.

Later, she told Andrea about the funeral.

"Oh, how sad. How goddam sad!"

"Those kids are awfully young to lose a father."

"Have you heard from Mark?"

"Not a word. He's due back at work tomorrow. Mark and his ghosts. But I'd rather talk about you. How's Ira, the battling astrophysicist?"

"He came over to apologize. Debbi made him do it. Maybe the little fly-girl isn't all that bad."

"And Tex?"

"Tex-Mex is off to a good start. He's as happy as a pig in swill. Notice that little down-home saying, Jess. God help me, but I'm starting to talk like Lyndon Johnson."

"Hey, hey, LBJ, how many ribs did you eat today?"

"God, Jess, do you realize that was nearly twenty years ago? We are getting on. By the way, Tex has asked me to marry him when the divorce is final."

"Will you?"

"Yeah, I think so. My mother even came up and met him. He charmed the pants off her. Would you believe she's going to use Tex-Mex recipes for a Hadassah lunch?"

"This is the woman who was threatening to impale herself because her daughter was sleeping with a cowboy?"

"The very same. She's now planning a family trip, she and Dad, the kids, Tex and me, to the Holy Land. Can you see them trotting down the Via Dolorosa: Bubbe, Zeyde, and Tex?"

"As long as she doesn't make him carry a cross, Andrea."

"No, just the American Express card. She thinks 'Don't leave home without it' was one of the original ten Moses brought down from the mountain."

"Well, I'll dance at your wedding. Again."

"Will I dance at yours, Jess?"

Jessie wanted to say something bright and cheerful but thought better of it. This was Andrea; she'd never pull it off. She shook her head.

"I may have done it again. Found another man who can't love me."

"Jessie, I know Mark loves you! I've seen the way he looks at you."

"I think he wants to love me. I think he wants it very much." She rubbed the ring on her finger, not even realizing she was doing it. "But all the warning bells are going off inside his head. They're saying, 'Danger! Danger!' God, I know that feeling."

"But he's the one who's always talking marriage."

"Was. Past tense."

"Come on, let me make you some tea. You'll feel better." Andrea got out the good china and poured them both a cup. Jessie leaned back in her chair and sipped the tea, trying to feel better. It didn't work.

"Oh, Andrea, if this one doesn't make it, that's it for me. It's my last chance, I think."

212

"Jessie, don't say that!"

"It's not going to work. I can feel it. And I was such a jerk. I'm hopelessly, desperately in love with him. More so than any man I ever knew. I'm going to get clobbered again, Andrea. Shit. Shit, shit, *shit*!"

Andrea poured more tea, the Margolis remedy for everything from gout to infidelity. "Oh, dammit, I thought this one was going to be the one that worked."

"So did I. I wasn't smart. He said 'Trust me' and I did. I let my guard down. I should have known it was too good to be true."

"He's coming back," Andrea said, trying to sound hopeful.

"Yes, but he's not coming back to me. He's going to find a way to leave, because if he doesn't, he's going to have to face everything that happened in Vietnam. Ghosts. I don't think he can do it."

"That fucking war. When is it going to go away?"

"I don't know. Maybe never."

After she left Andrea, Jessie wandered for a time through Harvard Square, looking at the faces of young people who didn't have a war. Lucky them. Mark and Eliot were like them once: B.G., Before Ghosts.

A young mother walked by, holding the hands of her two children. Jessie felt a pang. She had already started to have fantasies about their children, hers and Mark's. She had even picked out names, talk about dumb! For a girl, Caitlin, after her grandmother; and Mark Junior for a boy. And now they would never be real. They would only be wraiths, curling through her imagination like smoke.

She walked on, sticking her hands deep in her pockets for warmth. He would be back, but she was going to lose him. She was not a woman a man took risks for, and to love her, Mark would have to take the greatest risk of all: face a past that had the power to tear him limb from limb. Could he do it? She would not put money on that one.

It was a sucker bet all the way.

TWENTY-ONE

He had walked, how far? He looked behind him and saw only the silent woods and his own tracks, one foot starting to drag, now, in the snow. His thigh was beginning to chafe badly, his fingers and toes were numb. He wondered if Nichols had been this cold, as he went down, down, into the quarry.

Eliot would join him there now. They would both swim through his dreams, two bodies in the dark green water, moving slowly, with cold, empty blue eyes.

"Eliot," he said, "why the fuck didn't you call me? I am just so pissed at you, Hebe. We could have beat it. Together, we could have."

It was the one thing he had never expected, not Eliot. Eliot would always be there, thumbing his nose at the odds. "We're fucking going to make it, Redneck."

The cold was getting worse, chilling him through his parka. He turned around, to retrace his steps. He barely noticed the cold beauty of the day.

214

The tar pit. If anyone could have licked it, it was Eliot. But it waited. Deep. Quiet. Terrible. It was always there, so you just had to keep running. Maybe it would get you, one day. Scratch the maybe. Keep moving, buy a little time. *More power to the shields, Mr. Scott.*

He walked more, the chafing on his thigh getting worse. He would have a sore. Jessie. He hadn't called Jessie.

He stopped and took a deep breath of air. A jolt of panic shot through him. When he thought about her, he was in a dark closet, trying to suck air. At night, staring into the darkness of the hotel room, he saw her, in her white dress, with her pale shoulders. She was standing on the far side of the tar pit. If he tried to go to her, it would just close over his head and he would disappear. Be obliterated.

He took a deep breath.

Over and over in his head he ran the scene, like the instant replay of the images you saw so often they were burned into your brain: John Kennedy slumping in the backseat of the car; Lee Harvey Oswald grimacing in pain; Reagan getting shoved into the limousine as the shots rang out. Mark saw Eliot walking into his office, closing the door, using one foot to slide the heel out of his other shoe, taking off both shoes that way. Sitting in the chair. Picking up the gun with his toes. Eliot Feldman and his erotic extremities.

And what did he see in that last awful moment? The haunted eyes of a child, quietly bleeding to death? Eyes that had followed him for fourteen years? That he had never been able to outrun?

The valleys are gone
And only death awaits
And *I* am the evil.

"Dammit, Hebe, why didn't you call? Why didn't you just say, "I can't fucking hack it anymore!' I would have been on a plane. Dammit, Eliot, why did you give up? You owed it to me not to give up. Dammit. Dammit, Eliot!"

Another stab of panic ran through him. He was outdoors, nothing but trees and woods as far as he could see; why did he feel like he was in a box and there wasn't any air? His lungs struggled to draw it in, there was air all around him, a sea of air; why did he feel he was drowning? Was he in that place Eliot had described, that tiny, tiny place where none of the rules applied? Where he could suffocate in the open air?

Move. Just keep moving. *More power, Scotty.* He forced his tired limbs to work. His thigh was a burning ache, now. He came to a bend in the trail and saw the roof line of the hotel come into view. He thought of her, her face very pale and small, with the chipped tooth and the little white scar.

"I'm sorry, Jess. Oh, Jesus, I'm so sorry!" He said it to no one, to the cold air. He had thought it wouldn't happen with her. He shivered again and tried to breathe. He wished he could run.

Keep moving. Just keep moving. His lungs were rasping now, from the cold air and the exertion. He wondered what it would be like, just to lie down in the snow and let it stop. Let it all stop. Dammit, Eliot!

Keep moving. Just keep moving. Buy some time.

Beam me up, Scotty.

TWENTY-TWO

"I'm worried about Brian," Jake Siegel said. "He really seems depressed, Jessie. I can't even get a rise out of him when I say I'm for the MX and Star Wars. I say I'm going to lead an expedition to Nicaragua to fight with the contras, and he just sighs."

"Don't mention anything about an expedition to the students, Jake. They'd think it was a fun way to get summer credits."

"Yeah, their whole idea of war comes from *Rambo*. They think you spent half the time shooting people and the other half on a Nautilus."

"You think Brian is really down?"

"Oh, yeah. He just sits and stares. It's not any fun without Brian to fight with," Jake said. "Not any fun at all."

"I'll go see him," Jessie said. She made it a point to drop by his office at a time she knew he would be there. He was seated behind his desk, drinking coffee, staring morosely out at the street.

"Brian. How are you doing?"

He swiveled around in his chair. "Oh, hi, Jess," he said. His

217

eyes lacked the old fighting sparkle. His ponytail drooped. Brian Kelly looked like a beaten man.

"Jake tells me you've stopped doing your radio show on WKIN, 'Social Justice Today.'"

He shrugged. "What's the point? Nobody cares anymore. All people care about are their cars, their pads, and the next raise. Who's listening?"

"Brian, maybe now's the time when we need your voice most. When things are bleakest."

"It's going to happen all over again, Jessie. The neglect, the poverty. And when the cities burn again, people are going to say, 'How did it happen?' and there will be a presidential commission and we'll spend a few bucks and then it will all begin again."

"That doesn't mean we stop caring, Brian. Or stop speaking out. People listen to you."

"People don't remember who I am. I'm a relic. Jake has the right idea. Go with the flow. Enjoy yourself."

"Brian, you're not that kind of person. You believe in what you worked for."

"Was I just a clown, Jess? I could get on the cover of *Time*, but what did I do?"

"You helped stop the war, for one thing. And Brian, now you may be just about the only voice kids hear that speaks of social justice. And compassion. That tells them there's something more to life than tape decks and computers and VCR's."

"How much of it registers? I'm only a momentary diversion, then it's back to 'General Hospital' and the management training programs."

Jessie gave Brian her best pep talk, but it didn't take. He was as gloomy when she left as when she had come, and she was usually able to perk him up, at least for a little while.

After seeing Brian, she had a meeting with the head of Buildings and Grounds for a final showdown over the condition of the campus. There was no excuse, she said, for such a mess. He ranted and raved that the students were pigs and didn't deserve cleanliness, but she laid down the law. Things had to improve, pronto, if he wanted to keep his job. He left, muttering under his breath—cursing her, she was sure. Then there was the *Globe* story to deal with. An education roundup had cited Kinsolving's tuition for next year as $3,000 higher than it actually was, and anguished parents had been lighting up the switchboard. She called the

218

ombudsman and insisted on a full story to correct the error, not just a little box. He was resistant, but when she explained the damage the error had caused, and let a hint of legal action float in the air, he agreed to a prominent mention in his column. With that taken care of, she turned to the matter of the fund drive, which was not going as well as it should. She had to take a panicky phone call from the trustee who was heading it up and reassure him that he was doing fine. These things always started off slowly. When the phone call was completed, she conferred with the lawyer on the matter of the irate parent who was suing the campus cops because one of their number broke his kid's nose trying to disperse a rowdy beer party. Should they settle? Yes, she said, it was expensive, but the publicity would be even more damaging. The father was a big wheel at GM.

And Mark was back.

He called her and said he needed to talk to her that night. His voice seemed cold and distant, just the way she had feared it would sound. She said she would come to his apartment at seven. It was a meeting she was dreading. She needed all her womanly wiles for this one. Unfortunately, as far as she could tell, she didn't have any. Other women could raise an eyebrow or wiggle a hip and men fell at their feet. Jessie had never learned how to manipulate men. She just came straight out with things; it was her way. It didn't work, a lot.

When she entered the apartment he was standing in the living room, and his body language was sending out a clear message: keep away. His shoulders were rigid, his body tense and strained. There were furrows in his forehead.

"I'm glad you're back," she said. He nodded. "You didn't call me," she said.

"No."

"Where did you go?"

"New Hampshire. I just stayed in a hotel. Walked a lot. Thought a lot. Tried to work things out."

"Work what out, Mark?"

"You know what was happening to me. The flashbacks. The nightmares. I wasn't holding it together."

"So you went up there to make some kind of a decision."

"Yes."

"And did you?"

"Yeah."

219

"What is it?" she said, feeling suddenly cold.

"There's a spot open in D.C. Information officer at the Pentagon. A guy called me about it a week ago. It's mine if I want it. They want me."

"I see."

"I think—maybe a change of scenery is what I need. New job, some new challenges. I think I'm getting stale."

"What about your degree? The book? All your plans?"

"I can come back to those. I have to get away from all the Vietnam stuff. It gets in my head too much."

"You think you can run away from it?"

"I'm not running away. It's just a change of scene."

"You never let yourself face all those feelings, Mark. Never let yourself get angry about what happened to you. Or mourn. You have to do that, to be free."

He shook his head. "No, that's not it. That was fourteen years ago."

"It has a name, Mark. Post-traumatic stress disorder. PTSD. Flashbacks. Nightmares."

His eyes flashed with sudden anger. "I'm not some goddam psycho, Jess. That's what you want to do to all of us. You think we're wackos, that we're all going to get rifles and start picking off people from bedroom windows."

"I never said that."

"It's what you all think. All you people who weren't there."

"And in Washington, it will all go away? Poof! Like that?"

"I'm in a rut, Jess."

"Oh, for God's sake, Mark, you know that's not true. You can go to Washington. You can go to the moon. It won't make any difference."

"It'll be different," he said.

"You don't have to go to Washington to get away from me."

"We can still see each other."

"Oh, sure. You can fly up for Patriot's Day. I'll drop by for the Inauguration. You're running from me, Mark. You think you can jerk me around like that? One minute you can't live without me and the next minute you don't want me anywhere near you."

"I didn't want to do that, Jessie. I really didn't."

"Mark, I know there are a lot of things you have to wrestle with. I can be patient. I can wait. But I have to know you want to work it out."

"How very saintly," he said acidly.

"Don't be snide."

"I don't need you playing Florence Nightingale."

"That's not what I meant."

"Isn't it? Pity the poor veteran. He's a little dotty, but let's humor him."

"You're putting words in my mouth. You're doing it on purpose, to fight with me."

"I told you, Jess, the one thing I can't stand is pity."

"No, the one thing you can't stand is somebody getting close, really close. You thought it was what you wanted, but then you backed away. Because to love me, you have to face all those other feelings. All those things that happened in Vietnam. You don't want to do that, do you?"

There was a long silence, and then he said quietly, "I can't." The pain in his voice tore at her. She had wanted to take the pain away, and instead she was the cause of it.

She was quiet for a minute and then she said, "You'll have to do it sometime, Mark."

"There's a big tar pit out there. If I fall in it, I'll never come out."

"Are you sure?"

He nodded. "Eliot knew it was there. He ran. He ran hard. But everywhere he turned, there it was. So he stopped running."

"What are you saying, Mark? That you're going to do what he did?"

"I don't have the same kind of monkey on my back that Eliot did. I just want to get back to where I was: keeping it in control."

"You were all alone. Not letting anybody near you. Is that what you want?"

"Not what I want. What I have to have, I guess."

"So that's what you came up with, out there in the woods. The Macho Man plan. Do it alone. Be Clint Eastwood."

"Jess, I've been coming apart. I saw what happened to Eliot, and I realized it could happen to me. I could get so crazy that one day I might just take a gun and blow my brains out. Unless I control it."

"Mark, don't run away. Dammit, face it. I'm here. I can help."

"Eliot said talking didn't do much good. He just went around and around in circles."

"Did he ever really try to get help? Ever go to anyone who understands these things?"

"He said there is a place, you can only see it under a microscope, where none of the rules of the universe apply. And that was 'Nam. Nothing made sense."

"Is that what you feel now?"

"Sometimes. I could get stuck there too. And once you're there, it's over. All she wrote."

"Mark, they have people at the VA who know all this. They have rap groups. You're not the only one who's faced this."

"Oh, right, we'll all just sit around and chat and everything will be A-OK. You go to the VA, and they label you some kind of nut case. It's a lot of crap they dish out."

"Not if you get to the right people. There *are* good people at the VA."

"Pop psychology. That's not for me. I've always done things on my own. It's how I work things out."

"And what about me?"

He looked away, and he was quiet.

"Remember what you said, Mark? 'Trust me, Jess.' And I did. 'Love me, Jess,' you said. And I did. Damn you, I did!"

"I know," he said quietly.

" 'Wear my ring, Jess. Have my child.' You said that. Want to hear something that will give you a big laugh, down in D.C., when you're out of your 'rut'? I picked out names for our child. Mark Claymore Junior. Caitlin Claymore. Isn't that funny? I did trust you, Mark. That much."

"Jess, when I get my head together, maybe it'll work out."

"No. Dammit, don't hand me any bullshit. You're dumping me. Be honest with me. You owe me that. At least that."

"Jessie, I'm no good to you like this! I'm no good to anybody."

"You'll find somebody else. I'll be replaced, like a microchip. And it'll be fine, for a while. Then she'll try to get close, and off you'll go again. It's a pattern. You think you're the only one?"

"So I should stay around so you can psychoanalyze me?" he snapped.

"No," she said. "You should stay around so I can love you. I do love you, Mark."

He looked away. She saw his face, etched in a misery so intense she could hardly bear to look at him. It was her best shot, and it wasn't good enough.

She sighed. "Well, Major, I guess we should talk business here. The catalog copy goes out this week. Do you want me to have them take the Vietnam course out?"

He nodded.

"It will take a while for me to replace you on the Provost's Council. Can you come to the next few meetings?"

"Yes."

"Oh, one other thing." She slipped the jade and pearl ring off her finger and put it on the table. "It's hardly been used. You can recycle it. Or hock it. Nobody would guess it's secondhand."

"Jessie, you keep it. Please."

"Why? So I can get my daily jolt of rejection? My little reminder that yet another man didn't want me? No, thanks. I'm not into pain that much." She laughed, mirthlessly. "You taught me a good lesson, Mark. Men are like streetcars. They run right over you."

"Jess—"

"Well, no more. The next time I hear the *ding! ding! ding!* of my heartstrings, I am going to run like hell the other way."

"Jessie," he said, "don't. Don't. You're a wonderful woman. You're warm, you're kind—"

"Write me a commendation, Major. You ought to know about that. I deserve a medal. The Distinguished Service Cross for Stupidity. Christ, I ought to have a whole closetful of those!"

And she walked to the door, giving it a good hard slam as she closed it behind her. She walked quickly down Marlborough Street. He wouldn't be coming after her, that was for sure. She wanted to weep, but she clenched her teeth and blinked the tears away. It would not be good for student morale to see the provost walking down the street blubbering. They might think she knew something they didn't, and transfers to BU would take a jump.

"Well, Jess," she said, "here you are again."

She was, she thought, like London after the Blitz, always digging herself out of rubble. She needed the bracing voice of Winston Churchill to stiffen her backbone: "We will fight them on the beaches, we will fight them on the streets, we will fight them in the discos and the dating bars and the backseats of cars."

One more time, Jess. Dig yourself out. You did it before, you can do it again.

A wall of grayness had dropped like a curtain, covering the night sky, the houses, probably the entire East Coast. It was going to be a lot harder this time. Every time, it got harder. How many bootstraps did one woman have?

She looked at the newly naked finger on her left hand. It looked small and white, pathetic. The finger of a woman nobody wanted. She expected to see it turn green, shrivel, and drop off right before her eyes.

"Oh, Mark," she said. "Dear God, I do love him. I do. That really sucks, doesn't it?"

She wondered if the Deity was offended by scatological references in what might be considered a prayer. If so, let him zap her with a bolt from the blue. "Go ahead, make my day," she said.

She stopped in her tracks. Maybe she should just turn around, march right back there, and tell him that it wasn't that easy; dumping Jessica McGrath wasn't such an easy thing to do. But she heard the voice of the VA psychiatrist: "Remember, you can't change him if he doesn't want to change. Don't kid yourself."

And he didn't want to. That was the bottom line. "Not all your piety nor wit can change that, Jessie McGrath. Nor all your tears wash out a word of it."

She walked into her own apartment, which was dark and silent. Grace was spending all her time with her new lover; she had hinted that they were going to be married and she would be moving out. Jessie flipped on the light and looked around at the room. It looked so pathetic—that word again. Perky little prints and quilts and baskets full of fake flowers. A pad trying to masquerade as a home. She walked into her bedroom and looked at her bed. It was just like her life—small, empty, barren. The images danced in her head like sugar plums, Mark and Caitlin, small and sweet, little never-would-be's. They held hands, swung each other around, then faded away.

She felt a sudden stabbing emptiness in her womb. That was the worst of it, this time. She had let herself trust him, and trust had unlocked all sorts of maternal feelings she had not known were there. She found herself looking at children on the street, marveling at how small they were, how vulnerable. She tried to remember how it was, being so small. All she could remember was feeling that she was the right size. Children don't think they are small; only adults do. She watched the children and thought how brave and how sturdy they were. She found herself wanting to stroke their hair and pinch their little cheeks and tie their shoes and do motherly things for them.

There was something that would have to stop. Getting arrested for molesting toddlers on the street would not do her academic career any good at all. The *Herald* would have a field day: Moppet Mauler, Tot Toucher, Pervert Provo. The possibilities were endless.

She undressed quickly and climbed into bed. The sheets were cold. There was no one to touch when she stretched out her hand. There was something so lovely about having a man in bed beside you: firm muscle and warm skin, the sound of breathing in the middle of the night. It was so quiet, her bedroom. The damn digital alarm didn't even tick. When the wind howled or a branch scratched against the window, awakening the primordial fears of childhood, there was no one to huddle against until the child inside was soothed. She had forgotten how it was, sleeping alone all the time.

She was just going to have to get used to it. One more time.

TWENTY-THREE

Nights. He hated the goddam nights.

He wished Jessie were in bed beside him, warming him. He loved her body, her long, pale legs and her lovely, gentle breasts, her body that made him feel so accepted, so alive.

He picked up the phone, heard the dial tone. He held it for a minute, then put it down. He heard the echo of her voice as she left him, coated, like a fried chicken leg, in bitterness. "The Distinguished Service Cross for Stupidity. Christ, I ought to have a closetful of those!"

He had hurt her beyond imagining, and she was no stranger to hurting. He had wanted to love her and he ended up wounding her, a real warrior. His lance pierced the heart of the one woman who had loved him as he was, who would have twined her life with his, who would have had his children.

Oh, Jessie. *Jessie.*

He called out her name in the dark, and only the silence answered. He held her now only in his fantasies, and in his dreams, and they were laced with nettles. They were walking by the sea, and he pulled the coat around her and he could hear the beating of her heart. But she cried out, in pain, and she was bleeding, from something sharp and terrible inside the coat, and he would reach out to touch her face and it would decompose, melting like wax, and it would form into the death's-head face of Nichols, staring at him with the terrible eyes.

He turned and tossed, needing to sleep, not wanting to dream. Finally he got up and hobbled around the apartment on his crutch. He opened a drawer and found a pair of her panties, neatly folded. He picked them up and held them against his cheek, wanting the musk of her, but all he could smell was the detergent. In the bathroom there was her powder and a box of Tampax. She left a trail of things, like Hansel dropping bread crumbs in the woods. She was not tidy. There was a jar of Noxema on the top of the toilet; in the kitchen, her jar of decaffeinated coffee and her diet breakfast drink. On the coffee table, where she had left it, was her jade and pearl ring.

He picked it up, rubbed it with his fingers, thinking of the day they had picked it out together in the little jewelry store on Charles Street. Her pleasure had been his. It seemed so small and lonely, as he rubbed it with his fingers, as if by warming it he could warm her, alone in her bed in another house, on another street.

"You asshole, Claymore," he said to himself. "You fucking asshole."

He sat down and thought of her in the long white dress he had imagined for her. Her hair was loose and curly, and little tendrils of it curled around her forehead, the way it did on humid days. He kissed her, his tongue deep inside her mouth, and she tasted of grapes.

He groaned as his penis hardened and he thought what a coward he was; he had no right even to the phantom image of her, he had hurt her too much to keep anything at all. So he banished her from his mind's eye as he had banished her from his life. She would not go, of course, from his dreams.

There was one dream that came often, with many variations. She was always in some terrible danger; she was drowning, or being attacked by huge beasts, and he would hear her calling his name and he couldn't move and then she would begin to scream. In one dream a horrible beast was reaching for her, his talons raking her small white throat, and the red blood spurted and

227

spurted, the way it happened to the man next to him whose jugular had been cut by shrapnel. He saw the beast turn and smile at him. It had his face.

He went out of his way to avoid seeing her, but there was a Parents' Night he had promised to attend, and with a dull and trembling heart he walked into Kinsolving Hall. He saw her smiling and greeting people, wearing a dark red jersey dress with a V-neck that exposed the whiteness of her throat. He walked up to her and she said, "Hello, Mark." Her eyes were cool, guarded, closed as marble. "I appreciate your coming."

He nodded and looked at her throat. It was still cool and white and lovely, there were no marks from bloody talons on it. Only he—and she—knew they were there.

"Are you—OK?" he asked.

Her shoulders went back, a gesture of defiance. It made her seem achingly vulnerable. "Oh, yes, I'm fine."

"I saw Andrea on Commonwealth Avenue," he said. "She told me you went to Eliot's funeral. I didn't know."

"Yes. I did."

"How were they? His family?"

"In shock, I think. Still dazed. This won't be an easy thing for them to get over."

"No. I know it won't."

"How are your plans for Washington coming along? I'd like to make sure we get somebody good to take your place."

"I have to go to D.C. next week. Talk to a couple of people."

"It's a nice city. You'll enjoy it."

"Yes, I suppose."

They were chatting like polite strangers. It was absurd. He knew every inch of her body, the freckles that dotted her pale bare back, the scar above her knee where she fell off her bike when she was eleven, the little red tracks that even the softest bra made on the skin of her shoulders. He wanted to yell at her, Stop this! This is crazy. We're not strangers!

But he said, "Andrea tells me you're going skiing with them next weekend."

"Yes, Tex wants to try cross-country. Are you going to be using the place at Gunstock?"

"No."

"You won't mind, then, if we use it?"

"Of course not."

"I'll write you a check for my half of the rental. I've been meaning to do that."

"No, you don't have to do that."

"I always pay my way," she said, tilting her chin a centimeter higher.

"Well, be careful," he said.

"There's nothing *there*," she said, injecting little needles into the word, "that can hurt me, Mark."

But it was only a tiny acknowledgment of pain. Liz Hailey came over, with a pair of parents in tow, and Jessie smiled at them, and Liz tugged her off to another group of parents. He watched her as she smiled, chatted, was the gracious hostess. *Class,* he thought. Don't let them know you're hurting. She would do her job, do it well, no matter what. Jail hadn't deterred her. Or swinging nightsticks. She was that kind of woman. He could see her driving an ambulance as the bombs fell in Spain or, in another century, shepherding her covered wagon across the plains, her children in her arms. *Class.* She deserved the best there was. Deserved more than a one-legged soldier, a coward who couldn't face the phantoms of the night for her. Who was running away. Who always would.

The next day he took a Delta flight to Washington, and after his session at the Pentagon he took a cab to McLean, for an errand he had neglected too long. Diane Feldman greeted him warmly. She looked gaunt and there were hollows under her eyes, but her smile was real.

"Oh, Mark. I'm so glad you came."

"I'm sorry, Diane. About the funeral. I—it hit me pretty hard. I guess I didn't want to believe it."

"I know. You two were friends for so long. Mark, come have a drink."

He went into the living room and she made him a bourbon. He asked her if Eliot had ever told her the story of what happened to him in Vietnam.

"His arms? Just the outlines. I never asked about the details."

"No, the little girl."

"The little girl? No. Nothing about a little girl."

"I think you have to hear this." He told her the story, as Eliot had told it to him. She watched him intently, and when he was through she shook her head and said, "He never told me. Never."

"I don't think he could. I think he told it to me because I had

229

been in 'Nam, I knew how crazy it could get. I think maybe he was afraid you would call him a murderer."

"I never would! It was an accident. I never would!"

"I know."

"All those years, he never told me."

"He didn't tell me until a couple of months ago."

"All the time, I blamed myself. When the marriage failed. I thought it was me."

"Why?"

"What else could it be? He was a successful businessman. He loved the children. He had made an asset out of his handicap. I thought it *had* to be me."

"No. It was what happened fourteen years ago. He said to me that life didn't make sense after Vietnam. He tried to make it make sense. But he couldn't."

"Mark, why didn't he go for help? Oh, if only I'd known. He must have been so alone."

"Eliot was always good at making things happen. I guess he thought he could make the world make sense, all by himself."

"He mentioned you, in his note. Do you want to see it?"

"Yes."

She went to the desk in the hall and opened a drawer. Removing a piece of Feld-Tech stationery that had been folded in four, she handed it to him. Mark felt a tremor run through him when he saw the writing; Eliot's large, looping letters, written with his toes. It seemed impossible that the man who wrote those large, bold, confident letters was dead. That he knew he would be dead minutes after he wrote them.

Mark read the note.

My dearest Diane,
I am just so sorry. So, so sorry. The valleys are gone. Everything is getting dark for me. I love you and the children. This is for the best. Tell Redneck I'm sorry I couldn't come. He'll know.

"Do you know what he meant?" she asked. "The valleys are gone?"

"Yes. It's a poem. About Vietnam. About things not making sense. He was going to come up and visit me. We were going to go skiing. God, if I had thought, the way he was talking—but we were smoking dope and things got so fuzzy—"

230

"Did you have any idea?"

"No. Oh, God, no. He was down, but you know Eliot. He always bounced back. Oh, jeez, if only—why didn't I pick up on it? Maybe I could have stopped him."

She shook her head. "No, don't blame yourself, Mark. I'm glad you told me all this. It's like—like somebody just took a big rock off my chest. I felt so guilty. But it was beyond me, wasn't it?"

"Yes. It's an old story. From a long time ago. It wasn't anything you did. Vietnam killed him. It just took a long time."

"Oh, what he must have gone through. All inside his own head." She sighed. "At least he's at peace now. He hadn't been, had he? Not for a long time."

"No. Peace is hard to come by. For a lot of us, Diane."

"I hope you find it, Mark. But not the way Eliot did. Not that way."

He went back to his hotel, and that night he slept deeply and did not dream. He was up early the next morning and hailed a taxi to take him to the airport. But on impulse he asked the driver to drop him at the Vietnam Memorial instead. He had seen it in so many pictures, he was curious. He wanted to see it for himself.

It was a cold winter morning in Washington; the sky was streaked with high, hard skeins of clouds and the sun inched up into the sky, but its rays did not warm the air. He stood, at a distance, and looked at it, a huge dark V of black marble embedded in the hillside. The "black ditch" it was called, by those who opposed it. But from where he stood, it looked like a bird, an enormous night bird, wings spread against the sky, which had for some unknown reason become trapped against the earth. It seemed right for *his* war, somehow. White marble would have been a sham, but then, wasn't white marble a sham for any war? This black marble bird seemed to carry with it a heavy load of grief and death. He imagined it rising very slowly, ripping up great clods of earth as it struggled free. The idea was so real that he almost expected to see it happen, to see the great bird rise like some alien spacecraft, slowly, majestically, rising over his head until it blotted out the sun and the Washington Monument behind it, soaring higher and higher until it vanished, a huge black bird disappearing into the sky.

He shivered, but not from the cold. He had not expected the monument to move him. He had seen so many of them, tributes

231

to other wars, and he had been mildly curious about the men who fought them, but unstirred. The bird was not like them.

He walked closer, and the names swam into focus: fifty-five thousand of them, carved into the side of the bird like so many scars. He thought of a line from T. S. Eliot he had read, "I had not thought death had undone so many."

He walked close and put his hand against the marble. It seemed to burn at his touch. Cold, he remembered, often felt like heat to the nerves of the fingers. So many names; so many. He walked along the length of one wing. The grass and sky were mirrored in the flank of the bird. So many names. *James Nichols.* He raised his hand to touch the letters, expecting, somehow, that they would move beneath his fingers like living tissue. He walked some more. *Roger Wolfson.* Who had died in the same mine blast that had mangled his own leg. *Tom Webber.* Webber, dead? He hadn't known. All these years, he hadn't known. He reversed direction. He was alone, except for an elderly couple standing by the far wingtip of the bird. There were bouquets, small flags planted into the earth at intervals along the length of the monument. Names. So many. *Carl W. Jennings. August D. Johnson. Paul R. Karas. Fernando Leal. Harold E. Lee.*

So many names. He listened. Was it his imagination, or just the winter wind, or could he hear them whispering their names? *Howard Barden. David Berkholtz. Gary Bullock. Don't forget me. Please don't forget me.*

He trembled again. He felt he was in a sacred place, like an Indian burial ground. It was a mistake, coming here. They were all around him, the ones who didn't come back. Who were shot or blasted or burned and slid into body bags. They were here, and Eliot was with them; Mark could sense his presence, because he belonged with them, whispering *Please don't forget me.* A piece of his own body was there, mangled, and how much of his soul was with them too, forever gone?

He put his hand against the marble and suddenly, without warning, he began to cry, and he hadn't cried since he was a child and his mother died. It was quite unexpected. He tried to bring it under control but he couldn't, and so he just stood there, sobbing uncontrollably, his breath coming in huge tearing gasps. The elderly couple stared at the strange sight, a man in civilian clothes, wearing a gray raincoat and navy blue slacks, standing in front of a black marble slab, sobbing.

"Damn!" he said. "Oh, *damn!*"

The tears would not stop, and he stood there, letting all the feelings wash over him. The huge black bird drew them out of him, like some magical creature whose centrifugal force he could not combat. He stood there weeping for all of them, for Wolfson, for Nichols, for Webber. For Eliot. For a boy who had gone off to war and come back as a man with one leg, with moods and angers and nightmares.

He let his head rest against the marble and said, to no one, to all of them, "It hurts. Oh, shit, it hurts!"

And he sobbed against the cold black wing of the bird until there was nothing left inside, until he was dry and drained. He looked up and saw the elderly couple avert their eyes, politely. Then he turned and began to walk away from the monument, quickly, letting the cold air sting his face and his reddened eyes. He did not look back.

Later, on the airplane, he looked out the window at the mashed-potato mounds of clouds and the cool blue sky and knew he was going home. Not from Washington but from another place entirely. At last, he was going home. It was over, for him. The war was over.

But his journey had just begun.

Three days later, on a Thursday night, he walked into a small room with a couple of couches and some hard metal chairs. He looked around the room, at the faces. The men nodded, smiled at him. There was no need to explain. Eliot could have come here. *They* knew about the valleys.

He sat down in a metal chair and someone handed him a cigarette. He hadn't smoked cigarettes since 'Nam, but he took one, lighted it, and inhaled.

"My name's Mark Claymore. Yeah, like the mine. I didn't want to come here."

Heads nodded around the room.

"But I'm a Vietnam vet too, and I thought I was going crazy. I mean, it was fourteen years ago, for me, and I thought I was going nuts."

There were more nods. "Oh, yeah," said a man.

"I got my leg blown off." He looked around. "You know the drill. I guess I tried to pretend it didn't matter. Everything that happened to me. But it does."

233

"Shit, yeah," said another man.

"I think I'm just so pissed. I think I want to kill people, sometimes. I'm afraid I will, so I have to keep it under control. All the time. I think there's a lot of shit I have to get off my chest."

He inhaled again, took a deep drag.

"I don't want to be here. But I think I got to talk about it. Shit, I don't want to, but I think I got to."

"Yeah," said a voice.

There was silence in the room for a minute, and the voice came again, decisive.

"You got to."

TWENTY-FOUR

Jessie woke and walked to the window, staring out at the street below her bedroom window. The bleak winter day matched her mood. She picked up the tape recorder that she kept on her dresser and pressed the record button. She had long since abandoned her youthful diary, but she had retained the habit of speaking her thoughts into the Sony. Perhaps, she thought, it was only a legacy of the self-importance of a generation that believed everything it did was charged with significance. But it helped her to sort out her feelings, her ideas.

"I wake in the morning and it's there," she said. "The grayness. It covers everything, like a fine ash. I see colors dimly. Food has lost its taste. I eat only so that I won't fall down.

"I've been here before.

"It's temporary. I know that the colors will return. Food will taste like food instead of cardboard. It's temporary.

"I wonder how Mark is dealing with it all. Are the phantoms still drifting through his dreams? It was not good to see him at

235

Parents' Night. Like ripping the bandages off too soon. I walk along the street, sometimes hoping I'll see him, sometimes dreading the idea. It will be better when he's gone. I keep trying to think of him in the past tense. When he begins to fade, like the Cheshire cat, I can get on with my life.

"I think of Eliot and the demons that pursued him. I still see the face of his little girl, those cold, closed-up eyes.

"I wonder, too, what he saw in the eyes of that little girl he killed. We called them 'baby killers' so glibly. We were so angry— at the government, at the stupid war—that we didn't have much compassion to spare for them. I remember what Mark said, It's a fraternity you never escape. The gunfire never stops, entirely. I wonder if I will ever stop loving him. I don't think so.

"I've been thinking lately that I'd like to adopt a child. Vietnamese or Cambodian. There are so many children living in camps, shuttled around. So much of my life has been involved with that war, one way or another, I want to see something good come out of it.

"I don't think I will ever marry, but I want to be connected, somehow, to the future in a deep way. Mark opened up all those feelings—all that mothering stuff I didn't know was there. I want to use them. I just don't want them to fade away into nothingness, like my never-will-be children. I've already started on the paperwork. Hell, I can't let all that free tuition go to waste.

"They never tell you how tough life is going to be. Good thing, probably. People would want their money back.

"I am going to survive. I always do. There's work to be done, thank God for that. I want to make sure we don't get involved in any crazy adventures in Central America. I don't want to see another generation of young men maimed the way Mark and Eliot were, for another misguided political adventure. I am going to make a speech about that at the next Massachusetts Deans' meeting. I think it will get some notice. God, the wounds of Vietnam are still so raw, after all this time. It's easy to overlook them, for people who don't want to see. Mark and I are casualties. The women who love the men who have the scars get marked as well.

"You don't see the gashes, of course. But they are there. They certainly are.

"I wonder if they will ever go away."

236

TWENTY-FIVE

Andrea was fifteen minutes late for her lunch date with Jessie at the Harvest. She came hurrying in, wearing a stunning pink suit with enormous shoulders. Jessie looked at her friend.

"As I live and breathe. It's the Refrigerator, in drag."

"Sorry I was late. Meeting ran over." She picked up the menu. "I got tired of gray. Why can't a power suit be a little feminine?"

"Sure. A little girlish blush before you kick 'em in the balls."

"They'll never see it coming. What's the salad?"

"Crabmeat and endive."

"Ugh. I think I'll do the quiche. I'm not very hungry. I spent an aggravating half hour this morning arguing with the guy who's going to do the knishes and egg rolls for the wedding. Tex-Mex will do the main meal, but we need somebody who does Jewish."

"Is Tex still going ahead with his plans to convert?"

"Yes. It's not *my* idea, believe me."

"He's really getting into Judaism, I gather."

237

"Yes. He's taking Hebrew lessons. He's even picked out a Hebrew name."

"What's Tex in Hebrew?"

"There isn't any exact equivalent, as you can imagine. His real name is Elmore, and that's not big in the Talmud either. But his father had a biblical name: Joshua. So Tex is going to be Elihu Ben Joshua."

"Good grief, he sounds as if he's right out of the cast of *Exodus.*"

"You think that's a joke? The trip to Israel turned Tex into a raving Zionist. It's getting out of hand. When I call General Sharon a fascist, he says I'm an anti-Semite. I thought I was going to be marrying a cowboy. How did I wind up with one of the Elders of Zion?"

"Your mother must be happy. You got yourself another nice Jewish fella."

"Remember when Ira was a Jewish saint? My mother now refers to him as the Putz. Tex is her boychick now. They dragged me into every goddam Roman ruin and Crusader fort in the state of Israel. Tex doesn't have to convert. He and my mother already share a religion: Tourist."

"You like to travel."

"Travel means you get a nice hotel, you sit by the pool and sip white wine, and now and then you go out and look at something. The Crusaders didn't make as many forays as Tex and my mother. And the drek we brought back!"

"The bracelet you brought me was lovely."

"Every con man spotted Tex and my mother a mile away. The Arab hustlers and the Israeli hustlers were trampling each other to get at them. They bought a piece of the Wailing Wall and an icon of Mohammed's third cousin."

"Was it really a piece of the Wailing Wall?"

"Sure. They had plastic back in King Solomon's day. Solomon said, "The east wall of the temple shall be made of Formica.""

Jessie giggled. "Who's Mohammed's third cousin?"

"Mohammed Ibn Saud. He runs a car dealership in Detroit. That's why the icon was a hubcap. And it only cost a hundred-fifty."

"Tex promised to show me the slides."

"Jessie, we are talking an epic here."

"I *like* slides. People who don't even know me call me up to see their slides. I'm the only person on the East Coast who really likes slides."

"On to a subject that's even worse than slides. Have you seen Mark lately?"

"Yes. We can hardly avoid one another. He's going to be here till the end of the semester. But the scar tissue is forming, I guess. I don't feel so raw."

"Do you guys talk to each other?"

"We're polite. Super polite, actually. It's like walking on eggs."

"It's not great, is it? Better if you didn't have to see him."

"Well, maybe it all worked out for the best."

"How do you figure that?"

"I wonder if I would have had the patience. He has so much stuff to work out. Fighting the war all over again in his head. His moods shift so suddenly. One minute he's there, and another he's a million miles away. Maybe we'd never have made it, even if he'd stayed. Maybe we'd just have caused each other more pain."

"Women don't get sent off to war. They just get stuck with all the shit for years afterward."

"It's time for me to call a cease-fire. Get away from that damn war. Get on with my life."

"If we forget it, Jessie, that's trouble too."

"I know. Maybe I just want R and R."

"Do you read what they're writing, some of the guys who didn't go? All this mea culpa about missing out on the true test of manhood? All the glory shit, it's coming back, Jessie."

"Not from the vets. Not from the men who did go. The ones who have nightmares. And flashbacks."

"No, but I think there's a conspiracy of silence out there. After every war, when the killing is over, it all gets papered over with confetti and Technicolor. The reality of it."

"Eliot is the reality of it. And Mark."

"Why do we do it, Jessie? Why do we keep sending kids off to be maimed and killed, and why do we forget so fast? I don't want it to happen to my son. To Noah."

"*We* don't send them, Andrea. Women don't send their sons off. That's one of the reasons I want to get into politics. We don't always think 'Send in the Marines.' Sure, there are times when you have to fight, but not so often. Not so fast."

"Your speech caused quite a stir, I hear."

"Yeah. I told the women in the audience to get off their asses and to get involved. You know, there are studies that show that women legislators vote differently from men. They're more often opposed to the use of force to settle disputes. And it figures. We're not taught to punch somebody in the nose if we disagree. We learn to talk things out."

"Yes, and in some ways we're more connected to life than men are. We're built for giving life, not death. I used to bristle when I heard men say that, because I thought it was a put-down. And it was, the way they were using it. But I think it's our strength. Times are changing. Even the kids are conservative. Do you think the kids will just go quietly? March off to another dumb war?"

"We can't let them. You said that to me, remember?"

"Oh, Jessie. I'm just getting my personal life settled down, my job is on the track. Where are the damn kids, it's their turn."

"They're all in law school or getting their MBAs. When they say 'Hell no, we won't go!' it's because somebody offered them less than forty grand."

"It isn't fair, is it, to think we might have to do it twice."

"Who said life was fair?"

TWENTY-SIX

Mark walked into the conference room, where the meeting of the Provost's Council had just begun, and slid into his chair.

"Major, we had just about given up on you," Jessie said.

"All present and accounted for," he said.

She nodded and said, "Good." Her eyes met his for an instant. They were still closed and cold, like an iron door. His heart felt like a lead ball inside his chest. Love, he thought, was like putting up a rocket. The angles, vectors, and velocities all had to converge at a certain time. There was a tiny window that opened to let you through. When that window had closed, you had missed your chance. It was gone.

He looked at her face; it seemed pale and drawn. She kept her eyes away from his. *She'll be glad when I'm gone,* he thought.

There was an empty chair next to his and Jessie said to Jake, "Are you sure Brian knew we were meeting?"

"I saw him yesterday. He said he was coming."

"I'd really like to have him here, because there's a tricky

tenure issue we have to discuss. It's in Brian's department, so it's critical that we get his input on this."

"I'll call him," Jake volunteered, and he picked up the conference room phone and dialed Brian's office. He waited for a minute. "Not there," he said.

"Damn," Jessie said, annoyed.

Liz Hailey said, "I'll send somebody over to see if they can scout him up. Let's put the tenure case as the last item on the agenda."

"It's going to take some time, we've got a lot to do. Can everybody stay through lunch?"

They all nodded.

"OK, we'll get some sandwiches sent up."

"Not from food service, please, Jessie," Jake said. "Last night there was a food fight when they served porcupine meat balls."

"Porcupine meat balls?"

"Yeah," Norman Wineberg said. "Old hamburger balls with toothpicks in them. When used as projectiles, they're deadly."

"I am told," Jake said, "that they had to use triage at the clinic last night. The mortally wounded were just left in piles with toothpicks sticking out of their bodies."

"Food service is one of the things on the agenda," Jessie said. "We're thinking of changing companies."

"I can get you a good deal on cans of Spam, unopened since 1943," Mark said.

"Oh, God." Jake groaned. "Just think of the casualties the kids could inflict with those. *Apocalypse Now*, right in the dining hall."

Then Liz Hailey's secretary stuck her head in the door. "Sorry to interrupt, but there's an urgent call for you. Want to take it in here?"

"Yes, thanks, Ellie."

Liz picked up the conference room phone. "George? What's happening?" She was quiet for a minute, listening. "In the square? Oh, good God! George, are the media there? Channel Five? Natalie *and* Chet. The WBZ copter. Oh, God. We'll get someone right over."

"Liz, what is it?" Jessie said.

"Brace yourself for this one, Jessie."

"Liz, what on earth—"

242

"Brian has taken over the Puritan Trust bank branch in Kenmore Square."

"What?"

"Good God!" said Wendell Phelan.

"He apparently has a list of nonnegotiable demands."

"Liz, what do you mean 'taken over'? Who was that on the phone?"

"My friend George Cotter from police headquarters. He says Brian and a group of people entered the bank, pulled out rifles, and took two tellers as hostages."

"Who were these 'people'?"

"George says they were wearing white robes."

"The Reverend Mr. Kinsolving!" Jessie said.

"And the Merry Mushrooms!" Norman Wineberg groaned.

"There was an older woman with them too. From the description, it sounds like Edith."

"Edith the bag lady?" Mark said.

"Brian has been very nice to her," Jake said. "He has such a soft heart, Brian. Gives her quarters for the cracker machines."

"I got her a food service card," Liz said.

"You think your average bag lady is going to eat that slop?"

"I don't believe this!" Jessie said.

"Just like the old days." Norman Wineberg sighed. "I remember when the Black militants took over the president's office. Took eight days to get them out."

"I didn't think Brian had it in him!" Jake said, with a grin. "There's some of the old spark left. What do you know?"

"I'd better get right over there," Jessie said. "Maybe I can talk some sense into him. Oh, my God, what a time! The fund drive was just starting to move."

"My van's outside," Mark said. "I'll drive you to the square."

Liz called the police to notify them that Jessie would be at the bank in five minutes. Mark and Jessie hurried out and climbed into the van. Jessie chewed on her nails nervously as they drove.

"You're really worried about Brian, aren't you?"

"I only hope nobody gets hurt. Brian could end up in jail for this. And that would be so unfair. He's a little nuts, sometimes, but he does care about people. He really does."

"So do you, Jess. You really are good at what you do, you know? You can make the tough decisions, but you care about what happens to people. I can see you in the Senate one of these days."

"So I have your vote, do I, Major?"

"Yes. And the name is Mark, remember."

"I remember."

When Mark pulled the van into the square, the whole area had been cordoned off, and curious onlookers had gathered behind the police sawhorses. A whole phalanx of men in blue uniforms were positioned outside the bank, and there was a fire engine and an ambulance as well. Three camera crews were on the scene, grinding away.

Mark and Jessie climbed out of the van and a policeman allowed them through the lines when Jessie explained who she was and showed her Kinsolving ID. The policeman pointed out the captain who was in charge of the operation. They walked over to him.

"Captain, I'm Jessie McGrath, the provost at Kinsolving. This is Major Claymore."

"Major, I don't think we need the army in on this."

"No, I'm head of ROTC. I know the man in there. What kind of weapons do they have?"

"M-16s, as far as we can tell."

"Good God, where did Brian get those?" Mark said.

"Captain," Jessie said, "Brian Kelly is not a criminal, he's just a political science professor. He's a very peaceful, gentle man. He's against war. He's a pacifist."

"Lady, this guy just took over a bank with his own private army. This is not Mahatma Gandhi we've got in there."

"What does he say he wants?"

"He's got a whole list of demands. But he's insisting he has to talk with the president of the bank. In person."

"Can I go in and talk to him? I'm his friend. I'm sure we can get this thing settled. But please, *please* don't go in there shooting."

"Ma'am, believe me, that's not what we want to do. OK, you get on the bullhorn and talk to him."

Jessie picked up the bullhorn and said into it, "Brian, it's Jessie. Jessie McGrath."

Brian's head appeared at the first-floor window. "Jessie," he called out, "it's time for action! We're striking a blow for social justice!"

"Brian, I'm coming in there. I promise, no tricks."

"OK, I trust you, Jessie. Come ahead."

"I'm going in with you." Mark said.

"It's all right, Mark. I can handle Brian. He'd never hurt me."

"Yes, but who knows about those other nuts."

"I can take care of myself."

"Jess, if anything happened to you, and I was out here—"

"A little guilty conscience, Major? OK, come on. Brian respects you, even if he doesn't like you a lot. Maybe you can help talk some sense into him."

They walked across the cleared space in front of the bank, slowly, their hands held high to show that they had no weapons. Flashbulbs blazed as they walked. The front door of the bank opened and Mark and Jessie hurried in. Brian, wearing his jeans and love beads, was hefting an M-16. Four of the Mushrooms had guns as well. Edith the bag lady, clutching a rifle like Stallone in full charge, moved up behind them, her rifle aimed at their backs menacingly.

"Edith," Jessie said, "don't point that thing, please."

"You gave *her* a gun?" Mark said to Brian.

"She was a WAC. Actually, I think she's the only one of our troops who knows how to use it." He leaned over and said, sotto voce, "Don't worry, they're not loaded."

"Where did you get this stuff?" Mark asked him.

"In a raid on a National Guard Armory in sixty-nine. I kept a few for sentimental reasons."

"Brian," Jessie said, "where are the hostages?"

"They're in the back room. They're fine. Don't worry, we won't hurt them."

The Reverend Mr. Kinsolving, who had been standing in the tellers' area, walked out to the center of the room. With his graying beard, he looked vaguely like Moses, and he raised his hands and said, "Beware the wrath of God. Beware Armageddon."

"Brian," Jessie whispered, "these people are not exactly stable."

"I know," he whispered back. "That's why I didn't give them any bullets."

"Brian," Mark said, "you could wind up behind bars for a lot of years for this."

"I just couldn't sit around idly anymore. If nothing else, this will help to dramatize the plight of the poor. People need to be made to see. Jake and I were always pretty good at using guerrilla theater to get attention."

"But this isn't the sixties anymore," Jessie said.

"Read my list of demands, Jess. Are they unreasonable? Is this the raving of some crackpot?"

Jessie took the photocopied list Brian handed her. "Disinvest in South Africa. Begin a ten-million-dollar neighborhood development plan for Roxbury-Dorchester for housing rehabilitation and enterprise zones."

"See, Jess, I even used Reagan's phrase: 'enterprise zones.' What could be more middle-of-the-road?"

"Brian, you captured a bank!" Mark said. "I do not think that is what President Reagan had in mind."

"And signs and wonders shall appear in the heavens!" boomed the Reverend Mr. Kinsolving, to no one in particular. "Repent! Repent!"

"Keep it down, buddy," snarled Edith, "or I'll bust your butt."

"Brian, you didn't really think this could work, did you?" Jessie said.

"I'll get on 'Today,' Jessie. I'll get on 'Twenty-Twenty.' I'll talk about kids going hungry and families living in deserted cars. I'll be a media star, Jess, for a while. The longer the siege goes on, the bigger the story we are. So I go to jail. So what? I feel *useful,* Jess. And it's been so long."

"Brian, they're going to come charging in here with guns. They aren't going to just let you *keep* a bank, indefinitely. People could get killed."

The sound of the policeman's voice on the bullhorn drifted in through an open window. "Come out of there. Throw down your weapons. Come out now and no one will get hurt."

"The end of the world is at hand!" said Kinsolving Junior.

Mark moved to the window and called out, "This is Major Claymore. It's OK in here. No one has been harmed. We're talking. Just give us some time, OK?"

He went back to Jess and Brian and listened as Jessie patiently tried to talk Brian into ending the siege. But Brian's jaw was clenched. He was not being moved.

Mark said to Brian, "Look what they did in Philadelphia. They dropped a goddam bomb!"

Brian chuckled. "On a black neighborhood, sure. They're not going to bomb a *bank*. Ray Flynn doesn't want to be a white Wilson Goode. Say, is he here yet? He usually goes to all the fires."

"The mayor's outside," Mark said. "I saw him as we came in."

246

A woman wandered out of the back room and stood very still, looking around, wide-eyed. "Oooohh," she said. "The colors are *so* bright."

"Who's that?" Jessie said.

"A hostage."

"She looks like she's stoned," Mark said.

"Oh, shit, I bet they're giving her mushrooms," Brian said. "I told them not to."

The bullhorn sounded again. "Major Claymore, what's going on?"

"It's OK. The provost is talking with Professor Kelly. Give her time. Hold your horses. I repeat, everything is all right in here. No one is going to be hurt, if you keep it cool."

He went back to Brian and Jessie. "They've got the SWAT team. There's a guy with a sniperscope on a roof across the street."

"Is the NBC color truck out there?" Brian asked.

"No," Mark said.

"Oh, well. They can get the feed from BZ. We'll hit the top of the news at Five, Seven, and Four, maybe second lead on the networks. Is Mike Barnicle out there? I bet Alan Lupo would do a column for the *Globe* on the neighborhood angle."

"Brian, you have to stop this!" Jessie said. "Innocent people could get hurt."

"Good visual, you and the major coming in. Shit, I bet Peter Jennings *opens* with that. Slow news day. I made sure of that. I was just hoping the Russians wouldn't shoot down another jet or something. Then we'd get shoved down after the stock report."

"Brian, for heaven's sake—"

"I'm not going to give up, Jessie. I'm making a statement here."

"Think of the college, Brian. We'll be all over the front pages."

"You couldn't buy this publicity, Jess."

"Oh, God, Brian—"

"Attention, in there," came the bullhorn. "We have a person who says he has to come in."

Brian moved to the window. "Who is it?" he yelled.

"Mr. Jacob Siegel."

"Jake?"

"Oh, Lord, what's *he* doing?" Jessie groaned.

247

"Let him in," Brian called out.

Jake, who had changed his clothes since the council meeting and was now nattily attired in his best silk dress-for-success brunch suit, trotted up to the door as more flashbulbs blazed away. He was carrying a leather briefcase.

"Shall I let him in or shall I drill him, chief?" asked the bag lady.

"Let him in, Edith."

"Roger Wilco."

She opened the door and Jake came in. He looked around, grinned, and said, "Hey, Brian, are those from the armory?"

"Right."

"Yeah, I have a couple too. Well, Brian, you really pulled it off. The mayor wants to talk to you."

Over the bullhorn came the voice of Mayor Ray Flynn.

"Professor Kelly, listen to reason. Bring your people out safely. The president of the bank will be here in a minute. I repeat, the president is on his way!"

"I'll be damned," said Brian.

"I called him," Jake said.

"You did?" Mark said, astonished. "And he said he'd come?"

Jake chuckled. "Not without a little persuasion."

"Behold, the Armies of the Night come hither," said Mr. Kinsolving Junior. "Behold, Armaggedon." Nobody paid him the least attention.

"Jake," Jessie said suspiciously, "what did you tell the president of Puritan Trust?"

"I just dropped a name."

"Which one?"

"A certain North End family. They have—interesting entrepreneurial habits."

"The Mafia?" Mark asked, surprised.

"Your word, not mine," Jake said archly.

The bullhorn sounded again. It was the mayor. "Professor Kelly, the president of the bank is here. He's coming in."

"We hear you," Brian called out the window. "Send him in."

A tall, silver-haired man walked briskly to the door. John Crowninshield Baker, Harvard, '52, Harvard Law, '55, a member of the Somerset Club, a prime mover in the Vault, the small circle of businessmen who controlled the city's financial destiny, always

248

walked briskly. His aristocratic brow was furrowed into a scowl.

"Wonderful," Brian enthused. "We'll hit the lead on all three networks and CNN. Maybe the cover of *Newsweek.*"

Edith opened the door, and the bank president strode in.

"Mr. Baker," Jessie said, "I'm Jessie McGrath, the provost of Kinsolving. Major Claymore, Professor Kelly. You—ah—know Jake Siegel."

Baker glowered at Jake. "Siegel, what is this nonsense you're talking?"

"It's not nonsense. You know that, or you wouldn't be here."

"See here, Siegel—"

Edith hefted her rifle and stuck it against the bank president's ribs.

"No tricks, Buster."

"It's OK, Edith," Brian said.

"Who is that woman?" Baker demanded.

"Specialist Fourth Class Edith Mahoney, Women's Army Corps," barked Edith.

"The volunteer army is *not* a good idea," Baker said, glaring at Mark.

"Actually, she's Libyan," Mark said, annoyed. "Qaddafi hit squad."

Jake, meanwhile, had opened his briefcase and took out a photocopy of a memo. It was on Puritan Trust letterhead. Silently, he handed it to Baker. Baker's pale skin got even paler as he read it.

"Where the hell did you get this?"

"Very interesting, a certain company that's on your exempt list of customers."

"It's not illegal," Baker said.

"What's that?" Brian asked.

"It's a special list that banks have, of their most reputable customers. The ones they do business with a lot. They don't have to file a report with IRS on cash transactions with these companies." He looked at Baker. "How do they bring in the money, in violin cases?"

"There's nothing illegal here. Perhaps—a small error in judgment."

"The press would have a field day with that small error in

249

judgment. There's also the matter of a slight delay in reporting certain international cash transactions."

"We're correcting that," Baker said. "A clerical error."

"One the IRS would be very interested in."

"Goddam it, Siegel, you could be arrested for stealing that stuff. That's confidential."

"Oh, I didn't steal it. It came from inside your own organization. A little insurance for some folks."

"What do you intend to do with it?"

"I always wondered about that myself. I do have an idea."

"I can imagine," said Baker.

"What I think happened here," Jake said, "is a misunderstanding. Professor Kelly didn't know when he began his crusade that the bank already had a major redevelopment program in the works for Roxbury-Dorchester."

"God is coming!" intoned Mr. Kinsolving Junior.

"You son-of-a-bitch," Baker said.

Jake smiled. "It would be a great story for the media to have the two of you shaking hands as you made public your community program. Five million?"

"Seven," Brian said.

"You son-of-a-bitch," Baker said again.

"Actually, Mr. Baker," Jessie said, "I think we are talking about a very good investment in public relations. Don't you think so, Major?"

"Yeah, it does seem that the press would be playing the story so big that they might not even get wind of certain—clerical errors."

"Well," said John Crowninshield Baker, known in the Vault as the ultimate pragmatist, "I think some—accommodation can be made here."

"What about disinvestment," Brian asked. Jake glared at him. "Brian, don't push your luck."

"What about amnesty? For my troops."

"With your cooperation," Jessie said to Baker, "the police commissioner might agree to misdemeanor charges. The guns aren't loaded."

"They aren't?" Baker said. He looked at Brian. "You mean you did all this with empty rifles?"

Brian nodded. "I'm a pacifist."

"We can't just let these people off with a slap on the wrist,"

Baker said angrily. "Think of the precedent. People all over the country will be charging into banks with cap pistols."

Jake hummed the theme from *The Godfather.*

"Mr. Baker," Jessie said, "it will not do my school any good to have one of my faculty members charged with a felony. I have enough damage control to do as it is. You have certain information which would best be kept private. Professor Kelly is not a criminal. The Puritan Trust is not a criminal. Shall we keep this among ourselves?"

"Yes, Ms. McGrath, shall we do that, indeed."

And so a deal was struck. It made for great TV, the president of Puritan Trust and Brian Kelly facing the cameras together. Brian graciously said that he had misjudged a progressive financial institution and that his only motive was to make a statement about the plight of the poor. John Crowninshield Baker said that while Professor Kelly's tactics were indeed misguided, Puritan Trust shared with him a great concern for the disadvantaged. Which is why he had been planning to announce, shortly, a community rehabilitation program amounting to several millions.

"Of course, Ted," he told Ted Koppel on "Nightline," "I'm not free to discuss the details, but we're in the completion phase right now." Brian chatted with Barbara Walters about the problems of the poor. The producers of "Today," and "Good Morning, America," and "CBS Morning News" fell over themselves trying to get exclusives. Finally, they all planned segments featuring both Baker and Brian. Phyllis George promised not to ask them to hug. *The New York Times* prepared an editorial applauding Mayor Flynn for handling the crisis with populist aplomb, and the two tellers huddled with *Herald* reporters for a dramatic first-person story: HELD CAPTIVE FOR HOURS. Edith the bag lady would clip a photo from the morning *Globe* of her holding an M-16 (taken by Pulitzer Prize–winner Stan Grossfeld). She would place it in her Filene's bag among her prized possessions.

"Jake," Jessie said, as they watched the six o'clock news in her office, "where in the hell *did* you get that memo?"

"From a regular at one of my seminars. She knew some funny stuff was going on at the bank, and she was scared. It was in her section. She thought she might get nailed someday, while the higher-ups got off."

"So you told her to make a Xerox."

"Two Xeroxes."

251

"Do you teach blackmail to your management students these days, Jake?"

"Hell, yes. Blackmail, bribery, industrial espionage, computer fraud, and cost overruns."

He smiled.

"It's called 'free enterprise.' "

TWENTY-SEVEN

Jessie watched herself on "Nightline," walking with hands held high across the clear space to the door of the bank. Jeez, why did she have to be wearing last year's tweed skirt? It was too short and it looked decidedly tacky. Twenty million people were watching, and there was a run in her pantyhose.

Shit.

The doorbell rang and she went to open it. Mark was standing on the doorstep. She felt a pull, somewhere in the region of her chest. Scar tissue ripping away. She took a deep breath and said, "Come in, Mark."

He walked in and she told him, "You look good on TV. Good posture. I have a run in my pantyhose."

"Well, it all could have been a lot worse."

"Don't remind me. But it was not great. How many parents are going to want to send their kids to a school where the faculty takes over banks with M-16s?"

"Barbara Walters told Brian he was gutsy. I think he's going to become a folk hero. Robin Hood."

"Jake told me a lecture bureau has already contacted Brian. Would you believe that?"

"Celebrity is what counts. Gordon Liddy is big box office. People forget what you did, exactly. They just remember you were on the cover of *People*."

"You may be right. Oh, Lord, what a day. Major, the Pentagon is going to be pretty dull compared to Higher Ed."

"I guess so."

They were quiet for a minute and then he said, "Jess, I'm talking about it."

"It?"

"The war."

"You are? With whom?"

"A bunch of guys. At the VA."

"I didn't think you wanted to do that."

"I didn't. I don't. But there's so much. More than I realized. Terrible things got so—commonplace that they seemed normal. You thought you'd built up this wall against them, but your mind was whirring along, recording it all. I'm remembering so much stuff I'd repressed."

"That you tried to will away. Just make it go."

"Yeah. Like Eliot. He ran and ran, but it was always there. When it happened to him, I was scared shitless. Eliot was the smartest man I ever knew. The strongest. Had the most energy."

"But even he couldn't run fast enough."

"Yeah." They were silent again and then he said, "I hurt you, Jess. I'm having a hard time forgiving myself for that."

She smiled tightly, her lips like wax. "I'm a survivor. Tougher than I look."

"It was the one thing I didn't want."

"How many of us get what we want, Major?"

"We're back to 'Major'?"

"I think that's best."

"At the VA, Jess, we talk. About what we saw. What we did. We cry sometimes. And it's OK. I had this sense, for a long time, that I was a bystander in life. After 'Nam, I was out there just watching the parade go by. And that was OK, because I didn't have to sweat life. But I couldn't be like that with you. I had to feel again, with you. And so many of the things I've felt in my life were so goddam bad. Pain. Death. So you want to run. We're all like that, the guys in my group. Always with our sneakers on."

254

"And now you don't want that?"

"Oh, yeah, I do, a lot. A lot of times I want to get up and walk out of that goddam room and never come back. To hear the things those guys went through, what they did—but at least I'm not alone. And it's worse when you run. Facing it, you have a chance for some peace. I don't want to be a bystander for the rest of my life."

They were quiet again, and to break the silence she said, "Do you want a drink?"

"Yes, please."

"Scotch and water?"

"Right."

Her hands, she noticed with some satisfaction, were steady as she poured the drink. It was a point of pride with her not to let a man see the devastation he had wrought inside her. She had always been civil to Herb, even through the divorce proceedings, when in fact she wanted to squeeze out his eyes and drop them in the blender and feed them to the cat. With Mark, she was a Potemkin village, painted bright and shiny on the outside, so the passing entourage could not see the emptiness inside.

"I had to get up my courage to come here," he said.

She was quiet.

"I know I haven't got any right to ask anything of you."

"No," she said, "you don't."

He looked down into his drink. The silence stretched out until it had a sound: a high, thin buzzing.

"Maybe I shouldn't have come."

"Well, you're here."

"Yeah, I'm here. If you want me to go, right now, I'm out of here."

She said nothing. It had taken a long time for the scar tissue to congeal and toughen. Weeks and weeks. All that healing could be ripped away in a minute.

"What do you want, Mark?"

"I want to stay. Try to work things out."

"Stay for how long? The pause that refreshes?"

He winced. She felt an instant thrill of victory at his pain. Only an instant. Then she was ashamed of herself.

"I'm sorry," she said. "That was nasty."

"I deserved it." He shrugged. "Life is timing. Mine is lousy."

He took a sip of his drink. "You've probably got some other guy, anyhow."

"No," she said. "I don't."

"The other night, in my group, I heard one of the guys saying that he only loved one person in his whole life and he kept doing things to drive her away. Ran around with other women he didn't care about, drank himself blind every other night. But inside there was another part of him asking, 'Why are you doing this? Why are you making her leave?' And she did. I heard him talking, and it was me, too. I didn't want to believe it, that night you told me I had a pattern, that it was delayed stress. But there was someone inside me who knew you were right. The other guys at the VA—they're so much like me. Do the same things. I thought it was only me."

"It's not only you."

"I see the other guys. Some of them have started to change things. Once you know, maybe it's possible. I didn't think so. Now I do. People change. I can change, Jessie."

"I trusted you once, Mark. And I got clobbered."

"I'll be honest with you. That's one of the things we have to do in the group, can the bullshit. I can't tell you it will be easy. It won't. There are times I'll be rotten to live with. Christ, I'm so angry sometimes. There's a lot of shit I have to shovel."

"That's your deal? We shovel shit together?"

"I guess that's it. I love you, and the truth is, I don't know if I'll make it without you. But I don't want to give you any crap about how I'm this suddenly changed person. I get moody. I get pissed. I get the feeling that it's so damn unfair, other people didn't have to go through what I did and nobody gives a damn that I did it."

"And I'll have to live with that?"

"Yes. I won't lie to you. Yes."

"Now tell me the good news."

"I do love you. More than anyone in my life. Ever. I guess Eliot was the only other person I ever let get really close." He sighed. "The good news. I'll always be in your corner. I like the way you go at things. You're tough. You're ambitious. I like that. And I'll make you laugh, Jess. I really like it when you laugh."

"The thing I couldn't bear was when you shut me out. When the door slammed and there was no one home. That was the worst thing."

256

"I had to slam the door because I was scared shitless of what was out there. I'm not great at opening up. But I'm learning."

There was quiet again.

"Do you love me, Jess?" he said.

She walked to the window and looked out at the dark street. The scar tissue was almost like armor, now. She'd be crazy to go back. What she told Andrea was true. She didn't know if she had the patience. There were men out there who didn't have flashbacks and dead men floating through their dreams. There were men who would be witty and charming and who would ask nothing of her but a passable white wine and a reasonable fuck, who would leave her energies intact for other things. Life would be so simple. All she had to say was no. Inexplicably, she remembered the day—she was ten years old—when she threw a baseball, her only genuine major league baseball signed by Ford Frick, through Mr. Davidow's living room window. The other kids all ran. She stood there, shaking, and Mr. Davidow came out and started to shriek. He was nervous about children. She stood her ground and said, "I did it."

There were two kinds of people in the world, the runners and the stayers. She was, God help her, a stayer.

She turned to face him. "I tried to stop loving you, I really did. It didn't work so good."

He walked over to her and put his arms around her. He made the move. He came to her. A good sign. She rested her head against his chest, wearily.

"I was so scared that you'd tell me to go. That I'd fucked it up for good."

"I know."

"I'm here, Jess. I'm not going anyplace. I'm here."

He led her to the couch and they just sat together, not talking, for a long time. Then she said to him, "After you—left, I decided I wanted to adopt a child. There are a lot of kids. Vietnamese and Cambodian, who don't have any families. Could you handle that?"

"A kid?"

"Yes. Thinking about having children with you gave me the idea. I've started the process. It will take about ten months, maybe a year."

"Those kids have problems, Jessie. It won't be easy."

"I know."

"But it would be something good, wouldn't it? Out of the whole thing."

"Yes, I think so."

"Something coming full circle. Death, but life again. Life going on."

"Do you have any feelings about those children? Some of the ones who killed Americans were so young. Is it something that would bring it all back?"

"I know it happened. I told you about a buddy of mine. But I liked the kids. They were beautiful. I used to pick them up, hold them, a lot. There was something about them. Maybe it was because they were real, and alive, in that shithole of a war. They'd laugh, like kids anywhere."

"I tried to ask myself, Was I trying to be a do-gooder, did I have any unconscious motive? But I figured, what the hell, no parent is a saint. It's something good to do, that's all," she confessed.

"I think I could be a good father. It's something I've been thinking about a lot. I think I need people to take care of. I was good at that in 'Nam. It's what kept me sane, knowing I had those guys to take care of. That was the most important thing in the world. There are people who are alive because of me. And that's good. Maybe that's my real talent, taking care of people."

She thought of how good he was with the ROTC kids and she pictured him with the kids in the rotting, lethal jungle—no more than a kid himself, herding them like stray sheep through the valley of death. The Good Shepherd of the Grunts.

"It's funny," he said. "Eliot said Vietnam made him ambitious. Me, it's the opposite. I don't want to run my tail off. I want to write, I do want to be good at it, but I don't give a rat's ass about making a lot of dough."

She smiled. "Are you saying I am going to have to support you?"

"Naw, I can always get my hands on Spam. If you want prime rib, that's another story." He was quiet again, and then he told her, "It's just my way of saying that I'm not like a lot of guys you'll meet. Upwardly mobile. Movers and shakers."

"Those guys, Mark, they never stay in anybody's corner. It's the center of the ring or nothing. I was married to one of those. I'll pass."

She ran her fingers gently across his lips, the full, sensual lips she liked so much, traced the square line of his jaw. She felt him tremble. She thought perhaps she ought to go slowly; sexual aggression was going out of style these days, for women. Pretty soon they'd be back to Doris Day, frat pins, and padded bras. Christ!

So she ran her tongue across his lips—that always made him wild—and started to unbutton his shirt and he didn't seem to mind too much, except when he bumped his head on the arm of the couch.

"Are you going to keep this up," he asked, "until we're eighty?"

"Yes."

"Christ, I'm going to be tired."

"Oh, shut up and take your leg off and let's do it."

"Here? Right here?"

"Do you want to?"

"Fucking-A," he said.